The Devil to Pay

DAVID DONACHIE

Allison & Busby Limited
12 Fitzroy Mews
London W1T 6DW
allisonandbusby.com

First published in Great Britain by Allison & Busby in 2014.
This paperback edition published by Allison & Busby in 2015.

A CIP catalogue record for this book is available from
the British Library.

10 9 8 7 6 5 4 3 2 1

ISBN 978-0-7490-1663-0

Typeset in 10.5/16 pt Adobe Garamond Pro by
Allison & Busby Ltd.

The paper used for this Allison & Busby publication
has been produced from trees that have been legally sourced
from well-managed and credibly certified forests.

Printed and bound by
CPI Group (UK) Ltd, Croydon, CR0 4YY

To my grandson,
Lewis Nelson Donachie,
who was born when this
novel was in its infancy.

PROLOGUE

John Pearce found it easy to be irritable in a place like Palermo. The weather, even in early September, was searing hot during the day and scarcely less so at night without a breeze. With a broken arm in splints, held in place by heavy bandaging, the amount of itching it caused was enough to drive him near mad with frustration. Added to this physical discomfort, he was required to deal with the folk who undertook the repair of ships in the harbour, there being no dockyard in the proper sense, while he had in HMS *Larcher*, after his recent battle, a vessel in need of much restoration before it could be considered fully fit for sea.

The damage to the hull and upper works he could, in the main, leave to his own men, at least those who had survived whole, while much of the ship's tackle, like blocks and sheaves, if torn from their usual location, were serviceable. Canvas to repair sails too shot through to be of any use was something to be bought in bolts and fashioned by those same hands. Likewise cordage, albeit much time was spent in bargaining for a fair price, a restraint imposed on him by limited funds, much of which was expended on those woodworking tasks beyond the skill of the ship's carpenter and his mates.

It was in the article of an upper mast and especially the bowsprit that he was struggling to get the armed cutter ready for sea and this in an island not short on timber, though it seemed to lack anything of the required length and shape. He had some suspicion that the wily locals knew very well what was needed, knew as he did not, where to find it – and were holding out for an excessive price – aware he was in a poor position to bargain.

All his rigging had suffered damage and in the case of the long bowsprit the lack of it left *Larcher* bereft of her major asset when it came to manoeuvrability. In his short and unusual naval career the dockyards in England had figured low to non-existent in Pearce's experience, though he had heard much through wardroom gossip regarding the practices and speculations of those who both ran and laboured in them, tales of theft and corruption so comprehensively murky that he was left to wonder how the nation ever got a fleet to sea.

Even with such outright chicanery they must be paragons compared to the Sicilians, who seemed to see physical labour as a crime against the person and payment for what amounted to scant effort as rightful reward. The whole process was rendered even more trying due to the slothful behaviour of the man supposed to represent King George in what was the second city of the Kingdom of Naples. His inaction – he rose late, lunched long and biliously in the article of wine, before taking to his bed – was surpassed only by the lack of his willingness to pay the necessary price demanded by the local chandlers.

'Signor di Stefano, I must have both a mainmast and bowsprit whatever they may cost while you must recognise that any monies you advance to repair a vessel of King George's Navy will be met and reimbursed in full.'

'But when, Capitane Pearce?' came the reply, in dramatically accented English, this before the consul produced from a desk drawer an untidy sheaf of papers. 'Here are copies of bills I have incurred on behalf of King George, some over two years in age and yet to be satisfied. My credit is not so good that I can run up the level of expense you demand, for in doing so I face ruin.'

Di Stefano was good at theatricality of the outré sort and he did the misery of impending penury well, both in his wretched facial expression and the way his plump body slumped, as if suddenly afflicted by a great weight, to the point where even his knees, giving way slightly, played a part. It was a hard case to argue against, it being no mystery that His Majesty's Government was notoriously tardy when it came to meeting the expenses incurred by its agents abroad.

'Sir William Hamilton may undertake to reimburse you.'

Now the mobile di Stefano countenance – puffy from imbibing and dark-skinned from the climate – morphed into an image fitting to the burial of a dear friend; one to which John Pearce had been witness to on the day he and di Stefano interred the ten men he had lost in the recent fight and one which took him back to that desperate battle that had occasioned the damage, which, if it could be counted as an ultimate success, was not much of one.

'I must question whether the income from Sir William's estates, which he uses to maintain his own position in Naples, are sufficient to bear as well the cost of my duties.'

John Pearce suspected there was something of a lie in that; Sir William Hamilton was the Ambassador to the Kingdom of Naples and had to be a direct link between Sicily and London, even to the cost of the consul's duties here on the island. If he thought it, he could not say for certain he was being misled. For all he knew, Sir William, a man he had met on only two brief occasions and a seeming gentleman, might be as sluggish at meeting his obligations as the clerks working under the Secretary of State for Foreign Affairs in London.

'Might I point out, sir,' Pearce said, in an emollient tone, 'that costs do not diminish with time. I am running out of ship's stores and with what I am obliged to buy locally I am low on the funds needed to keep my crew fed—'

'Added to your other obligations, Capitane,' di Stefano cut in with an oily tone, unable to keep a sly look off that mobile countenance, unwittingly preventing Pearce from mentioning another expense: the bill for those wounded and still accommodated in the *Lazaretto*, 'for you have too the burden of your *Bella Signora*.'

Was the reference to Emily Barclay's married state a dig? Pearce could not tell, but he was not going to let any comment on something that had already caused difficulties pass unchallenged and this time his reply was quite brusque.

'The lady of whom you speak meets her own obligations, sir!'

'Then you are doubly blessed,' the consul sniffed, adding a toss of the eyes that indicated his lack of belief that what was being imparted to him could possibly be the case.

'It would be better if we stick to the subject at hand, signor, which is how am I to get my ship into a fit state to sail back to join the fleet of which I am a part and on whose behalf you are tasked to lend every effort consistent with your office. I might add that I am required by my station to note every difficulty I experience in my log which will, in time, come to the attention of others, both the Fleet Commander and the Admiralty in London.'

Di Stefano now chose to play the part of a man deeply offended, pouting in an exaggerated fashion as if he were being threatened in a meaningful way, which Pearce, even if he had hinted at the possibility, thought absurd. What harm could a mere lieutenant in the King's Navy, and one that was less than loved in the places of power that mattered, do to him?

He huffed and puffed a bit, as well as rolling his eyes, and pulled out a large square handkerchief with which to wipe his brow. Pearce was tempted to tell the consul he had missed his true calling; given his comedic abilities he would have had them rolling in the aisles if he had chosen a career on the London stage.

'I must leave you, sir, to consider which is the lesser of two evils, the crew of my ship begging at your door for sustenance or you meeting the requirements for the necessary repairs.'

Seeing the consul now swell up to a proud puffball, Pearce added quickly and with faux sympathy, for he knew he had been too critical for his purpose; without di Stefano's aid he might be stuck in Palermo till eternity, a total falsehood designed to take the wind out of his sails.

'And please be aware I am not in ignorance of the problems this presents to a man of your abilities, commitment to exertion and your sterling reputation.'

Interview over, Pearce left the consul's house to exit into the heat of the day, which, approaching noon, seemed to be trapped by the narrow confines of the streets through which he walked. It was made ten times worse by the fact that any visit to di Stefano required that he do so in uniform. The heavy blue naval coat he wore was singularly unsuited to any climate other than that of the British Isles and points north, while the sword he wore – but would struggle to employ with a dud right arm – slapped against his thigh as he moved.

His dignity did not allow him to remove it so by the time he reached the *pensione* where he and Emily Barclay were staying, his shirt was like a dripping rag. Her room at least overlooked the harbour and the wide bay, while the open shutters admitted a bit of a breeze that, once he had his coat and shirt off, allowed him some relief. She, sitting and wearing a single loose garment, was busy sewing for a fully occupied group of tars, repairing clothing suffering from the wear and tear of the work in which they were presently engaged.

'You do not have the air, John, of someone who has succeeded in his undertaking.'

'Signor di Stefano has a tight grip on his purse and I doubt he will loosen it. We may have to seek to get to Naples if we are ever to fully refit the ship.'

'Naples?' she said, in a soft and uncertain tone, before putting aside her needle and thread to come and join him by the open window.

Pearce turned as she came closer, struck as he ever was by her beauty, and even more taken with the way the breeze from the sea was pressing the thin garment she wore against her skin, revealing every contour of her body: her breasts, the outline of her thighs and the slimness of her waist. If he had troubles aplenty, even if Emily Barclay was another man's wife, John Pearce was happy to have her as a burden.

'From there you have more chance of passage home, Emily, so very few British vessels call at Palermo by comparison.'

It was in one such rare vessel she had come here, brought by a captain who, ever grateful for the services John Pearce and the crew of HMS *Larcher* had rendered in saving his ship from almost certain seizure by pirates, had chosen to continue his voyage without her, refunding the monies Emily had paid for her passage.

The hand that he reached out was taken, Emily allowing herself to be pulled close and into his embrace, her head resting in the crook of his naked shoulder as he kissed the top of her fine auburn hair. Outside the window, what had been a noisy, bustling quayside was winding down as the locals headed to wherever they lived to escape the zenith of the broiling midday sun, to first eat and then sleep until late afternoon.

For two such young and ardent lovers slumber was not the first object of their taking to bed and such was their familiarity with each other that John Pearce's stiff, splinted arm was no impediment to what followed.

CHAPTER ONE

It was the itching of trapped skin that woke him and, careful not to disturb a still-sleeping companion, Pearce sought with his fingers to get between the splints to gain some relief. Yet if his arm troubled him, his thoughts were equally taxing for he knew that the notion of any more delay was to court a very poor alternative, namely he might be required to leave his ship here and take passage to Naples, where he could make his case to Sir William Hamilton for the funds he needed.

An even more troubling thought surfaced: that he would meet resistance there and would then be required to return to the fleet and explain his actions, hardly attractive given he had no right to be in Palermo at all; his mission had been to take despatches to Ambassador Hamilton and return with, in the navy's favourite phrase, 'all despatch'.

Those orders did not mention Emily Barclay who became, as she had been on the voyage out from England, an unofficial passenger, he harbouring the hope that he could find her accommodation, as well as protection with Sir William and Lady Hamilton. The ambassador's wife, being a lady of an uncertain pedigree and a chequered past, was someone, he was sure, who would be non-censorious regarding her present situation.

The first part of his orders he had fulfilled, delivering not only his despatches but also a private letter to Lady Hamilton from Commodore Horatio Nelson, the latter carried out with a degree of misplaced apprehension – the ambassador was privy to the regard in which his beautiful wife was held and not only by that particular officer. Having dined and spent the night at the Palazzo Sessa and with arrangements made for Emily to stay behind, he set off from Sir William's home intent on fetching her ashore, only to find she had fled his ship and taken passage in a merchant vessel bound for England.

As he set off in pursuit and, angry as he was, Pearce could comprehend her motives: to be a married woman at large in Italy with an acknowledged lover was to court much condemnation and even downright hostility, as had been proved by a brief stay in Leghorn, the base from which the Mediterranean Fleet drew its stores. Emily's husband was a serving post captain, known personally to a number of the officers come to the port to re-victual and by reputation to almost everyone else, and that rendered her innate discomfort doubly difficult to bear.

That many did not love Ralph Barclay, he being a man of little humour and a lot of barely disguised resentments, made little difference; the collective of the navy would, Emily surmised, feel the implied insult of his cuckoldry, making it impossible for her to remain in Leghorn and that was before such problems had been confounded by John Pearce's own difficulties.

Cruel coincidence had seen an old problem resurface, one which could only be laid to rest by a duel, one in which, in his darker moments, he wondered if what he had done to win the contest could be counted as honourable. Certainly the military officers who had supported his opponent did not think so, which had seen Emily in receipt of vocally expressed insults that went beyond anything that could be considered tolerable. It had also left her lover troubled by his inability to do anything about it. Those same officers, when challenged for their behaviour, had refused to give him satisfaction.

Staring out at the sparkling Mediterranean, the jumbled thoughts induced a complex set of feelings. How had he come to be here in Palermo, indeed how had he come to be entitled to the blue coat he owned and the command he enjoyed? Ralph Barclay was the prime cause and there was some lifting of the gloom at the thought, indeed the beginnings of a quiet smile, that such a dark-hearted bastard as he might, in moments of like introspection, damn himself for his own actions.

It took little to lift Pearce's spirit and the sweet, melodious singing of a young girl, passing underneath his window, was enough to shift his mood to a happier plane; too many times in his life, when matters had looked desperate, the ultimate upshot had been of benefit. For all the turmoil of his being a one-time pressed seaman, how could he complain of how his life had turned out? By the personal order of King George, he was Lieutenant John Pearce and he had enjoyed in that role a degree of independence denied to most naval officers, while still sleeping in the bed behind him was a woman he would never have met had her husband not sought to press hands for his undermanned frigate.

Inevitably his mind returned to the main difficulty and the consideration of a possible solution: surely to get HMS *Larcher* to Naples was not impossible, the distance being, even in far from perfect weather, not much more than two days' sailing on a fully functioning vessel. Right now he was looking out at a benign sea state and a wind that, if it could be felt on his skin, carried no great force.

Could his master rig enough sail to undertake the journey? *Larcher* would take longer but that was not a problem if the weather held. Naples had a proper dockyard well supplied with masts and timber, was a strong ally with Britain in its fight against the French Revolution, so would surely advance him any aid he needed.

The more Pearce thought on it the more attractive the idea became, yet it was not without risk: the climate in this part of the world could be fickle, with winds that could spring up in the turn of a glass to change a benevolent sunlit day into a nightmare of gales and raging seas. The route was also a potential hunting ground for pirates and it was in fighting a pair of Barbary brigantines, in company with the merchantman on which Emily had taken passage, which had brought on his present dilemma.

They too had suffered in the encounter and would no doubt, like him, be seeking to repair the damage. Any place a Mussulman could do so had to be well away from the shores of Catholic Sicily, so he had nothing to fear from them, though there could of course be others, even French Privateers. Risk and reward lay at the very core of the life of any man in command of a vessel of war and, small as she was, HMS *Larcher* was that. John Pearce had the choice to leave his ship and crew to rot in Palermo or take a chance that good fortune would favour his attempt to get her away.

His daily duty took him to HMS *Larcher* twice; he cheerfully ignored the Standing Order that a captain must sleep aboard his ship. Firstly, to the cock's crow to ensure all was shipshape and hear a report on what work would be undertaken that day, then again in the evening to see delivered those fresh foodstuffs he had bought in the market. For, on such a small vessel, Pearce was not only Master and Commander but his own purser, with all the problems and paperwork such a position entailed. Accounts which had to be, like his own captain's log, filled in by Emily if they were to be legible.

It was no good sitting here by this open window, enjoying the cooling breeze on his skin and waiting till the appointed hour. He needed to get back aboard the ship to come to an informed decision, so quietly Pearce donned a fresh shirt and his breeches then, carrying his shoes and his hat, he tiptoed out of the room.

There was no more activity aboard HMS *Larcher* than on the rest of the quay, a place so deserted Pearce could hear the crack of his own heels on the cobblestones. If he was not hot as he had been earlier in his broadcloth coat, it was still a damp-shirted individual who came aboard to no ceremony whatsoever; there was no whistling pipes or eager-to-oblige faces as there would have been once the heat went out of the sun.

The lack of respect to his rank he cared for not a jot, what upset him was that he could get onto the deck and do as he wished without anyone noticing; in short it could be pilfered at will in a country where the light-fingered locals were particularly adept at thievery.

'Where in the name of Lucifer is everyone!'

A young hand who went by the nickname Todger, in response to that shout, sprung up from what amounted to the only shade available, a bolt of canvas slung over two of the ship's cannon, where prior to this somnolence he had been in the process of cutting and stitching to turn it into a sail.

'Weren't asleep, your honour,' Todger barked, knuckling his forehead, his young face deeply troubled.

Pearce knew it to be a lie and the necessary rebuke was just about to be delivered when he recalled that he too had recently been abed and asleep. Todger, unlucky to be left on watch, was a man to whom he owed a slight obligation, a fellow who had been the first to feel his wrath on this commission. The offence in question had to do with the presence of Emily Barclay on a ship too small to properly accommodate her needs.

Todger had regaled his mates with a scabrous tale about the certain ability of a Portsmouth trollop called Black Cath to perform a less than salubrious act, which involved a certain bodily function added to the distance it could be projected. This was overheard by Emily, indeed on such a small deck it could be heard by everyone, and clearly Todger had forgotten there was a lady present within earshot.

Pearce had reacted badly on her behalf only to be reminded by the person who ought to be offended that she had no right to be aboard in the first place and then she had insisted he withdraw the punishment he had imposed. The memory of the incident and his own reaction still left his commander troubled and because of that he decided Todger was due some leeway.

'Then you should have challenged me when I came up the gangplank.'

'Didn't see the need, Capt'n,' the youngster replied, with palpable relief, 'you bein' who you is.'

Not for the first time since his elevation, John Pearce was left thinking command was not easy; maybe it was for a tyrant like Ralph Barclay but not for him. He wanted an efficient ship as much as the next man but he could not abide the thought of an unhappy one, which had been the case on Barclay's frigate. Mind, half the crew on *Brilliant* had been pressed men and disgruntled with it; *Larcher* was different, being manned by volunteers.

There was balance to be struck here; Pearce did not want Todger crowing about getting away with being asleep or the way he had managed to lie his way out of trouble. For the offence of which he was guilty, dereliction of duty, a flogging, according to the Articles of War by which naval life was governed, was the appropriate punishment. It was also one John Pearce knew he lacked the will to impose. On the last occasion he had stopped Todger's grog.

'Then damn you, Todger, you better learn to use a bosun's pipe and some way to greet an officer coming aboard that meets the bill.'

The glance over his shoulder told Pearce that the rest of the men had come up from below, roused out by his yelling, and he turned to face them. At the same time Dorling, the ship's master, came striding up the gangplank, looking sheepish and slightly flushed, which had Pearce glancing towards the nearby buildings and wondering within which particular one he had been enjoying himself, given it must have been close enough to hear his angry demand.

Had Dorling been bedding a local doxie or had he formed a

more permanent attachment in the preceding three weeks? Not difficult when tied up at the quayside and the man in charge rarely aboard. Again Pearce felt a stab of inadequacy; he was in command so he should know. It was irritation at his own lack of knowledge that had him speak more harshly and with more confidence than was merited, while also singularly failing to outline what had driven him to the conclusion he proposed.

'Mr Dorling, it is my opinion we have rested here too long and that we have reached a point of diminishing returns. The natives are playing ducks and drakes with us and will, I suspect, happily do so while we decay. It is my notion that we should have those repairs we still require carried out in Naples.'

Matthew Dorling was a young man, as befitted his position in such a small vessel, but he was also competent and would, Pearce was sure, rise one day to become master of a ship of the line. He was also the fellow who had saved his captain from more than one folly in the time they had spent together, having been at sea since he was a nipper, and was thus the vastly more experienced seaman even before he studied to attain his present position. Pearce should have been asking his opinion not making his statement sound like a decision already arrived at.

'She will sail like a tub. Anything in the nature of a blow and we'll be clinging to what's left as wreckage.'

The doubt in the master's voice was as obvious as the gentle murmur that came from a crew who could overhear every word. With his slung arm itching like the devil, his shirt soaked with sweat and his face red from the sheer heat of the day, John Pearce, who could now envisage no alternative, was not in the mood to have his aims thwarted by excessive caution.

'The hull is sound?' That got a nod. 'Can we rig a suit of canvas to give us enough to steer by?'

'With respect, Captain,' Dorling responded, in a measured tone and with a direct look, 'it is not a course I would adopt.'

'Yet is it not one we are obliged to, Mr Dorling?'

'This is a judgement that falls to you.'

In the silence that followed, brief as it was, there was enough time to reflect on that reply, which stood in sharp contrast when set against the attitude Dorling had displayed in the past. Since taking over command, Pearce had enjoyed a relationship not only with the master but also the rest of the crew which was as close to friendly as such an association could be – based on the fact that he made no attempt to hide his lack of deep knowledge that went with a lifetime of naval service.

Initially he had been given HMS *Larcher* as a temporary command, the fellow he had replaced being too ill to carry out his duties, while he was required to undertake a mission to the Vendée on behalf of Henry Dundas, presently Minister for War and William Pitt's right-hand man. From what he could read and deduce, his predecessor had been a miserly sod that often, in the added role of ship's purser, cheated his crew of pennies when supplying their needs as well as being an officer, though not a flogger, only too willing to punish for minor infractions. Pearce surmised that he must have come as something of a relief, for which he had been rewarded.

He had relied on them and they had not let him down, having sailed into danger more than once before the recent battle. Pearce had, since their first voyage together and the fading of the natural caution extended to a stranger, felt the crew to be fully with him.

It was not like that now and such was apparent in the faces of the men behind Dorling.

Even more to the point was the most pertinent fact: the master, having proffered his opinion, wanted no part in deciding how they should proceed. Would Dorling note in his log that it was Pearce who had advanced the notion of sailing to Naples, so that if matters went awry he would not share any opprobrium? He might even write in plain words his objections to such a plan.

It was then, in what had become a brief locking of eyes, that John Pearce was assailed by the feeling that he had forfeited something very important since coming to Palermo and that led him to wonder at how it had come about. He had, of course, been groggy himself by the time they tied up at the quay, not only nursing his arm but a sore head, having been knocked out before the battle was finished.

It had been several days before he became fully aware of the damage HMS *Larcher* had suffered, which was extensive and so were the casualties; she had only made harbour by being lashed to the *Sandown Castle*, the merchant vessel they had come across, the very ship carrying Emily Barclay, and the one threatened by those Barbary brigantines.

Right at this moment he felt he was being challenged; leaving him to wonder later if it was a stubbornness to which he knew himself to be prone that had him issue the orders necessary to get the armed cutter ready to set sail, these delivered to a man who was the only person on board with the skill to make it so.

Dorling kept his face expressionless as he said. 'Aye, aye, sir.'

'Meanwhile,' Pearce continued, in a confident voice loud enough to carry to all, 'I will visit those still wounded and make sure they are fit enough to be accommodated back on board. It would be unfair that they should be left here.'

As something designed to encourage it fell visibly flat; there were no smiles or nods of agreement, which had him look to the one face that, due to the height of the owner, stood out clearly and one in which he might be able to read a positive reaction. Michael O'Hagan towered over all those around him and in girth was as wide as any pair combined; he was also a man John Pearce held to be a friend.

On his face, in some contrast to the rest, was a look that could only be described as quizzically amused. A swift look to either side of the Irishman picked out Charlie Taverner and Rufus Dommet, two others who had been pressed by Ralph Barclay at the same time as he and O'Hagan, and if not as close to him as Michael, still fellows he felt he could rely on. Asked to describe their expression Pearce would have plumped for embarrassed.

'O'Hagan, I wish you to accompany me.'

'Capt'n,' came the reply, with Pearce wondering if the rest would smoke his motives. He then added, in a deliberately cool tone. 'Meanwhile, Mr Dorling, I need some indication of how long you feel you will need to get the ship ready for sea?'

'Given there's not much we can rig, we should be able, wind permitting, to cast off tomorrow morning if you are sure that is what you want, sir.'

The way that 'sir' was delivered smacked of dissent, which rankled. 'Then it is best you start work now.'

Walking down the gangplank and back along the quay, even with the bulk of Michael O'Hagan at his rear, Pearce was sure he could physically feel the glares emanating from the deck; that last order had been delivered in a tone never before used. He was obliged to wait until he was sure he was out of earshot before he spoke and even then it was an over the shoulder hiss.

'What in the name of creation is going on, Michael?'

'Sure, John-boy, asking me won't get you far.' Pearce had turned into a shaded alleyway that cut him off from sight of *Larcher* so he was able to stop and face O'Hagan. 'The boyos know we are close and go back a way together, same goes for Charlie and Rufus, so they don't talk open when we are hard by.'

'Talk about what, for all love?'

'That we might be accursed.'

'And how long has that been going on?'

'It's been strong since we tied up here, or it happened after the burials.'

'Michael, you are nobody's fool.'

O'Hagan paused, as if he was reluctant to speak, which was in itself unusual. In the time they had known each other, which included many an up and down for both, they had formed a bond that transcended mere friendship. Michael was rated as his servant, a task for which he was both physically and temperamentally unsuited. It was a position fitting for them both, given Pearce disliked the idea of one in the first place while Michael, though observing in public all the proper respect, was adept at making any point he thought needed airing.

'Ten men dead, John-boy, and more wounded, in a fight that many think you brought on for your own reasons . . .'

In truth Pearce did not need Michael to spell out what was the cause; he had deep down sensed the reason that it was so while talking to Dorling, even if he had been reluctant to let it surface.

Uncomfortable with the look on O'Hagan's face he walked on, in his mind once more ranging over the event that had brought on such deaths. If he had not set off after the woman he loved, HMS *Larcher* would not have come anywhere near those Barbary pirates, there would have been no fight, no damage to ship and, most important, no casualties.

The burials had been a sombre affair – how could they be anything else – ten of his own men and another pair from *Sandown Castle*; a priest there to say the correct words over a trio of papists, while he provided the necessary words over the others. If Michael was right he had been so wrapped up in his own thoughts and his duties to notice anything amiss, which was to his mind reprehensible.

'If I was in the area for Emily, Michael, I was still obliged to intervene once I saw *Sandown Castle* under threat from those pirates. A British merchant vessel in trouble would expect aid.'

'That's not how some see it.'

'Not all?'

'It don't take all, John-boy, just one or two jigging signs to set minds a' fretting.'

There was a nagging question in that and one John Pearce had avoided asking himself. The odds had been against *Larcher* from the very first sight of the enemy, they being better armed and faster sailing vessels than the armed cutter. Added to that the navy was quite clear about what a captain's options were in a situation where the odds were so clearly stacked against him. He could accept or decline battle and the Admiralty would back such a decision if he chose the latter, given they hated to lose ships, especially by officers in search of glory.

The truth was plain to him: he could not have stood back and let the merchantman take care of itself in a battle it could not win and that had nothing to do with Emily Barclay. He would have intervened anyway and as to losing respect with his crew, how much of that might he have forfeited for refusing to protect their fellow countrymen? As he strode along, Pearce could feel himself getting angry, given he was being damned both ways.

'They are a tight bunch on *Larcher*, closer than most.'

'Which, Michael, was an advantage.'

'You should wheedle out the ones stirring matters up.'

'How?'

'Best ask Charlie that, John-boy, when it comes to eavesdropping there's none better.'

That got a grunt as well as creating an unspoken question: Pearce had a feeling Michael was holding something back. As for Charlie Taverner, he was London-born, a one-time sharp who had worked the Strand as well as Covent Garden and, according to his own telling, a master of his craft, able to dun the wise out of their purse as well as the innocent. Pearce had good reason to doubt the truth of that; had he not first met Charlie in a place where he was hiding from the law?

'How many would we be talking about?'

'At a guess, half a dozen, but you will have seen more are affected.'

'Say he names the culprits, Michael, what then?'

'You'd have to punish them, and hard.'

Pearce stopped once more, to look up at the Irishman. 'I cannot do that, Michael. When we sail we do so as one. If I have lost something I need to regain then it must be done at sea.'

'And will being at sea include your good lady?'

'I cannot leave her behind.'

'Sure, I'm bound to enquire if that is "can't" or "won't"?'

'Both,' Pearce snapped, 'and maybe when we get to Naples the crew of *Larcher* will be shot of the both of us.'

O'Hagan laid a gentle hand on his friend's shoulder. 'I never thought you would go without her.'

'Do the crew resent her as much as they now seem to resent me?'

Michael looked away as he responded to that, once more giving an impression of being evasive. 'She's not a snot-nosed blue coat like you are.'

'Thank you for that,' Pearce replied gloomily, as they entered the *Lazaretto*, their noses twitching at the strong smell of the vinegar used to keep the place clean. 'Spoken like a true friend!'

Michael's laughter at the discomfort he had created echoed off the bare walls; Pearce knew that joshing him was a game the Irishman enjoyed, though his merriment seemed loudly excessive for such a minor jest, the noise of it getting many a stern look from the nuns they passed. When they came to the room where the last four injured men were still accommodated, Michael suppressed his mirth so they would not witness it. He was punctilious when it came to never embarrassing, either in the presence of superiors or fellow tars, the man he was engaged to serve.

'Gentlemen, do not stand,' Pearce commanded as each rose at the sight of him, 'you will be going back to the ship today, but be assured you will be accommodated in as much comfort as you enjoy here.'

Which was bending the truth somewhat; the mere motion

of a ship could, he thought, in at least one case cause a relapse, for the fellow was recovering from a wound to the chest that was manifested in wheezing breaths. Had he been allowed to stand he would have struggled to do so, but the other three were ambulant and should be fine, albeit one required the use of a stick.

'Thank the Lord fer that, your honour,' said one who had his arm, like that of his commander, in a sling, 'the vittels here is not fit for any decent man.'

There was a temptation to reply with a rebuke but there was little point; the food, since they had come to Palermo, had been fresh and of good quality, as well as abundant, especially in the article of lemons, fish and corn. But it was typical of British tar to deride anything foreign, nourishment being the most particular followed by the need to drink wine instead of small beer. Nothing but beef and pork long in the barrel, as well as peas and duff, would fit their needs.

'I must go and see the Mother Superior and settle any outstanding expenses, but that done Michael here will escort you back to the quay.'

Once Pearce had left, another of the wounded, leaning on his stick, he looked at O'Hagan, clearly bent on asking a question, his voice low as it was posed. 'Does he know yet it were you that clouted him?'

'No, he does not,' Michael growled; he had knocked John Pearce out on the deck of *Sandown Castle* to stop him from trying to keep fighting with his sword arm broken, which could have seen him cut down and probably killed. 'And you'd best not be overheard talking of it, or you'll feel the same fist.'

'It were a nice punch, mate.'

'Never,' came the scoffed reply as a ham-like and much-scarred set of knuckles were raised. 'Sure, it were only half of one.'

'I heard one or two of our shipmates who came to call would pay well for a repeat.'

'Best grease that stick of yours afore you ever say that again, mate,' Michael hissed, 'for it will be disappearing up your arse if you do.'

CHAPTER TWO

The ease with which Emily acquiesced in the decision came as a relief; Pearce had been expecting innumerable objections but she packed her chest with seeming calm. This left him to wonder how much of her attitude had been brought on by the refusal of Captain Fleming, with whom she had come to Palermo, to take her any further, he having found out that she was a married woman as well as her connection to John Pearce.

In booking her passage Emily had used her maiden name of Raynesford, but that had not held after Fleming got into conversation with the crew of *Larcher*. Pearce had not been present when the merchant captain informed her of his decision, but he had gone to visit a man he felt owed him much when it was imparted to him, this despite the fact that Fleming's attitude suited him.

He had no desire that Emily should return to England; it was the implied insult that irritated him. The man was full of apologies but not willing to budge: the owners of *Sandown Castle* were High Church Anglican and would not stand for any scandal being attached to their vessel or their trading house; to take Emily might place his own employment in jeopardy and he had a wife and children to support.

'I will however, Captain Pearce, since I have no passengers, take back home those of your men who will no longer be fit to serve, even should they fully recover from their wounds and at no cost to you or the navy.'

That had knocked Pearce off his high horse, for that too had been a worry; he had lost enough men already to be comfortable with any dying from their wounds. To be at sea in a tightly packed man o' war was no place for a man bearing the kind of injuries that would render them unfit to stay in the service. They would be invalided home certainly, but only when HMS *Larcher* was back with the fleet and probably in a returning and crowded transport. In a spacious merchantman they would not only enjoy more comfort, but they might also live to collect a small pension, their due from the Chatham Chest.

'He is a good man,' had been Emily's response to that offer when it was relayed to her.

This did much more to drive home her predicament than any form of continued complaint at Fleming's behaviour. In short, she understood his thinking only too well, given it had formed the reason for her flight. Tempted to once more reassure her that things would be better in Naples, Pearce held his tongue, well aware that by speaking of such things he risked her taking up a position from which, experience told him, she would be unlikely to withdraw.

He had felt it best to go out on an errand he needed to fulfil anyway; it would be his last visit to the Palermo market to buy fresh produce for the voyage, which included several live and noisy chickens.

To say that HMS *Larcher* looked odd in the early morning light was an understatement, with her stunned mainmast now rigged with a jury yard, made to look no better by a triced-up square sail which was a good third short of the height it should be. What Dorling had contrived for a makeshift bowsprit did nothing to enhance it either, two spars gammoned together, with stays and the rigging for a jib that even John Pearce knew would not take much in the way of strain.

Any attempt to tack or wear would have to be carried out with great care or the whole assemblage might come adrift, which had Pearce harbouring more than a tinge of doubt about attempting the voyage. Against that he hated the idea of withdrawal and why would he when the weather had held. It was still sunny and warm, even at this early hour and the breeze, though not strong off the land, seemed favourable to both get them out to sea and provide steerage once there.

The deck was alive with men working as he and Emily approached, a pair of locals at their heels with their chests as well as his logs and purser's accounts. Ropes were still being reeved through blocks so that the makeshift yard could be controlled. Scraps of canvas were being bent onto the jib lines, the deck itself tidied to the standard required within the service, all of which seemed to pause for a split second as they were sighted. If it was imperceptible to Emily it was to John Pearce very obvious and, given the lack of smiles, it did not bode well.

Word had been passed to the bosun, Mr Bird, for unlike the day before he was on hand to pipe his fully attired captain aboard with proper ceremony, all toil being suspended until that was complete and Pearce had raised his hat with his one good hand to what was laughingly called the quarterdeck. Given he was present, it was necessary for Pearce to order Dorling to 'carry on' before he could make for his tiny cabin. A space small to start with, it was even less so given the presence of Michael O'Hagan.

'Michael,' Emily said, with genuine warmth.

'Ma'am,' came a formal reply that sat oddly with his grin.

Her smile disappeared to be replaced by a slightly quizzical look as she spotted the way Michael and her man then exchanged a brief glance. Emily knew better than anyone how close these two were. It was not too much to say neither would be alive without the other for, in what was an acquaintance of not much more than two years, they had been through and survived a good number of risky adventures – and those were only the ones Emily knew about. They shared many secrets to which she was not privy.

'All's as shipshape as I can make it, John-boy, and I have had Bellam boil up some water for coffee, which will be with you in a trice.'

Michael said this in a very soft voice; with not much between him and the deck, a thin bulkhead, it was necessary to be discreet in his manner of address. Pearce nodded, but still Emily thought with a look that did not match his acceptance.

'Is there something troubling Michael?' Emily whispered as the Irishman departed.

'What made you think that?'

The reply came from a man now deliberately looking away so

as not to catch her eye, making himself busy by arranging his logs and account books on what passed for a desk, his own sea chest.

'John,' she said in a firm tone, albeit still softly, 'you know as well as I do that a woman can cause trouble on any vessel and have I not done so, with all innocence, in the past?'

Pearce tried to bluff, tried to pretend he was unsure at what was she was driving at for it could be many things and he mentioned more than one; the way she had reacted to her husband's treatment of him aboard HMS *Brilliant*, for, against all the rules of the service, Barclay too had taken her to sea with him. Then there was the incident on the voyage out from England with young Todger; she would have none of it, forcing him into a quiet confession.

'But my unpopularity has nothing to do with you, Emily, it is entirely down to my behaviour.'

'In pursuit of me?'

The conversation was halted by a knock at the cabin door, followed by Michael appearing with the aforementioned coffee. He proved to be as sensitive to a strained atmosphere as Emily, seeking to get the tray down and depart with haste.

'Michael.'

This time the 'Ma'am' was larded with caution.

'You will be aware that at all times John seeks to protect me from any unpleasantness.'

'Is that not right and proper?'

'It may be so in certain circumstances but not now. I require you, as a good friend, to tell me if I in any way have acted to upset the men who serve this vessel outside the mere fact of my presence. Will you promise me you will do that?'

O'Hagan looked first at Pearce then back at Emily in a space between them so confined as to leave little chance of artifice; they were so close the warmth of each breath could be felt on another's face.

'I have told her what you told me, Michael.'

'Then,' the Irishman replied, looking at Emily and speaking, for him, very formally, 'you should know that the regard in which I hold you has not suffered at all, Charlie and Rufus likewise.'

'I am pleased to hear it, but it does imply, Michael, that a problem exists with the rest of the crew.'

Yet another knock at the door stopped that exchange, too, as Dorling appeared to inform his captain that if they wanted to make the best of the tide and the shore breeze, it was time to cast off. This required that Pearce go on deck to issue the necessary orders and he stood, hands behind his back, as the cables were lifted from their quayside bollards and HMS *Larcher* was pulled clear, running an acute eye over everyone working on deck.

Should he order the sweeps to be employed, heavy toil in any circumstances, doubly so in a morning in which the heat was already palpable and getting stronger by the minute? The great oars would get them clear of the mole more quickly than their gimcrack sails, for the breeze was still slight but he was disinclined to issue the necessary orders; time was not of the essence.

'Mr Dorling, I leave it to you to decide what canvas we can safely employ, for this so-called tide will not get us clear and into open water in less than a turn of the glass.'

There was truth in that; the Mediterranean was not really tidal, the sea only rising and falling a matter of feet, and while it would carry the armed cutter out it would do so at no great pace. Dorling acknowledged the order and began to issue instructions of his own. Ropes were hauled as canvas began to appear, some of it new, most heavily patched, with Pearce wondering if the men doing the pulling were happy at least to be on their way. It was an indication of his status as captain that he could not ask.

As they sailed slowly out they passed the night fishermen, who, having landed their catch were now drying and checking their nets, tasks which they put aside to watch this very odd-looking vessel as it made its way towards the harbour entrance. Its boats were being towed behind, one containing the chickens Pearce had bought, who in their cackling seemed to mock the whole endeavour. There was some laughter at the sight, but more shaking of heads in wonderment and even one or two who crossed themselves, which was not a ringing endorsement of the enterprise.

Pearce looked aloft at the limp flags that identified HMS *Larcher* as a vessel of the King's Navy, serving under the command of a vice admiral of the Red Squadron, who happened to be that irascible old sod Sam Hood. He felt that the lack of any vitality in those pennants was akin to his own, for being on his way had brought back to his mind misgivings he had too conveniently buried.

Would he have to face Lord Hood on rejoining the fleet to explain his actions, or had the old man gone home to be replaced by the even less inspiring prospect of reporting to that slimy article and his second-in-command, Admiral Sir William Hotham? On previous occasions what was happening now, putting to sea, had induced a feeling of pleasure: now it was one of dejection.

'You have shaped a course, Mr Dorling?' Pearce asked in a loud voice, posing a question that had more to do with personal distraction than need. 'Once we are clear?'

'Sir, a few points off due north.'

'Well let us hope that we can easily hold it and that we will be in Naples in good time, to have the ship restored to its former state. It will be a pleasure to rejoin the fleet in what looks like a proper vessel.'

No smiles greeted that either; no nods of agreement as of old, so feeling useless Pearce nodded to no one in particular and went to partake of his rapidly cooling coffee.

It was not necessary to be on deck to be aware that the ship was struggling to make headway; every dip and rise of the sea was exaggerated, every fluke of a different wind as well as every little alteration in the run of the sea, currents that *Larcher* would have previously been untroubled by, affected her progress and made her yaw off course, sometimes to the point where sails had to be struck and reset. Added to that the level of creaking timber, an ever-present sound at sea, seemed to be ten times more audible and prevalent, as the temporary rig made known the strain it was enduring.

The day went by without incident, falling into night in which the most telling thing was the lack of gathering on the deck, which had been a previous commonplace in any benign climate. The hands would come up to take the clean air – to talk and joke, to sing and to dance – often to be joined by their captain and his lady after a supper of toasted cheese. Emily had a sweet, melodious voice to add to their masculine timbres and sang of the land and green pastures as opposed to the sea and the lives of the men who sailed it. Odd how what had worked to make her popular was now being used to damn her as a siren.

There was no singing now but quiet talk that was prone to an unwelcome interpretation from a pair who needed to get out of a stuffy cabin just as much as the crew wanted to vacate the stifling t'ween decks. Having on this occasion eaten a good dinner made of fresh produce, prepared by Bellam the cook and delivered to them by an unusually uncommunicative Michael O'Hagan, they stayed well aft when it came to taking some air.

HMS *Larcher* ploughed on throughout the night, making at best three knots but often two or even less, the hands roused out before first light with John Pearce on deck soon after, as was required by all naval captains, to ensure that no threat had crept upon them in the hours of darkness, as if they could under a carpet of bright stars. He was there again once the planking had been swabbed and dried to inspect their work, no great hardship in these waters, before the whole ship took breakfast and their captain washed and shaved.

Pearce was called when any other sail was sighted to establish what vessel it was and to be sure it presented no threat, a duty only he could undertake – given any subsequent orders fell to him. He was there to see the bells rung, the glass turned and especially when it came to the change of watch, ordering the decks to be wetted in the heat, given the pitch sealing the joints in the planking, the devil in naval parlance, was prone to melting. Likewise the boats stayed in the water to protect their seams.

Seven bells on the forenoon watch required that he be on desk with his sextant, in the company of the master, to shoot the noonday zenith by which they could establish their position in what was now nothing but an empty seascape. On each occasion, he sought also to discern any level of obvious dissatisfaction in each crew member, not he later had to admit, to much avail. The only smiles he got, and they were given with some discretion, came from the trio he knew as his fellow Pelicans.

He could not think on that tag without recalling how they had come to wear it and also, despite the circumstances in which it had been gained, the way it represented a rebellion against the kind of authority he now represented. How odd it was in this glaring sunshine and just past midday heat, to imagine himself once more in a smoky London tavern on a freezing winter night, to forget his present rank and station and recall that he had been a civilian on the run from the law.

The thought that, Michael O'Hagan apart, he had fallen amongst thieves in the Pelican Tavern induced a slight smile; Charlie Taverner the street-hunting sharp, Rufus the runway apprentice; the wiser head, old Abel Scrivens, dead now, running from a ruinous debt. The last of the original Pelicans had been quiet, unlucky Ben Walker, thought to have been lost overboard but last seen as an emaciated slave, beyond rescue, toiling on the waterfront at Tangiers and also probably dead by now.

All, again excepting Michael, had been on their uppers and each one avoiding a writ of some kind, none of the magnitude facing John Pearce. Where they had encountered each other had protected them, the Liberties of the Savoy, a stretch of the Thames riverside from which the bailiffs were banned due to ancient statute. He had hoped that it would protect him too but fate had decreed that the hand that he felt on his collar, as well as those of his fellow Pelicans, was not a King's Bench Sheriff but the clasp of a hard-bitten tar, one of the press gang employed by Captain Ralph Barclay.

Right at that moment he felt the loneliness of being in command; he would have loved to talk to those he considered his friends at any time, more especially now, so as to find out how to counter what was troubling the crew. It was all very well sharing his cabin with Emily but she was not someone with whom he could discuss such matters and that was not the only subject best avoided.

The whole area of her husband and their own relationship, if it was not out of bounds, was fraught with difficulty – so much so that Pearce had to consider what he was going to say before he said it, lest blurting out some unpleasant reminder of her predicament drove her towards a resolution he was determined to avoid. It was like walking barefoot on broken glass.

'Sail Ho!'

'Where away?' was the automatic reply and one that drew him from his melancholy reflections, to withdraw a telescope from the bulkhead rack by his side, freeing his arm from its sling at the same time, just as it seemed every man below, including those off watch, found a reason to be on deck.

'Dead astern, caught a flash of topsail.'

With some difficulty due to his injured arm, he adjusted the glass and laid it across his splints in the required southerly direction. This was not carried out in any great hurry, given he had no great expectation of getting sight of anything immediately; the man aloft could see things many miles further off than he.

'Two sail, your honour,' came as a near shriek.

That produced a knot in Pearce's gut, it being the same call that had come before his recent battle, one that he was just as quick to dismiss as mere fancy. But he did call aloft for early clarification;

non-fighting ships sailing in company were rare and when they did it was not in pairs but in convoys of dozens. Were they friendly or not? Time stood still with no more information forthcoming, which was not a cause for concern either; it often did at sea.

'Brigantines by their rig,' came the eventual reply, from a voice that seemed to find a higher pitch.

Every eye on deck was suddenly trained on him, Pearce was sure he could feel their concern and that had him say out loud just one word. 'Impossible.' How he longed to go aloft himself and make a judgement but he was one winged and that made it impractical so, more for prevarication than purpose, he ordered the raising of the private signal hoping that identifying his as a King's ship would get a like response from a friendly and similarly designated vessel.

Surely they could not be the same pair he had fought before! Dorling had been off deck when the first cry came but he was, like everyone else, there now, alternately looking through his own telescope mixed with worried glances aimed at his captain. What would happen was down to John Pearce who, as of this moment, was lacking in any idea of how to react. A gesture brought the master closer.

'An appreciation if you please, Mr Dorling,' he said quietly.

'We struggled to contest with Barbary afore.'

'I know that,' Pearce replied. 'Now I need to know if they are the same pair or even of the same ilk.'

This was imparted with scant patience; he did not need to be reminded that without the aid of Captain Fleming, who had put his own merchant vessel at great risk to aid him, they could not have survived the previous encounter. What was germane now was not what had gone before but what they presently faced. If these were the same two sea wolves, they each carried more weight of shot than *Larcher*, added to which they would likely sail with more speed and the ability to manoeuvre, even when damaged. As to numbers of men in close combat, given they were two and individually better manned, that spoke for itself.

Dorling had clearly decided on the worst case and that was reflected in the slightly desperate tone of his voice, and added to a look of downright scepticism that the man in command should think anything other than the worst.

'Who else would they be, Capt'n? A pair of brigantines and on our very course, minded to put right where they failed afore?' Then his voice took a slight note of panic. 'If we seek to fight, we will be taken this time.'

The temptation to tell him to pull himself together had to be avoided; it would serve no purpose and he needed to know what his options were. 'And if you are correct, can we run?'

'Too early to say.'

Pearce lifted his bandaged arm and responded with cold disdain. 'Which should tell you, Mr Dorling, that I need to know as soon as possible whether what you fear is truth or mere fancy.'

There was no need to add an instruction; Dorling knew he was the only one who could get aloft to see what they faced and judge the chance they might have of escape. He made for the shrouds and began to climb, an act observed and not happily so by the crew. Even Bellam, the one-legged cook was there now, a man who rarely came up at sea except to chuck out his swill, his eyes fixed over the stern, which irritated Pearce.

'Anyone not employed, get below until you are called to your duty.' The response was slow, even when Pearce added in as kindly a tone as he could manage. 'Please recall I have as much, if not more, to lose than you, now do as I have asked.'

The amount of murmuring that induced sounded, to his acute hearing, like a very active beehive and as it faded he was left with nothing but the disturbing facts. He had risked the lives of these men before and now, due to his insistence of departing Palermo, he might be doing so again and in much worse circumstances. The temptation to curse himself had to be put aside for it would do no good. It was a solution he required, not self-castigation.

'Am I allowed on deck, John?'

That had Pearce turn to face one of his major concerns: what to do if it looked as if they were about to be boarded, for he would never just strike his flag and let *Larcher* be taken. That meant Barbary and slavery for any man taken; for a woman what would happen to her did not bear thinking about.

'Best stay in my cabin for the moment.'

A swift nod saw her retreat, leaving Pearce to return to his thoughts; given there was nothing to report for what seemed an age, the sandglass needed to be turned and it ran again till half full, they went deep. Yet the silence from aloft continued, allowing him to begin to see that as a positive: those ships could not be gaining on them at any great pace, which had him register once again the lack of a strong breeze, further evidenced by the slack and near to drooping flags aloft. Dorling called finally and looking to where he was perched and seeing, even at a distance, his unsmiling face, Pearce knew the news was not good.

'If you have something to report, Mr Dorling, I would rather it was imparted with a degree of discretion.'

If the master's broad face had looked unsmiling aloft, it was positively doom-laden on deck and there was good reason that it was so. Astern of them, and they could not have avoided being likewise spotted and maybe even identified, were, he was sure, the very vessels that had inflicted the previous damage. He had stayed up there longer than necessary to be absolutely certain, worse than that they seemed to be, as far as Dorling could tell, in a state of good repair, with all their masts and a full top hamper of sails.

'Where in God's name could that have been refitted so quickly?' Pearce demanded, invoking in his case a rare reference to the Almighty.

'How many ports are there on the coast of Sicily?'

'Any number, but not open to the Saracens!'

That archaic description got a raised eyebrow, as if Dorling did not know that was how the folk of Sicily still referred to an ancient enemy. 'Money talks, Capt'n, even to a papist and how ever it were done, we are – like it or not – going to have to pay for it.'

CHAPTER THREE

John Pearce was disconcerted by the attitude of his master, whom he had always thought to have an optimistic streak, more so now than he had been in Palermo. British tars were, as a breed, a confident lot, often too much so for their own good, sure in their boastful way that they were worth ten times any Johnny foreigner when it came to a fight, be it on land or at sea. Against that he had never met a bunch of people more prone to superstition and he guessed it was that which was afflicting Dorling now, the feeling that somehow the fates had decided on retribution for some perceived sin and that it was imminent.

'I think,' he said softly, 'we are required to examine the charts, Mr Dorling, don't you?'

'Sir.'

'And a good pair of eyes aloft, I would suggest.'

The time it took the man to react and move to comply was annoying; some kind of torpor was now upon him making the reply both slow and low. Yet the need was obvious; over that gimcrack bowsprit lay Italy and a coastline full of ports, one to two large and well-defended, with fortresses and cannon to protect their harbours, which surely represented the only means by which they could escape. What was their position now and where lay the best chance of a safe berth?

They must establish the relative speed of the pursuit against their own so as to make some calculation of the odds of successfully evading capture based on the distance to shore, both factors Pearce felt he should not have any need to emphasise. Having told Dorling to join him in his cabin he went there to ask Emily if she could vacate it for the time being.

'Are we are in danger, John?' Getting in response a raised eyebrow she added, 'I heard the cries from the masthead.'

The natural instinct was to say no, to minimise any notion of risk, but that would not wash with Emily so it was with a bit of a forced smile that he replied, 'We may be in need of some providential assistance.'

'It must be serious if you are relying on divine intervention.'

'That is not what I meant,' he replied, for that would stray too close to religion, a subject on which they fundamentally disagreed, 'and please don't engage with me. Right now I have no time for theological dispute.'

The appearance of Dorling, with his rolled-up charts, killed any chance of that and giving him a smile, Emily eased past the young master. Pearce wondered if she had noticed what he had observed; the smile had not been returned which, if it was worrying, had to be put to one side as the appropriate charts were laid out. Dorling had fetched his logs as well as the slate bearing the latest information on course and speed.

They had to aid them a pair of chronometers, one set to Greenwich, the other to the local noon they had just established and if the instruments were far from new, they were, as far as Pearce could guess, accurate. Certainly the latter was so, having been regularly checked in Palermo harbour against the noonday gun. It took no great time in looking at maps, nor much use of the dividers, to form an obvious conclusion.

'What would we lose by changing our course to due east?' Pearce asked.

'What wind we have is sou' westerly.'

'So it would be better over our beam?'

'What there is of it.'

'But we might gain a fraction of speed?'

'As will those devils who have waited for us all this time.'

'Mr Dorling,' responded Pearce in an exasperated tone, 'we are not so much of a prize that two fellows who make their way in the world by thievery would take so much trouble. What happened, their being in the same patch of ocean as us, is mere coincidence.'

'You really think that?'

The tone was larded with both pessimism and a lack of the required respect. Just as depressing was the way the master kept his eyes on the chart, refusing to engage with his superior, as if Dorling was wondering at him not being able to discern the obvious truth. This encounter was fated to happen and what would follow could not be avoided. Pearce was having none of it.

'We will alter course and make the quickest landfall open to us south of Naples. As to a final destination, that will have to wait. And, Mr Dorling, I think it best that I have possession of the key to the spirit store.'

Dorling's head came up sharp enough then and there was at least a degree of hurt in his look. A wounded and otherwise occupied John Pearce had handed over to him the task of giving out the daily ration of grog, which Dorling had held on to given the captain was living ashore. It had been a mark of respect that it should be so and the man had carried out the duty properly. This task was not being withdrawn for any lack of faith in his honesty or ability, but for an absence of a different kind of trust. Worn on his waist, along with the keys to the cubicle that passed for his cabin, it was removed and handed over.

'Please ask my servant to attend on me at once.'

The charts were slowly, indeed deliberately, rolled up as though by the action Dorling was trying to communicate something. What Pearce saw was a man in a brooding mood and that had him speaking in a growling way that was at odds with the words.

'If you have something you wish to impart to me, I hope you know that however unpleasant it may be you are free to do so.'

A violent shake of the head was all Pearce got before the master departed. As the cabin door closed, Pearce turned to look at one of the other artefacts that cramped the interior space: the padlocked rack of muskets and pistols over which he had sole control – the thought that they might be needed a disturbing one. He was still lost in that when O'Hagan entered and, since he could not stay in place without being bent near double, sat down, to be subjected to a straight look from his friend and captain.

'Michael, I want to know what is going on right now, what the feeling is below decks, and no beating around. I have a very strong feeling you know something and you're not telling me.'

The response was not immediate and when it came was far from reassuring. 'Jesus, can you not guess, John-boy?'

'Is it Emily?'

'Who else?' O'Hagan replied, with a slow regretful shake of the head. 'I thought it was all shite and would die out once we got to sea.'

'Not now?' There was no need to mention the vessels closing in on them.

'There were a couple unhappy about having a woman aboard before we left Buckler's Hard, no, even afore that, given you fetched that mistress of yours from France.'

'One-time mistress,' Pearce replied sharply, for he could recall that he had been afforded scant chance to refuse.

Michael kept his voice low, to tell that there were those who had harboured the superstition that a woman aboard presaged bad luck from that very moment, doubly so when they set out on the subsequent voyage to the Med. But they had kept their thoughts close, nothing more than an occasional murmur, scoffed at in the main, seeing as how most of the crew thought they had struck good fortune.

Pearce was a better man to be in command than the fellow he had replaced, added to which, after that first mission to the Vendée and a skirmish off Portugal, he came across as lucky, another manifestation, albeit a reverse one, of their present superstitions. There was nothing to hang any worries on until the day they had set off in pursuit of Emily, with all the consequences in death and damage that entailed, which had given the doomsayers meat on which to gnaw and the rest of the crew a cause to first wonder and then be swayed.

'You staying off the ship didn't help either, bein' seen to be putting your pleasure afore your duty, which others were unhappy about. But it was the lads we lost and buried that gave the moaners the air to spread their talk of devilry, to say that it would never have happened without the curse of Mrs Barclay.'

'And you let this nonsense pass?'

'I told you they never sought to include me, John-boy, nor Charlie and Rufus, and even I can't fight them all. The doomsayers was free to say that as long as your lady and her siren ways was aboard *Larcher,* it was only a matter of time till Old Nick sought his due and one by one our shipmates began to fall in with it.'

'Siren ways?'

'She has a sweet voice, does she not?'

'Which I have seen much appreciated.'

'It was, John-boy, but not as we sit here.'

'And now they are a majority in this nonsense?'

'Hard to know who the doubters are, since they stay quiet.'

'Do you believe in devilry, Michael?'

That had the Irishman crossing himself hurriedly. 'Jesus, you know I do.'

'So I am bound to ask if you believe in this.'

'As I am bound to be offended that you should.'

Pearce dropped his head onto pointed fingers so he could think; Michael was aware that his friend required silence, the time to make sense of what he had been told, not that he was unable to guess as to his thoughts. If there was the suspicion aboard that Emily was a curse then he, her lover, had not only given it credence but also, by his own behaviour, allowed it to fester.

If he had spent more time aboard he might have sensed things and perhaps would have been able to nip in the bud the Jonahs spreading foul gossip. But he had not and was now paying the price. The silence was held as both listened to the orders being issued, as well as the running of feet as the change of course was carried out.

'It's not the devil chasing us, Michael,' Pearce said finally, 'they are, at worst, Barbary pirates.'

'Right at this moment there's few on this barky who would be willing to lay a finger on the difference. The doomsayers were making ground afore, made even more on your resolve to sail when we was in no fit state to cast off, predicting tempests and the like with all of us drowning.'

'While the sight of those sails . . .' Pearce shrugged; it was not necessary to elaborate. 'Who can I trust?'

'The warrants, maybe, seeing them as a breed have a speck more sense than most.'

'Maybe?'

'Can't say better than that an' it would do you no good if I did.'

'Dorling is one and I am not sure I would place much faith in him right now. Charlie and Rufus?'

That got a sharp nod from Michael and a grim smile, Pearce not even bothering to enquire further; the Pelicans would stay together as they had in the past. 'Mind, it would help to get Mrs Barclay out of plain sight, she's on deck being something of a red rag right now.'

'Make it so,' Pearce said, grabbing his hat and standing up so abruptly that Michael winced, fearing for his crown on the low beams. But he had been aboard a long time now, had cracked his head too many times and so stopped before his hair made contact. 'Be so good as to fetch her, Michael, while I go below.'

'Is that a good notion?'

The smile was a grim one. 'If there is a devil, then he is best faced.'

Emily was by the stern again, hands resting on the taffrail, looking aft, able to see when they rose on the swell the tip of the sails of ships that might be their nemesis, they too having changed course. He declined to call to her, leaving Michael to do as he had requested, making straight for the companionway that led below, aware that the act came as a surprise to the few men on deck.

As usual the smell of packed humanity and bilge, so very obvious when set against the clean tang of the sea, made his nostrils twitch but that was not the only thing that made an impression on him; what rose up was an almost palpable feeling of resentment made even more manifest as he met the looks of men who seemed to think his presence an intrusion. True, he rarely went below, except on Sundays for his weekly inspection after he had read the Articles of War, which under his command was what the men got in place of a biblical sermon, their captain being neither religious nor a hypocrite.

It took a real effort to meet every eye with a cold stare, especially bent over near double, for his height was against him, even harder to try to discern the varying levels of anything that could range from mistrust to downright loathing. How had he let matters come to this? The feeling he had was one of utter inadequacy. To traverse from the companionway to the manger was no great distance, the whole lower deck only a few paces more, and it being crowded meant actual physical contact was unavoidable.

Normally the crew made every effort to get out of his way; not now, so that if he was never actually jostled, then he was made aware that his passage was lacking in the kind of respect he had come to expect and was in truth, even if he felt something of a fraud in receipt of it, his due. Did they see his eye take in the spirit store, to make sure the padlock was in place and secure?

Pearce was thinking what to do about that, for it was a commonplace tale that faced with certain doom, especially drowning, sailors wanted to meet that fate utterly insensible from drink.

The safest way to secure against that was to put an armed man in front of the padlock, yet he was conscious of how that would look. It might so infuriate the men that it would produce the very reaction he was desperate to avoid and then he would be dealing with men too drunk to reason with. Three sheets to the wind, who knew what they would do and it was not beyond the bounds of his imagination to think of them casting Emily over the side and him with her.

It was a real relief to get back on deck and to walk to the now vacant stern, his gaze centred on the towed boats. Could he put Emily in the cutter with a stepped mast and sail to get her away? Pearce thought not, for that would require the crew to haul the boat alongside and empty it, which would act as a signal of both his intentions and their fate; he would not be seeking to save his lady if he expected the ship to survive.

Added to which she would need men to sail it, who would

they be and what would the remainder say to a couple of their shipmates being given a chance of life? Added to that, the only people he could trust her with were his Pelicans and the sight of Michael, Charlie and Rufus making for the cutter would cause a full-scale mutiny and a fully justifiable one at that.

He only had to lift his eyes to now see the topsails of the pursuit, but that brought some reassurance, for they were not gaining, as he feared they might. The Mediterranean day was short so they would have no chance of catching HMS *Larcher* before nightfall, and that might give him a chance to humbug them and at least gain some extra advantage. Looking at the sky, it was still clear and showing no signs of clouding over, which he would need if he were to change course unobserved. The first thing Pearce must do is try and put a different interpretation of matters to the crew, which had him spin round and yell.

'Mr Bird on deck.'

Birdy, as he was known, was a compact, muscular and quick-witted fellow and he arrived with proper alacrity added to which he at least, if he shared the opinion of his shipmates, had the wits to keep it hidden. There was nothing in those bright questioning eyes to hint at despair or even concern.

'We will need to lighten the ship and the first thing we can do is start with the water barrels.' Again Pearce was faced with that split-second pause, which meant the man was considering the wisdom of compliance, set against what should have been automatic. 'So get the pumps rigged to get it out of the bilge.'

'You reckon we can get clear, your honour?'

Lie, say 'of course', was the first thought that came to mind, only to be dismissed. Instead Pearce said, 'All I know, Mr Bird, is that we will not do so carrying a full load of water. Ensure we are left with enough for two or three days and get rid of the rest.'

'Cannon weigh more?'

'In time, perhaps,' Pearce sighed, 'but before we come to that I must be sure we will not need them.'

'We'll fight?'

The grin that accompanied the question cheered Pearce mightily. 'Of course, we'll fight and we will take as many of those bastards to perdition as we did the last time. Now, send me the carpenter and the gunner so we can establish what they can do without.'

Pearce spoke with the Kempshall twins while the pumps were being rigged – two fellows so dissimilar it was more like they had no relation to each other at all; Sam having straw-coloured hair while his brother had black. Nor were their features in any way similar. In the past they had been models of efficiency, which they were far from now, being sullen instead, showing a good indication of where they stood on the ladder of superstition.

'Any spare timber I want it on deck ready to be slung over the side.'

'Don't amount to much in weight,' replied Brad.

'No, but it floats, which sends a signal to those sods chasing us that we intend to outrun them.' Next he turned to Sam the gunner. 'We need to keep the powder, but it would aid us to ditch any more cannonballs and chain shot than we will need for a short, sharp encounter. If they do come upon us they will seek to board quickly so we are not looking at any great number of salvoes.'

He stared into less than happy faces as he explained about

keeping the ship's cannon. 'But they will go too if it comes to a race for shore. Report back to me when you have carried out my orders.'

The pumps were working now, sending a stream of water – it had only been in the barrels a day – into the blue sea, the sound competing against the groaning of the ship, for Pearce had insisted that as much sail as *Larcher* could carry be raised, not that it was extensive or impressive. Other sails were being brought up from below, heavy canvas that also was to be thrown over the side to lighten the ship when the decision was made, cables too. The log was being cast continuously by the man in the chains, who was able to say that they were at least making as much speed as previously, while the lack of breeze was removing from those brigantines the natural advantage they normally enjoyed.

Back in the cabin Pearce faced Emily, knowing he had a difficult task to perform, as first he took from his sea chest the key to the rack that held the guns. 'I need you, my dear, to help me load a pair of pistols, which I cannot do one-handed.'

'Can you fire with any accuracy using your left hand?' Emily asked.

'I doubt with what I have in mind accuracy will be a problem.'

'Do you have it in mind that I should be given one?'

'Yes.'

There was no mistaking her look and she knew exactly what he was driving at when she responded. 'Then know that whatever comes I will not use it. Life, any life is better than death and, besides, it is a mortal sin.'

'You think it is to protect you against Barbary pirates, to give you that choice?'

'Who else?'

'It saddens me to say, my dear, that you may need to protect yourself from the members of the crew.' He handed over the key, ignoring the shock on her face. 'Now please do as I ask.'

CHAPTER FOUR

There are occasions at sea when the entity of time loses all meaning, the only passing indicators being the ship's bells and the creeping movement of the sun, arcing from its zenith and dropping towards the western horizon. The enemy topsails were occasionally visible from the deck now, as both *Larcher* and the pursuit rose simultaneously on the swell, while to the east, where safety lay along latitude thirty-nine degrees, there was nothing.

Dorling was on deck too, but staying away from the quarterdeck, issuing his instructions to move and adjust their top hamper in the hope of getting an ounce more speed out of the armed cutter, listening intently, as did everyone, as the cast of the log revealed if he had been successful. It was rare that his efforts made much difference in such light airs and that impacted on everyone aboard, though Pearce took some reassurance from the fact he was trying.

The tension seemed to grow as the heat of the day began to diminish, with Pearce acutely attuned to every whispered exchange that was within his hearing and vision, at the same time well aware that there were many more taking place out of it. So many of the crew would not look at him, or if they did it was when they were sure his attention was elsewhere, occasioning that sharp snap of the head if he suddenly caught their eye.

It took him back to the feelings he had harboured as a boy, when passing round the hat to collect money from those listening to his father, Adam, as he lectured his audience on the way the world was constructed to hammer the poor and favour the rich. There had always been lads his own age eager to steal his collection and that added to the inherent danger of being in the company of his radical father, who was not one to flatter those who came to hear him.

Indeed he made it plain to all that if the world in which they eked out their existence was corrupt, if their lives were constrained by laws that did them down, edicts that kept in place a useless and blood-sucking monarchy and an aristocracy that supported them, they only had themselves to blame. There had been more than one occasion when his strictures had been so ill received that they had been obliged to make a hurried exit from whichever town in which Adam was hectoring.

'Can I come on deck, John? I cannot stand being so confined.'

'Do so, Emily,' he replied.

The sight of her could not make matters worse, added to the fact that with the crew at their dinner, the deck itself was near deserted and soon theirs would be brought up from below. He could observe the reason she wished to be outside as she approached, no great distance, but a few steps from door to binnacle. Her brow and upper lip were both damp, as was her dress.

'I would dare say your accommodation is ever comfortable, John, but the heat seems to get trapped within it as the day progresses.'

'Don't ask me to conjure up a cooling breeze, my dear, for it is the lack of one that is keeping us from perdition.'

'Would it aid matters if I were to apologise?'

'For what?'

'My presence.'

'You are here because I want you to be here,' came the reply, in a tone that brooked no disagreement.

Realising his response had caused some hurt, he decided a change of subject would help and so he referred to those thoughts on which he had been ruminating before her interruption. Emily could not help but be drawn into talking about a life so very different to her own provincial upbringing, where a journey of ten miles from her native Frome was a major undertaking.

In contrast the Pearces, *père et fils*, had traversed it seemed the whole kingdom. Her man could talk of places and people she had never even dreamt of; his own fellow Scots and the Welsh, the folk of the northern regions who if they had spoken to Emily would not have been comprehended, so different was their argot and accent. Adam Pearce had set out to change the world in which he lived, taking his motherless son with him.

'Only to end up in gaol for our efforts, or scuttling away to Paris from a writ for seditious libel and the possibility of Tyburn.'

'It will do no good to brood on such matters now,' Emily replied.

She had heard many times of the way the government had

reacted to Adam Pearce and his pamphlets and radical speeches. If many welcomed the French Revolution as a bright new dawn, such sentiments were not shared by the government of King George or the monarch himself; they saw it as a threat to their position and reacted with venom.

The first arrest had seen them incarcerated in the Fleet prison, an experience which coloured and altered the way John Pearce thought about his fellow humans. They had shared their cell with the dregs of humanity, folk who would steal your eyes and come back for the holes. Release came in time, but Adam Pearce was not one to heed it as a warning; if anything it made him bolder in his attacks on unearned privilege and given he put his views in writing, and such pamphlets sold well, that led to the writ for seditious libel and flight from the country.

Paris, initially welcoming a fellow spirit, had turned out to be little better; those who assumed power in France were just as disinclined to let pass harsh criticism as their British counterparts. If their stay there had been the making of the son – he had enjoyed coming to manhood in a world of sensual freedom – it had eventually been the death of his father that broke him.

Michael appeared with their dinner for, much as Pearce believed it nonsense, the ritual of the naval day said it must be eaten in broad daylight instead of the civilised evening, this made doubly unpleasant by the need to reoccupy his cabin. He had a quiet exchange and one that told him matters had not improved, but it was not a good idea to talk for any time, given the Irishman was far from trusted already.

Neither he nor Emily had much appetite, even if the food was still fresh and good; there was too much danger, it was too hot for comfort, so much was left as they once more made for the deck and air they could at least breathe.

'What will happen next?' Emily enquired, seeing it as her duty now to draw her man away from a return to gloomy recollection.

'Night will fall and then perhaps present us with a chance to change course unseen.' Pearce then looked at the clear blue sky, with scarce a cloud in sight and sighed. 'Though we will need something to change in the weather to make such a thing possible.'

Knowing Emily would speak and wishing to think, he held up a restraining hand; there was scant chance of help from the conditions so he had to think of something else. If he could not evade the pursuit, how could he slow them down, which would increase the time available to make a land fall?

As of yet, nothing really serious had been done to lighten the ship; he had been waiting for darkness to act on that so as to increase the gap between him and the brigantines, which would become apparent at dawn, the idea being that the sight of the greater distance might persuade them the pursuit was useless. It was not a boundless hope, more a desperate one.

'Mr Dorling, your presence if you please?'

The master obeyed his loud call at no great pace, as Pearce called for the gunner and the carpenter too, Emily moving to the stern so as not to cramp them.

'Mr Kempshall, what is the supply of slow match?'

'Yards of it,' Sam Kempshall replied, with something close to a sneer, the lack of any acknowledgement of Pearce's rank very obvious but the temptation to check the man had to be put to one side. 'Don't use it so, seein' as we got flintlocks.'

Pearce nodded, for slow match was only carried as a precaution against flints not working, or to cause explosions ashore when the navy went raiding. 'And slow match burns at a steady rate, am I correct?'

'Can be timed to near the minute.'

'Good,' Pearce said, before turning to the master. 'The water barrels?'

'Empty,' Dorling replied, 'and broken up.'

'Well,' Pearce said, addressing Brad, the second of the twins, 'I want them reassembled and let's have them filled with seawater to seal the seams.'

The looks he was getting were of a fellow who had lost his wits and, oddly, that cheered Pearce; he loved nothing more than confounding his fellow man and he was clearly doing so now.

'I want bases made for rafts, to be supported by those barrels and then we will put powder and lengths of slow match upon them.' They did not get it. 'Do you now see, gentlemen, how we might give pause to our pursuit?'

Dorling got there first, though even he was not swift to the conclusion and when he did it was with a look of doubt that the plan would do any good. Pearce knew what he was thinking: the chances of a raft of powder blowing up near enough to damage either of the brigantines was wishing for the moon.

'And I agree with you,' Pearce said, when he too had advanced that thought. 'The aim is to give them pause. Would you sail blithely on with what amounts to bombs you cannot see going off around you?'

'You reckon they will heave to?'

'They must, for they will have no idea of how many there are in the water. Now I suggest that matters be put in hand at once but out of sight, for it may be that they will have a good view of our deck from their tops. This has to come as a surprise so it will do no good if they can discern what we are about to do.'

Pearce nearly added, 'And perhaps we will blow one of them to hell, and that will lay to the same place as your damned superstitions.' But he held his tongue.

These not being tasks the warrants could undertake themselves, they had to be explained to others and it was obvious whatever doubts affected their superiors, the crew shared them. This made the work painful to watch, given it was carried out with little enthusiasm and him being below decks was seen as unwelcome. There is nothing more frustrating than the desire to interfere, to chivvy the men along, while at the same time knowing it would be likely to slow not hurry them.

Pearce had to go on deck once more, to occupy himself with a telescope, damned hard with one good arm, seeking to give the impression that he was making fine calculations about speed and distance when in fact it was merely serving no purpose. Yes, the Barbary brigantines were gaining, but it was not so swift that matters changed with anything approaching drama, quite the reverse.

The next task was to seek to time the run of the current, a fickle beast at best, so as to calculate the amount of slow match that would be needed to set off the powder barrels at the right time. In truth that was pure guesswork, for Pearce's rafts would not move at the same rate as bits of cork thrown over the bow and tied to the stern, even less an empty but sealed wine bottle.

Pearce reckoned they would move little; that the best calculation was to reckon them near stationary and time them to go off on that basis, which had Dorling seeking to make sense of the necessary numbers with his now habitual lack of enthusiasm. His figures done, Sam Kempshall was set to cutting the required lengths of slow match.

At last the sun was closing in on the eastern horizon, dropping in what was a band of haze between sky and sea, which obscured any chance of observing the enemy deck. It had to be the same in reverse, a fact he checked with the fellow placed aloft for that very purpose. It was frustrating to then have to order the making of the kind of slings necessary to get his bombs into the water, something that previously would have been done without a word from him.

It was a relief to see the great golden orb first touch water, to begin to go red as it picked up the dust that existed in the air, even at sea, the residue of desert sand carried on the wind all the way from the Sahara. Then it was gone, leaving a short glow, the first stars already beginning to show, for the transition from day to night in the Mediterranean is swift. Soon the sky was a mass of them again, while the moon, huge and as low as had been the sun, was now the colour of cheese, changing to white as it rose.

The makeshift rafts lay on the deck, six of them, with half barrels of powder given that full ones might be too heavy and cause them to sink. Gingerly, and by the light of nothing but the stars and the moon, they were lifted over the side to sit on the water, before being gently pulled clear to ensure they did not snag on the ship.

At first they were obvious, the glow of the slow burning match visible. But that soon faded and, given they were as dark as the sea on which they sat, like their enemies they had no idea where those rafts were. Pearce was wondering if the Jonahs would now be predicting it would be *Larcher* that would suffer from this folly – that they would explode hard by to crack her hull. There was a new fellow aloft, but just as in daylight there was no mistaking the pursuit; their sails picked up the moon and starlight with ease, their bow waves the phosphoresce of the breaking water. To order a change of course would do no good, merely adding to the distance to shore.

The light on the binnacle had been shaded, likewise the stern lantern had not been ignited, so there was a ghostly feel to their progress, aided by a wind that was not strong enough to make their rigging whistle. Almost everyone was on deck, no one was in their hammock, some trying to appear indifferent, most unable to avoid staring over the stern, like their captain waiting – he with his watch in his hand – for the first barrel to explode.

As it was two went off at once and a goodly distance from each other, sending great flashes of orange light into the night sky. Pearce waited for a cheer and he waited in vain, nor did that come when the rest of the slow match hit the powder on another, blowing the barrel to matchwood. Had they gained what he had hoped? Had the enemy let fly their sheets and hove to? In the available light, there was no way of telling for certain but the indications of their presence, flashes of canvas and that bow wave did seem to disappear.

Five having gone off, the wait for the last seemed interminable; in the end it never came and neither did the prayed for miracle: that one would get so close as to blow in the scantlings of one of those brigantines. Perhaps the raft had sunk or the match had been extinguished by a freak wave – they would never know. Slowly the deck cleared as the men went below to their slumbers, or in some cases to their rumblings of discontent.

Pearce lay in his cabin, still stifling from the daytime heat, listening to Emily's even breathing. If he had succeeded in what looked like a hare-brained enterprise, how would that affect the crew? Would wiser counsels overcome the Jeremiahs predicting doom and would the level of trust they had in him be on the way to being restored? On consideration he doubted it; only when they were in a safe harbour would anything of that nature happen and perhaps not even then.

He was on deck before anyone was roused out, there to see the gun crews man their cannon as was required, though this time Pearce had ordered them loaded with powder and shot and the flintlocks put in place – normally a precaution avoided given the worming of a loaded cannon was time-consuming and wasteful. It was always silent on deck at dawn, yet this time it seemed oppressive as the first hint of light began to grey the eastern horizon.

Slowly it spread towards them and no cry came from the masthead. Then the first tint of gold began to appear, swiftly rising until it filled the sky with deep blue, then fading to duck egg as it rose. Still no cry came from aloft and that lasted until they could say with certainty the sun was full up. Pearce began to feel his chest hurt, so much was he holding his breath, and he released it in a thankful sigh; he had humbugged his enemies!

'Sail Ho!'

That cry dashed his hopes and that of all on deck, every one of whom was looking to see how he would react as the cry came to tell of the second enemy still on their tail, with Pearce forced to remind himself that the aim had never been to lose the pursuit but to delay it.

'Have we made any gain?' he shouted.

'Hard to tell, Capt'n,' came the reply.

This was nonsense; either those brigantines were as close as they had been the day before or not, indeed, if they had not hauled their wind they should be much closer. Again he was prevented from doing what he needed by his damned arm and he had to make a call that he would rather have avoided.

'Mr Dorling, will you please go aloft and tell me if the chase is as close as it should be? Indeed have they gained on us at all?' Looking around the deck he then shouted. 'The rest of you get about your duties.'

'You're going to hell, Pearce, and taking us with you.'

Having turned away, Pearce could not place the voice when he spun back, for every head was down and the order he had just given was being carried out. The guns were being run in to be wormed, the balls removed and the barrels cleaned. To stand and stare, to glare and let his fury show would do no good and he fought to make his tone humorous.

'Lucifer may be looking for your company, fellow, but he will scarce want mine for fear he might lose his kingdom.'

One or two laughed, not enough but at least some kind of reassurance that not everyone was wholly taken in. Dorling came to his aid when he called down that the enemy had lost way overnight; they were further off now than they had been at dusk, so his ploy had worked. That occasioned some nodding heads and a few looks at the quarterdeck that did not have within them any hint of animosity. But it was not all and, for once, upset by that shouted prediction, Pearce did nothing to supress the bile that rose within him.

'It is my intention to get us to safety, lads. That I will do despite the wiles of Satan and his naysayers. When I do, I promise you this: I will find out who has been spreading falsehoods and then they will discover that I am not the kindly soul you reckon me to be, for the sight you will see is their back entirely lacking in skin! I will have them flogged round the fleet for stirring up mutiny.'

CHAPTER FIVE

If there had been a gain it did not seem to persist for long and worse lay in the increased feel of the wind as it swung due west then to a few points north. If it had not sang in the rigging before it was beginning to do so now, not in any great way but enough to tell Pearce that any advantage he had was rapidly diminishing. Given the top hamper HMS *Larcher* was carrying, a low-slung mainsail, this change did not amount to much in the way of speed. Indeed, looking at the strain on the canvas and the effect that was having on the temporary upper mainmast, it seemed it might be necessary to lessen the amount they had rigged in case the pressure caused it to carry away.

The sight of a thin line on the horizon was a blessing indeed, for that indicated land; not the shoreline but the high peaks of the mountains that covered much of Italy and trapped the moisture at high altitude. Yet set against such good news was the one plain fact: the enemy were gaining a great deal more from any alteration in the weather than the armed cutter.

At least Dorling seemed to have set aside some of his lethargy, spending time over his charts and the slate to try to advise his captain what chance he had of making his landfall before those brigantines could close. His furrowed brow at every cast of the log was enough of a message to all that it was going to be so much nip and tuck that the lightening of the ship could no longer be delayed.

The water gone, next it was the supply of wine bought in Palermo, which occasioned one wry smile from Pearce; the crew seemed sad to see that go for if they pronounced it to be not much above vinegar it at least contained a measure of alcohol. Next came the last barrels of beef and pork before a derrick was rigged that would see over the side most of the cannon and their nearly as weighty trunnions, albeit the act was held in abeyance.

The increase in speed from what had been discarded was again minimal and there was a downside too; lacking that weight *Larcher* was higher out of the water and so even more likely to yaw off course on a fluke in the current, something that could only increase the closer they got to shore. It might be, once they hit the swirling flows that were common close to land, she would actually lose speed rather than gain it.

There was silence on deck now: no quiet conversations or murmuring, just exchanged glances intermingled with looks astern at the increasingly obvious pursuit and the clear sight of a complete suit of sails, all drawing well. It seemed whatever suspicions the men harboured had altered in its objective; no one wanted to look aloft at the man swaying on what was a less than wholly secure perch, his telescope trained mainly forward for the first sight of the shoreline, in case by doing so they damned the chance of it ever happening.

'They're splitting up, your honour,' came the cry, for the same fellow had the task of watching the pursuit.

There was no need to be so elevated in order to see the truth of that; it was as plain to everyone else with eyes. Both brigantines had made only a slight alteration but it was significant; it was a message to say that the endgame was approaching. The time was coming when HMS *Larcher* would, too, have to alter course; that the chance of safety lying ahead was diminishing.

Pearce had hoped, though with no great conviction, they might manage a change of course to the north so they could enter the Gulf of Salerno where lay two great cities, one of the same name and Amalfi. Both were important centres of trade and thus with harbours heavily fortified against raiding, perhaps even home to some Neapolitan warships that, seeing the danger they were in, would help to drive off the enemy. Mere proximity to such ports would be bound to make those brigantines cautious.

Out came the charts again and with them all the information gathered over years by the men of the British Navy; written reports and drawings, details of landmarks and hazards as well as soundings taken by any number of seafarers to tell those who came after them the depth of water they could expect under their keel – often made by officers and warrants for pleasure as much as duty. On examination of the options, Pearce, in discussion with Dorling, had alighted on two possibilities; slightly southward lay the ancient harbour of Scalea, little used now. The other alterative lay to the north-east, the small fishing port of Sapri at the apex of the Gulf of Policastro, the great bight into which they were being forced.

The former, Scalea, was the better option, given it might have some kind of defence. Sapri lay in a deep horseshoe bay and by all accounts possessed a mole but seemed too much of a backwater to justify any cannon, even less a garrison able to use it. Both suffered from the same drawback; once in their harbour *Larcher* would be trapped and any help would have to be sent for, that is if the enemy made no attempt to cut them out.

'Our friends have the same charts as us, your honour.'

'And may well have more local knowledge, Mr Dorling, given their predecessors have been raiding on these shores for centuries.'

'I take leave to doubt they are as diligent as the King's Navy.'

Said with pride it seemed to Pearce that it would be churlish to point out that at one time this had been a Saracen sea and one in which, even when evicted from the island of Sicily, they had plundered at will. When it came to the despoliation, Italy, with over 600 sandy bays on two elongated coasts, was indefensible.

'We are not yet forced to a decision, let us see what happens.'

Back on deck he joined Emily in looking over the stern – she had, as usual, vacated the cabin so they could examine the charts – and to him it was immediately obvious that what he had just said to Dorling had some resonance; the Barbary brigantine to the south was making a fraction more speed than his consort which, in time and if nothing was done, would remove the option of Scalea. In short, they knew the possibilities as well as he did.

'Is it permitted to ask how we fare, John?'

He looked aloft at the pennants, which if they were not stiff on the breeze had more life in them now than at any time since they had left Palermo. 'I would say our enemies have a plan while we are on the wing, which is not where I would like to be. But nothing is decided.'

'Are we worth the effort?'

It did not seem a good idea to mention that such people made a profit from selling slaves as well as captured cargoes. But Emily had raised a telling point: HMS *Larcher*, for those bent on piracy, was no great prize; indeed he had hoped that seeing the chase as lengthy and one of little return they would desist, but they had not. This led him to the unwelcome conclusion that they could be in search of retribution, a thought he had suppressed, it being not far off the superstition of the on-board Jeremiahs.

Could it just be for pride? Had that been so dented by their previous defeat that redress was essential? And what about Captain Fleming and *Sandown Castle*? Pearce had to assume the merchantman had got away but maybe he, too, had found these two waiting for him in a situation in which he could not avoid being taken.

'They think so, which is all that matters.'

'Land ho!'

The cry from aloft and a pointed hand told him, before the words were spoken, that their landfall lay right over the makeshift bowsprit. It was gratifying not to have to issue any orders to Dorling; he was already on his way as Pearce ordered the helmsman to alter course slightly north, which would take them close into the headland of the gulf. The way that southerly brigantine was behaving made any notion of Scalea too risky.

Walking forwards he laid a hand on the lower part of the mainmast, original and well seated in the keel that would hold. It was what sat above it that caused worry, for the only thing holding two bits of timber together were the thick laths lashed tightly with cables and it was now creaking so alarmingly that any notion of more sail and increased strain was out of the question; if they were to survive it would have to be under what they had.

The next positive sign was the presence of gulls, at first resting on the water, next in flight, birds that rarely flew out of sight of their land nests unless in the wake of a fishing boat. By the time the shore was in plain sight so were the decks of their enemy, the one closing in on the larboard beam, the other seeking to headreach them to the south, which slightly baffled Pearce; given their fire and manpower surely they should just be seeking to get close enough to engage then board. Was it a mark of respect? Had they suffered so badly in the previous encounter that they declined to risk a repeat?

He was watching the sky as well, but with no hope that night might come to his rescue; the sun was high and it was, through a telescope, illuminating the grey ragged and mast-high rocks of a shore that looked damned unwelcoming. Behind it lay what looked like densely scrub-covered land rising to thick woods circling the higher hills.

Having double-checked the course, he made sure they were heading straight for Sapri yet with no guarantee that they would find what they needed there. Given it was taking them closer to that rocky shoreline, the man in the chains was casting for soundings not speed; the latter mattered not at all, given the problem there was plain to see. These waters had been well charted but that did not mean they were without hazard; a rocky landscape indicated a like seabed and it would be too cruel an irony to have come so far only to founder on some unforeseen underwater obstacle, so he sent a man to the prow to keep an eye out for any water breaking over submerged rocks.

Again time became of no relevance and talk too; every possible outcome and move had been so thoroughly discussed there was no more to say, until the point came when everyone with sense, and that included John Pearce, realised the game was up. The southerly brigantine was now on course to get ahead of them and cut them off.

The derrick was still rigged and that would get the cannons over the side but if undertaken, with *Larcher*'s deck in plain sight, what message would that send to their enemies? Come on at will, you have nothing more to fear, added to which what would be the gain? It was unlikely to grant them the speed they needed to escape. Pearce knew he had delayed that particular gambit too long and that had him examining his own motives.

Was it a determination to be able to fight, even in an unwinnable battle? If it had been suggested to him that he cared for the ship as much as he did Emily Barclay, Pearce would have laughed. Yet there was some truth in the assertion, for he was not immune to a trait that affected every sailor. Prior to Palermo, he had been proud of HMS *Larcher* and the men he commanded and it was only now that he was beginning to realise how much that had been so.

He hated the notion of being taken by the enemy and not just for the sake of the preservation of life. If losing a ship was not a stain that particularly troubled him – it tended to have a negative effect on a naval career – losing this armed cutter did. Nor was he enjoying being passive in the face of the oncoming threat, which went against his entire nature.

'A whip to the yard,' he called, 'and something on which I can sit.'

It was not a command swiftly obeyed, which had nothing to do with ill-feeling, more to do with confusion and that was evident on every face he could see; expressions indicating a thought like, what the hell did the daft bugger want now? It was eventually obeyed and a sling was rigged on a line, lashed to a slat of planking that provided a seat, which was raised gingerly on his command so that he got halfway to the point at which sat the lookout.

If the man was better placed than Pearce to see, there was a judgement to be made that could only fall to him. Hooking his injured arm around one side of the sling so he could keep his seat as well as provide support allowed Pearce to employ his telescope, albeit adjustments to focusing were painfully slow.

Eventually he got it right and now he had better sight of the enemy, enough to bring into focus the bodies on deck, albeit without revealing clearly the features. Yet the impression was different from that he had experienced hitherto. Now, instead of seeing vessels fully restored he could see where they had been repaired, great sections of bulwarks that did not match the whole, places that should have been gun ports now had nothing but planking and that was cheering.

Clearly they had not been fully repaired, added to which, if he had lost men in their previous encounter it was a fair bet they had lost more; was that why they were behaving with what he could only see as caution? Perhaps the fellow who was the senior commander was suffering from the same problems as he; perhaps he, too, had a disgruntled crew. He certainly had fewer cannon than hitherto.

Much as it was pleasant to speculate that was not why he had had himself hoisted aloft. Pearce was up here to make a calculation and he set his mind to that, swinging his glass one way then the other trying to work out distances by a process of triangulation, which took time, enough for the watch to be changed below.

Looking at the shoreline he could see now it was not all rocks; there were inlets and small hemmed-in bays, even one or two with a boat hauled up on the beach, which told of human habitation. That was not what he sought and it was some time before he came across a possible solution to capture. When he did and was sure it met, if not all his needs, most of them, he had himself lowered to the deck where he started issuing orders.

'Mr Bird, I want the two rearmost cannon moved to the taffrail and set up with temporary tackle, the rest can go over the side once that is achieved.' Then he raised his voice to let all know what he intended. 'I am aware you all fear to be taken by Barbary, for we know what it means for our future. That is not going to happen and if HMS *Larcher* cannot fight these two swine as we did before, at least we can deny them a cheap victory. Mr Dorling, a change of course, if you please, to due north.'

'You intend to run us aground?' the master enquired, quick to see what the outcome of such words and such a course would mean.

'I do.'

The face clouded with renewed pessimism. 'We will be just as much at risk on an open beach as we are on this deck, your honour, maybe even more so.'

'If you have an alternative, Mr Dorling, I will be only too willing to listen to you. We cannot fight and you will now have realised as well as I have that we will be forced into that before we can make the mole at Sapri. Besides I have other hopes. Now please do as I ask.'

Dorling did hesitate for several seconds, but he finally yelled out the necessary commands in a manner that had men running to obey, for surely they, too, sensed a glimmer of hope. Falls were eased, the sails adjusted as the rudder was swung to take them towards what looked from the deck to be an iron-bound shore, Pearce watching to see how their enemies reacted. They, too, changed course so that now the fellow who had been astern was off their beam, the other coming up to chase, though Pearce reckoned he could be ignored.

The former represented the greater danger, he being able to cut the angle, while at the same time he would, at a fast approaching point, be able to bring what guns he still had to bear.

One separate difficulty emerged the closer they got to shore, for there was a current running from east to west and one that affected *Larcher* as soon as it became apparent, pushing her head off true. This was felt by John Pearce who was with Charlie Taverner up at the prow now, his friend on the duty to which another had been set to on the previous watch.

'You got us all guessing when you was up in the air,' Charlie whispered, so low not even those close could hear him, though his eyes never let off on his task, getting more vital by the moment, given inshore there was bound to be an increase in underwater hazards. 'Most reckoned you was seeking a different way to get us all killed.'

'No doubt with me and Emily surviving?' came the equally soft reply.

'Suggested,' Charlie responded, looking round enough for Pearce to see his grin. 'Though Rufus belted the one who said it.'

'Rufus!' Pearce could not keep the surprise out of his voice;

to him Rufus was still a young tyro, not yet a man and far from violent by nature.

'Michael had to step in, as he's been dying to do so for a while and it came in handy.' Charlie chuckled. 'Blood everywhere.'

The sight of that grin cheered Pearce as well as the words; it felt good to know that he still had men who believed in him, but that was set aside as the bows yawed to one side, which had him hooking his splints round a stay to avoid a fall and yelling that it was vital they hold their course.

'I keep telling them that youse a master of getting out of a fix.'

'Let's hope you have the right of it, Charlie,' he responded as the vessel yawed off course again. 'But it is all well to recall my gift for getting into them in the first place.'

Telescope up and focused anew he had it fixed on what he had seen from aloft. In among the tiny beaches and water-hewn caves he had spotted a narrow gap in the rock face, an inlet that at its shore end was no wider than the armed cutter. Where it met the sea was not much better and it was reasonable to assume there were other hazards below the waterline. Once in there, *Larcher* would be stuck, very likely holed and certainly doomed to eventual destruction by the power of the first heavy tide.

The inlet lay at the base of a scrub-covered and rock-strewn gully that ran steeply upwards to the hilltops, guarded by some kind of watchtower: an ancient construct, tall and round, set to overlook a whole section of the coast and, given it had no flag, probably abandoned, which indicated a shore that in times past was in need of defence. So there must be a set of paths leading up from the various beaches. He may not find one but surely they could hack out a route.

A swing of that glass showed just how narrow was going to be the gap between him getting there and his being cut off by the enemy, yet it drove home to Pearce that sentiment could not be allowed to enter into any of his calculations. The object now was to save the crew, not the ship and if he was engaged in a gamble it was time to throw the dice.

CHAPTER SIX

The shifting of the guns to the taffrail was proceeding apace, overseen by Mr Bird and gunner Kempshall. Others were called on deck to ditch the remaining cannon, for they were now of no use, Pearce reckoning if things were going to blow up in his face this was when it would happen; that it passed with no more than black looks he took as a bonus. It was time to tell Dorling of what he intended and explain the advantages – the downside required no explanation. They were about to try and achieve the sailing equivalent of threading a needle and to err was to run right into the rock face on either side of that narrow inlet and most certainly founder in waters that would lead to many being drowned.

'Before you tell me what we risk, I have to say we have no other chance of escape that I can see. If we sail on we will be cut off and taken. However if we can get ourselves jammed in that inlet it will be a brave commander who will seek to come too close in pursuit, for one fluke of wind could see them wrecked and whatever guns they can bring to bear we will match with our new stern chasers.'

'And then what?'

'We march inland and find some way of getting to Naples, either by boat or on foot and from there back to the fleet.' Sensing hesitation, Pearce added, 'It is called staying alive, Mr Dorling, to fight another day.'

Pearce was not insensitive to what he was proposing, for if he had something of a care for the armed cutter then he could multiply that a hundredfold for Dorling. The man was being asked to sacrifice his first appointment as a warrant, the very vessel from which he had hoped to so cement his reputation that he would be shifted to a series of post ships of increasing size.

'I realise this does not sit well with you and if there was an alternative I would be taking it. But there is not and, much as I value the deck on which we stand, I value the men we carry more, even if a goodly number of them reckon otherwise.'

A slow and resigned nod was the response.

'Now we need to get ready for what we face and we have little time.' Pearce handed him the key he had previously demanded back. 'Also, Mr Dorling, it would be a pity to sacrifice the rum and probably make me even more unpopular than I have been hitherto, but if carried it must be rationed ashore as it is afloat, do I make myself clear?'

'Best to arm those with charge of it.'

'When the time comes to abandon ship, Mr Dorling, we will all be armed, so you and your fellow warrants must rely on your standing with the crew to see that the necessary discipline is maintained. But rest assured of this, I will, myself, shoot anyone who gives you trouble.'

'Then I pray to the Lord it does not come to that.'

The man meant it, which further lifted his captain's spirits. 'The only way out of our present predicament is by acting in concert, which I'd be obliged to see told to the men. But as of this moment you have a more pressing duty to perform.'

The response, for the first time in two days, was brisk. 'Aye, aye, sir.'

Pearce then issued a stream of orders as the needs he anticipated occurred to him. The boats had to be hauled in and emptied, as much to provide portable food – a chicken coop weighed little – as to act as a backstop in case of disaster. Some would be able to get away if they struck the rocks, perhaps to a nearby beach. He put aside the notion that in a panic both he and those he counted as his personal responsibility might not be included in that.

If they did get ashore, some method of carrying the remaining water must be contrived; it would be too much of a burden for any one man and possession of such a resource he reckoned essential. Having looked at the far from fertile shore he had no idea how long it would be before they came across some hamlet or even a spring.

Likewise Mr Bellam must distribute things like the bread bought in Palermo and still near fresh, as well as contrive some way of allowing them to take sustenance enough to last several days. Each man must get out his shore-going rig, though it would be shoes that really mattered on the rough ground and he also must insist on heads being covered. As for their other possessions, short jackets and their fancy pantaloons, they could not to be allowed to overburden themselves; if it was warm at sea it would be ten times that on land.

Everyone not occupied was set to various tasks; the gunner's mates filling powder horns for the muskets, cutlasses being sharpened both for defence and what Pearce suspected would be a hard climb through wild undergrowth. Slings of rope were being fashioned for carrying what they would need and all the while, by the stern, the blocks and pulleys were being fitted to the deck that would allow them to run in and out the two remaining cannon.

Rufus Dommet was ordered to fetch from below every block of pitch and to line them across the deck behind the two newly rigged stern chasers. With the addition of rags around them ready to be turpentine soaked, he ensured the lantern in his cabin was alight and the tallow had plenty of time to run; everything proceeded as if there was no enemy closing on them at a telling pace.

That illusion was soon shattered: the first ball from the closest brigantine fell well short, more a signal of intent than a threat, as well as an attempt to kill the wind and slow the progress of *Larcher* towards the shore. What lay before her was easy to see now and far from reassuring, for if the rocks were not towering massifs they were high enough, while the waters at their base, in what was not much of a sea, showed a lively amount of spume, a clear indication of what lay beneath.

With every eye, at every opportunity, cast towards that it was not necessary to impart the obvious: if *Larcher* could not hold its course then the chances of success were slim. Pearce did not enquire of Dorling if he was aware of the risks; he had to believe, even as he watched with anxiety the master's actions, that if anyone could get them to where they wanted to be it was the man steering the ship, not him.

In the fine set of new calculations Dorling decided the makeshift jib was not aiding their cause. The pressure of the wind on that was constantly pushing the ship off course, so much so that he had set the prow well to starboard of the intended landfall, seeking to achieve the best balance between speed and direction. Even that was too risky, so he ordered the gaff shortened just as the next round of shot from the enemy was loosed off, which came a lot nearer to the hull than its predecessor, showing how fast the gap was closing, sending up a plume of water that on the wind swept a fine spray across the deck.

'Why we take that right kindly!' came the loud cry from Charlie Taverner, still up in the prow. 'Cooled me down a treat, mate.'

That got a laugh from a few, Pearce reckoning it to be the first he had heard in an age, which made easier his need to match the requirements of the ship, the necessity of allowing men in rotation to gather their belongings, while ensuring that any other tasks needing attention were carried out – on the whole a welcome distraction from thinking on possible catastrophe.

Michael O'Hagan emerged from his cabin to tell him that he had got together, with the aid of Mrs Barclay, two canvas ditty bags with which to carry their possessions and that his lady had obeyed his request that she cut off the lower section of a sturdy dress, put the most sensible shoes she possessed on her feet and to make sure she took along her parasol.

'The ship's funds,' Pearce asked, 'what's left of them?'

'Packed away as are the logs and accounts,' Michael replied, handing him a heavy bag. 'Private signal book, as you requested.'

There was a sense of finality to what Pearce did next, disposing over the side in a weighted sack the book that allowed any vessel of the Royal Navy to identify an approaching warship as friend or foe, a list of flags to be flown on specific days that would only make sense to another holding the same book. That could not be allowed to ever fall into the hands of an enemy so he took it to the side and threw it into the sea.

'Time to issue the muskets, I think,' Pearce said, rejoining O'Hagan, as another ball from the enemy dropped into the sea, short, but not by much.

'They'll land one or two on our deck afore we get ashore.'

'They will,' Pearce replied, wondering if that had been purposely said within earshot of the helmsman, allowing him to add a message that could be passed on. 'But not a full broadside unless they haul their wind and if they do that we will make it to safety well ahead of them.'

It was not that simple; close to shore there was an undertow slowing *Larcher* as it acted on the keel, making them lose a bit of way for every yard gained. Yet that would apply to the enemy too, perhaps more so given their deeper hull and it was obvious they too were finding it increasingly hard to hold a straight course, added to which they were sailing into an area full of breaking waters, which was a mite reckless. Pearce was anticipating abandoning his ship, but that did not apply to Barbary.

It was almost as if the thought communicated itself across the intervening stretch of sea, for the brigantine began to shorten sail dramatically, which told Pearce that his opposite number had probably misread his intentions, thinking perhaps he had come so close to the shore as a last gambit to avoid capture. Whatever, it now became clear that the armed cutter would run aground well before the enemy could prevent it and that, passed to Dorling, concentrating on what lay dead ahead, gave him some latitude in his final approach.

Pearce watched each face as a stream of men came aft to be handed a musket, glad that some at least were prepared to meet his eye rather than avoid it, which made more comfortable the order he then gave to each to get a horn of powder and a cartouche of balls from the gunner. Michael was handing out cutlasses to others while several had axes, so that now the crew was armed and potentially, to him, dangerous. The situation they were in being more so, that thought had to be put to one side.

They were close now, able to smell the mixture of disturbed seawater and the scents of the land, hot air and arid plants overlain by the smell of pine. HMS *Larcher* was beginning to buck like a horse, which made it necessary to have extra muscle to steer and hold the ship steady. If Pearce was holding his breath, he reckoned not to be alone as the ship's gimcrack jib swung wildly to crack and disintegrate as it struck the rocks.

That being to larboard actually aided Dorling as, with the stern lifting slightly on an incoming wave, the prow was forced into the gap, one that now seemed to the man who had observed it from a distance as akin to the mouth of a ravenous beast. The crashing sound came from below as the keel struck a rock, which had Pearce's heart in his mouth, that being the one thing that could prevent them making land. If *Larcher* got itself pinned on some underwater obstacle they could be too far from the actual shore to get anyone off.

There was a pause of seconds until another wave lifted the whole ship a fraction and drove it forward, though not by much. This, accompanied by a grinding sound as the jagged stone ripped into the hull, meant that water would begin to flood the bilges, not a positive as it would lower the ship and make it more difficult to get her to where Pearce wanted her to be. Then came the undertow and more grinding as it sought to drive the ship backwards.

'Enemy's across our stern, your honour, and making ready to fire, four cannon I reckon.'

'Is that poor soul still aloft?' Pearce cried as he looked to see from where the holler had come, his shout followed by a stab of guilt; if he was there, and to little purpose, only one person could be to blame. 'Get him down and the same for all of you. Lay flat on the deck. Michael, get Mrs Barclay out of that cabin.'

'Already done, Capt'n, below with Rufus at her side.'

That got a nod of gratitude and another stab of remorse; he should have ordered it before, the cabin being the most risky spot with an enemy across the stern. It was doubly remiss not to have noticed Emily as she exited their cabin and traversed the deck to the companionway.

'Join Rufus, Michael, and get Charlie out of the prow as well, you know why.'

They were at the mercy of both the sea and those cannon, one seeking to drive them to possible safety, the other intent on destruction. Along the deck most had obeyed his order and were lying down, others close to the companionway followed the

Irishman below, which seemed to promise more safety, yet that could be an illusion.

If the Barbary captain aimed his cannon right, the shot would blast through the flimsy stern of *Larcher* to wreak havoc as the balls swept along the lower deck. There was nowhere really safe on a small, armed cutter in battle, no deep cockpit where round shot could not reach. Worse for John Pearce, for the men steering the ship the option to do more than duck was not available; in his case he could not even do that.

As captain it was necessary to not only show an example of bravery and or indifference – a fatal panic could ensue if he did not – but in the situation in which they now found themselves he had to be fully aware of what was happening. He could not leave Dorling as the only upright figure on deck. All he could do was briefly close his eyes as he heard the crack of passing shot, feeling blessed as he realised that it had gone overhead, this evidenced by the splinters flying off the stump of the mainmast, which was hit with such force that what had been rigged above came loose and fell to one side, a skein of wood and rope that was arrested by its own tangle.

It mattered not, the sails had no effect on the ship now; it was the force of the sea that was driving her further in and what came next cheered him. The gun crews behind him had leapt up as soon as it was safe to do so and without any orders had trimmed their aim and loosed off a telling reply. Black smoke from the powder, like the seawater borne on the wind, swept over and past him.

Larcher was close to being jammed now, only moving forward in inches not yards, with high grey and jagged rocks to either side. Looking at the enemy, still on his own with his consort too far away to affect matters, Pearce could see and revel in his problems. Stationary on broken inshore waters, any accurate timing of gunfire was near to impossible.

He must have aimed at the hull with his opening salvo. That was the most effective thing to do in the prevailing circumstances, but a passing wave probably lifted his hull so it had gone high to where it would do little good. Yes, he had wounded the armed cutter, but to what purpose? Against that, the men manning the two makeshift stern chasers, now that they were within the maw of that inlet, had a more stable platform from which to take aim, plus the ability to reload their cannon at a speed no other navy could match.

They got their second shots off before Barbary reloaded and the balls struck the upper hull with an encouraging sound of ripping timber. Within seconds his men were hauling and swabbing their guns and might have got off a third before the enemy could match their second. Barbary did get off a salvo just ahead of them but this time it happened as an incoming wave caused the brigantine to down roll, which sent their shot into the sea yards from the stern, the intervening water taking out most of the velocity.

Dorling had called for hands to pole the ship using the sweeps. Men were leaning into one end while the other was pressed into any available fissure in the rocks. Initially ineffective, it became so when the master had them work separately so as to take maximum advantage of the minimal space off either beam, the result: a fractional move forward by first one side then the other, again aided by the incoming waves.

'Barky's taking water fast, Capt'n,' came the call from

the companionway, this before Brad Kempshall's dark locks disappeared back from whence they had come.

Pearce went forward to where he could see clearly there was still a gap between the now-naked prow and the end of the inlet, not much of one but just too much to bridge, which made it another kind of race. Would *Larcher* become waterlogged and get stuck where she was, or would there be enough buoyancy left to make that last few yards?

The clang of metal made him spin round in time to see one of his cannon upend and begin to roll along the deck, the trunnions below in bits as well as the taffrail, his heart sinking to think of more deaths and injuries laid at his door. It was in the nature of a miracle that this was not so; when he ran aft to count the cost, all of the gunners were alive, though two were wounded, yet not enough to render them unable to move.

'Get forward, all of you, those of you unharmed help the wounded.'

'One last round, your honour?' called Todger, who was gun captain on the remaining cannon and, given the grin that went with the request, it was one impossible to deny.

'Carry on, but abandon the gun as soon as it is fired.'

A shout from Dorling had him rush to the prow, to see that his use of the sweeps had made a difference. There was a small gap still, but it was now possible to get people over the bows and on to a section of flat rock on the larboard side. From there, albeit with wet feet, they could make their way on to dry ground and into the low bush-covered screed, which led to a command for all left on deck to get below and prepare to abandon ship. He was back to see the last shot from the armed cutter fired, a success, Todger having taken much time and such careful aim. Every head on the enemy deck went down as a very visible ball swept over their quarterdeck, which brought forth cheers and salacious gestures from the gun crew and then an irascible command from their captain.

'Belay that. Move, all of you, grab your dunnage but stay below decks until I call you up. Todger, spread that turps over those rags and then do likewise.'

Pearce went into his cabin, to see his sea chest open and half emptied. There was one thing he could not leave, something that even Michael would not know about, a small tin that he sometimes carried in his coat pocket, which contained earth from a Paris burial ground, the very place where his father was buried. There were other possessions, books and the normal souvenirs of his peripatetic life, but they would have to be abandoned without remorse; had he not had to do that so many times in his life?

His last act was to take the lantern from the wall, before he made to go back on deck, halting as he heard the thud of multiple shot and a raft of small balls struck various parts of the ship, which told him his opponent was finally using grapeshot. It was an almost spiritual reflection he had then; finding and pocketing that tin had delayed him and may well have saved his life!

'Too late, I suspect, my friend,' Pearce remarked to himself, reflecting on what had been employed by his enemy, 'should have used that on your first salvo.'

The enemy deck now had a line of men with muskets, the sight of his blue coat enough to bring on a ragged discharge, but at a range where they would be lucky to cause him any harm, not that he could hang about: another salvo was a near certainty. The tallow flared in the breeze as soon as he opened the glass door and he put a turpentine-soaked rag to it that caught light immediately. The rag was used to ignite the rest and by the time he made the companionway himself the blocks of pitch were surrounded by flames. It took little time for the thick paper that covered them to begin to burn and that set alight the pitch itself, sending up into the air a thickening pall of black smoke.

'You might guess what I am about, my friend,' was the next quiet remark, 'but by damn you will not see it.'

The crew abandoned ship in batches, Pearce first on to that flat rock so as he could supervise departure, timing his shouts to take advantage of the gaps in salvoes of grapeshot, coming now at regular intervals and firing on a deck they could no longer see. There were the wounded from Palermo to see to, those who had suffered on that overturned gun as well as the one-legged cook. The happiest moment was when he helped Emily off the ship closely followed by all three of his friends, O'Hagan carrying his few rescued possessions. Matthew Dorling, his own logs under his arm, as well as a map of this section of the coastline, was the last to depart.

'I have told everyone to hurry, Mr Dorling, and find a place where they will be protected from what will shortly happen. I say the same to you.'

John Pearce was right on the master's heels, to jam himself between two large boulders and to wait. It was not long, for those turpentine-soaked rags had set light to the sun-dried decking and the pitch in the seams. That had spread to the main timbers and the armed cutter was soon alight right across the stern. Eventually the flames reached the powder store and if there was not much left it was enough to cause a serious explosion, one that lifted the whole ship slightly and sent parts of HMS *Larcher* flying in all directions. When Pearce and the others stood up to look, she was aflame from end to end.

'Move out, all of you, muskets with me to the rear, just in case our enemies seek to come ashore.'

CHAPTER SEVEN

Sir William Hotham, acting C-in-C of His Majesty's ships and vessels in the Mediterranean, was closeted in the great cabin of HMS *Britannia* with the man who was now his chief clerk. He had inherited another clerk from Lord Hood as well as a pair of writers, making a total of three, to execute the mass of orders and correspondence he was now obliged to issue. He was the representative of his country in the region, a remit that ran over an area half the size of continental Europe and contained within it many conflicting communities and responsibilities.

He was required to keep the French fleet bottled up in Toulon, and if they should issue out, to then find and defeat them. Britain being part of a coalition of European states gathered to oppose the French Revolution, Hotham had to cooperate with the Austrian Empire, maritime city states such as Genoa and Venice, to keep in some form of order the various Beys and Deys of the North African littoral and treat with the Turkish Sultan as well as contain the activities of a mass of minor satrapies of that polity.

On the admiral's table lay the latest despatches, delivered that very day by one of the regular packets that plied the route between the Admiralty in London and the fleet base, presently in Corsica. If what the letters contained was of great import, a difficulty that had come in with the sacks of mail was more telling. Toomey was in possession of some unpleasant news and had set out to distract his employer with another communication, one come in from an unusual source, this so he would have time to think.

Hotham was reading what he had been given and wondering what to do about it, indeed why he should even react to it landing on his table. The missive came from a Major Lipton, in command of a group of bullocks who had gone to Leghorn for a spot of leave and relaxation. He claimed that he and his officers had suffered a serious assault in the port of Leghorn, visited upon them by midshipmen who made no attempt to hide the fact that they were from HMS *Agamemnon*. Indeed the name of their captain, Horatio Nelson, had been shouted many times, the implication being that the attack was some kind of retribution for insults they had heaped on his name.

In addition, and Lipton made this sound worse, the Agamemnons were aided in their assault by a number of common seamen, Liberty Men from half the navy vessels presently in the anchorage, it being a double slight that an officer holding the King's commission should be manhandled by the lower orders. The army men had been beaten and ducked in the harbour so severely that one or two had come close to drowning while the rest were rendered unfit to undertake their duties for several weeks due to the injuries they sustained.

Lipton's description was fairly graphic in its detail, which caused Hotham to allow himself a quiet smile, to recall that it was in many years past he, too, had once been a midshipman and, like all of his fellows, had taken part in a number of onshore brawls if ever they came across bullocks. In his present rank he was, of course, obliged to frown on such behaviour but in his heart he found it difficult. What his clerk put down to Hotham's habitual slow thinking was in fact this reverie, which was finally broken by a lazy drawl.

'When did this happen, Toomey?'

'Near a month past, sir. It has taken some time to get here.' Hotham looked up, the blue eyes his clerk thought to be vague posing a question. '*Agamemnon* was in harbour at the time stated by Major Lipton and the young gentlemen of that ship are known to be a mite full of themselves, so the complaint has some credence.'

'It does not surprise me that Nelson cannot control his mids berth,' Hotham growled. 'Damn me, he can scarce control his own damned servant and as for the men he commands, well?'

Captain Horatio Nelson, presently ranked as Commodore, was not popular in this cabin nor the breast of the man who occupied it. He was an officer too independent of mind, too lacking in the keeping of discipline and not just in his own private quarters. Even worse for Sir William Hotham, Nelson was much admired by Samuel, Lord Hood, the man the admiral had only recently taken over from as temporary C-in-C in the Mediterranean and one he saw as an enemy in both politics and tactics.

'Hood overindulged Nelson, Toomey, but I will not. As soon as he rejoins he will hear of this. I have the right to remove his blue pennant.'

There you go again, Toomey thought, letting your irritation run ahead of itself. The clerk knew his employer to be a man preyed upon by perceived slights and imagined concerns many of which, in keeping to himself, tended to magnify themselves in his thinking. Bad enough before Hood departed, it seemed to be getting worse, but right now it was not worth saying anything; best stay with the subject at hand.

'Major Lipton is demanding compensation for the medical bills incurred as well as damage to equipment and uniforms.'

'For which he will whistle,' Hotham responded after his usual gap for thought. 'The navy has better use for its coin.'

This was said vehemently, involving as it did money; apart from a regard for his reputation there was no subject closer to his heart. In the month since Lord Hood had sailed away in HMS *Victory* he had kept a weather eye on both, not least the sums coming in from the taking of prizes; Hood being, of course, still entitled to his eighth. Hotham might only be in a stand-in commander now, but he fully expected to be elevated to the full office; the temptation to calculate the difference in income when that day arrived and he had his full prerogative could not be avoided.

It may in fact have already happened, for Hood would be home by now and friends in high places were working on his behalf in London, people like the Duke of Portland who led a faction of Whigs that took their name from him as their leader. The Tory First Lord of the Treasury, William Pitt, needed the support of the Portland Whigs to prosecute the war with Revolutionary France and they had joined the government. Hood, a Tory to his shoe buckles, would be sacrificed by Pitt in order to appease Portland and hold at bay the main Whig opposition led by Charles James Fox.

Hotham, who had been relatively cautious up to now, was getting ready to put something of a stamp on his responsibilities by removing from command one captain whom he felt lacked the belly fire he knew would be needed should he bring the French to battle: a fellow called Frost, who had previously asked to be relieved because he was sick, only to stage a remarkable turnaround once the siege of Toulon was lifted.

Hotham had previously tried to have him replaced by Captain Ralph Barclay only to be rebuffed by Lord Hood. Now he was gone, HMS *Leander* would been given a new commanding officer and a whole raft of promotions would follow from what was a relatively small pool of officers. It was really too few to do justice to the needs of a fleet that had suffered, as any in action would, losses through death and the sheer attrition of naval service.

He would send for more – there were enough unemployed officers languishing at home to equip a dozen fleets – but not until his elevation to command was confirmed. Then he could demand men that he knew would support him as C-in-C: captains and lieutenants who had served with him previously, many of the latter as midshipmen.

He would also demand a draft of everything from warrants to common seamen, even landsmen if no others could be provided – this for a fleet now short on its establishment by near a fifth due to the same reason as his lack of officers – there was also the need to man prizes; indeed they were approaching the point where good warship captures would have to be sold rather than put into service.

He also had to decide which ship of the line was most in need of a full refit, something that could only be carried out at home. One of the despatches open on his table told him what he would get as a replacement: the newly built seventy-four gun, third-rate HMS *Semele*. The same message informed him that Captain Ralph Barclay had the command, which in normal circumstances might have been pleasing, given he was a client officer and thus a fellow to give him complete loyalty.

Yet Barclay was not without problems; not in the fighting line, there he could be utterly relied upon. It was his past actions that were a cause for worry and then there was his private life! Barclay's wife was a woman half his age and a rare beauty. There had been many instances, witnessed at the Siege of Toulon, of a less than harmonious relationship and thinking of Barclay brought to his mind the tangled web of problems his marital misalliance had created.

He had involved the admiral in a matter, which Hotham now wished he had left well alone and at the very heart of that problem lay the person of Lieutenant John Pearce. As a pressed and common seaman, which is what he had been, he could have been ignored; a stroke of good fortune followed by a piece of monarchical folly had made him an officer and subsequently a threat.

Toomey, acutely sensitive to the moods of the man who employed him, realised he had begun to brood on something unpleasant. In order to distract him further, indeed to put off what he was going to have to tell him, he pointedly pushed towards him a list of the capital ships under his command.

'The reports from commanding officers of the state of their vessels with addendums from their masters and carpenters, sir.'

'You have examined them?'

'I have.' Hotham did not respond, merely looking expectantly at his clerk and waiting. 'I have noted in the margins those vessels in the most desperate condition, having taken due note of exaggeration.'

Such a trait was not likely to come from the captains; they had spent their entire service life hoping to partake of a great fleet action in command of a fighting vessel and since there might be one in the offing here, going home was the last thing they sought. Added to that the Mediterranean was a place of opportunity, with vessels being sent off to re-victual in Leghorn with a wink that did not demand they proceed straight to the Italian port or back again, thus allowing a sweep in which they might secure a prize or two, a policy which was paying off handsomely.

Masters and carpenters of ships-of-the-line were a different breed: along with gunners and pursers were appointed to their positions by warrants from the Navy Board, a body often at odds with the Admiralty. They held their duty to be not to officers or their ambitions for glory, but to the condition of their ship and its ordnance, as well as to the Comptroller of the Navy Board. The holder of that office and the body he headed, commissioned and kept supplied the fleet. The warrants were prone to what their blue-coated peers saw as deep pessimism.

It was a coincidence that the first name on the alphabetical list was that of HMS *Agamemnon*, Nelson's sixty-four gunner and a veritable workhorse of the fleet, given the man had been so indulged by Lord Hood. He was presently in command of a squadron of accompanying frigates and cruising off Cape Noli. As a report it made sober reading, for the ship was not in a good state; some of its main frame timbers and futtocks were rotten, prone to give way when pressed by a strong finger, its masts loose in their seating and the deck planking near worn away.

Yet here was Nelson summing up to say she was the finest vessel in which he had ever set sail, a prize asset for her speed and manoeuvrability and that, despite the problems listed, he felt she was good for many more months of service. Given the Lipton letter, the temptation to read no further and just send Nelson home was one Hotham had to resist; there were ships in less good repair than *Agamemnon*.

'This will take time,' Hotham said, which was as good a way as any of asking if there was anything else Toomey had to say.

Toomey sighed. 'A grouse from Captain Lockhart—'

'What can he complain about?' Hotham interrupted. 'I have already tipped him the wink regarding *Leander*!'

'He has had a report that relations between the premier and the second lieutenant are so strained he worries for the efficiency of the ship, as well as the possibility that one or the other will demand their dispute be heard before a court martial.'

Such information could only have come from the man Lockhart was about to replace and it was a sign of why he, a very poor disciplinarian and idle in the area of command, would be removed. It would be he who took the vessel home that was designated as in most need of a dockyard and, if the report that went with him were acted upon, he would never be employed again.

'Names?'

'Premier is called Taberly and,' Toomey hesitated, knowing how his next words would be received, 'the second is Henry Digby.'

Hotham's shoulders seemed to slump; Digby, who was serving aboard HMS *Brilliant* at the time when Barclay had command, was another of those tangled up in the matter of Barclay versus John Pearce.

'You know, Toomey, there are times when I envy those dogs of revolutionaries their possession of a guillotine.'

That had to be ignored; the problem needed to be dealt with, not sentimentalised. 'Taberly has served as premier for over a year, sir, and his record is unblemished. Has the reputation of being a bit of a Tartar. Held things together what with his captain being so weak. I'd say it is certain he ran the ship.'

'Deserving of a step up?'

'Perhaps. The present premier of *Britannia* is too newly appointed to be so quickly promoted.'

Hotham nodded; one of his first commands had been to elevate the previous holder of that position, a cousin at the third remove, to the rank of Commander and the custody of a sloop. It was a common outcome for a first lieutenant serving aboard the flagship, a position seen as a guaranteed stepping stone and therefore one much sought after. The man taken in as a replacement was the son of an old comrade from the American War and would get his step up in due course, thus meeting a strongly held obligation. If they fought a successful fleet action he would get promotion automatically.

'Digby?'

'Captain Lockhart reckons Taberly would not take kindly to him filling his shoes as premier. You may recall you gave him temporary command previously, successfully completed, so he has the attributes to be elevated too.'

Hotham nodded, as though what happened to Digby was none of this Taberly's affair. He stood up and went to stand looking out of the casement windows, at a view of the fleet he commanded as well as the anchorage in which it lay, the wide sweep of San

Fiorenzo Bay and the mountains of Corsica that enclosed it. Experience told him the wardroom, however much it was overlaid by the need to maintain harmony, was bound to be split between Taberly and Digby for it was ever thus, people taking sides and if even one of them stayed put it would sour the takeover of one of his favourite officers.

'Safest we look to move them both. Let Lockhart appoint his own first lieutenant, it is usually the best way. I'll think on what to do with the two miscreants. I assume we are done.'

The clerk sought to compose himself as he responded; he had put off this matter as long as he could and in the prevarication had found no way to make palatable what his employer was about to hear.

'The packet brought in the mails also carried certain communications that require I report to you.'

'Go on,' came the guarded reply.

'There are letters from London to both Toby Burns and Lieutenant Pearce, both with the superscription of the same sender.' Toomey waited, hoping Hotham would save him saying the words; he waited in vain and he was sure there was something of a crack in his voice as he continued. 'That lawyer fellow engaged to enquire into the circumstances of Captain Barclay's court martial. If he is writing to Pearce, then that establishes beyond peradventure that he is the person who engaged him.'

'Did we not suspect it to be so?'

'We did, sir.'

'Does that man's malice know no bounds?'

'Both have other letters, Sir William: Pearce from his prize agent and Burns from several relatives. I feel it might be necessary that we are appraised of the contents of those lawyer letters before they are delivered.'

'You have them separate?'

'I have.'

All mail for the fleet passed through the flagship prior to distribution and this was the second delivery that had come to HMS *Britannia*. Toomey did not deal with bulging sacks personally – naval folk were great communicators and so were their relatives – that task fell to the letter writers transferred from *Victory*. Although because of previous problems he had made a point of checking on their efforts, supposedly out of a concern – and he knew it annoyed his inferiors who saw him as a fusspot – that it should be properly handled.

Hotham leant forward and rifled through his official correspondence. Toomey did not have to ask what he was seeking – the despatch telling him Captain Ralph Barclay, now in command of a HMS *Semele* seventy-four, was on his way – and he knew it was only the admiral making a point. It did not have to be stated that such a development was an additional concern.

'I have never taken much pleasure in surprises, Toomey.'

'No, sir.'

'Especially in a matter that should have been laid to rest long ago.'

The way that was said annoyed Toomey, though he had to hide it. If he had acted to aid his employer in what had become a deepening problem it was not he who had initiated matters; that lay squarely at the admiral's door. Not that such a fact was much use.

'I take it things will be seen to?' Hotham asked after a long pause.

That was not a request, but a command, which would have him apply hot metal to the sealing wax on those letters so that Hotham could be apprised of their contents.

'In the light of that, sir, should we proceed with the examination of Mr Burns? The person you have put to instructing him feels that the youngster is as ready as he will ever be.'

Of all the difficulties just aired, for all the banes of Hotham's existence, Toby Burns had proved to be the most persistent for the very simple reason of his close proximity as a serving midshipman aboard the flagship. He was a dangerous link between Barclay and Pearce as well as one who had the ability to be the most troublesome. The notion was that he should be promoted to a rank he scarcely warranted and sent to serve under a reliable captain in order to be controlled.

'Given it was your notion, Toomey, I think you should decide.'

'Sir.'

'No slip-ups, Toomey,' Hotham snapped. 'That little toad has wriggled his way out of things too many times, d' ye hear?'

'Survived' would be a better word, Sir William having sent him many times into situations of great danger where he could be injured or even killed. There had been a brief moment when the admiral thought the latter had happened and himself shot of the problem, only for Burns to reappear and once more ruin his equilibrium. Toomey had good reason to suppose the existence of Burns upset him to the point where it preyed upon his mind.

'He will be appraised of the nub of the questions before he enters the cabin where he will be examined. Even a dunce like Burns cannot fail.'

He left Hotham still looking out at the sparkling Mediterranean

Sea, which reflected the azure of the cloudless sky – it seemed as if summer this particular year would never end – his thoughts a jumble of memories and problems, not least that if the position of captain of a King's ship was a lonely occupation bringing with it endless challenges, being an admiral in charge of a fleet was doubly so. The information about those letters made him feel vulnerable and that was not a happy place to be.

Why the past event, which came occasionally to haunt him, should surface now he did not know, but surface it did: the huge mark that he was sure stood against his name within the ranks of the service. Not that he could be sure; no one ever mentioned the matter in his presence.

In command of a squadron of frigates during the American War and escorting a convoy of hugely valuable merchantmen, he had been intercepted by a group of French capital ships, two of them 100-gun Leviathans.

Unable to intervene – frigates could not fight ships-of-the-line – he had been obliged to watch as they filleted his convoy and took most of them captive. Hotham was sure that amongst his peers this was seen as pusillanimity. The Admiralty did not think so; indeed he had been praised for refusing to fall for the temptation of useless sacrifice; yet even that vindication left Hotham feeling exposed to behind-the-hand criticism that it was only his political connections that had spared him.

Sometimes he was sure he saw it in the looks he got from the officers who served aboard his flagship and gazing over that for which he had schemed so long, a fleet to command, Hotham was less than sure he was happy with the concomitant responsibility. To fail now would not be forgiven or understood; he must engage the French and give them a sound drubbing. Failure to do so could lead to the kind of disgrace that saw Admiral Byng, following on from his fiasco off Minorca, shot by firing squad on the quarterdeck of his own flagship.

The image of Ralph Barclay resurfaced to trouble him even more, especially in the light of what Toomey had just told him. Why had he got involved in the first place? Even as he castigated himself he knew he had enjoyed no alternative. Even before Toulon, Barclay had made no secret of his loyalty to Hotham, which put him at odds with Lord Hood, not an advantageous position for an ambitious officer, albeit the man had never been popular in that quarter so was unlikely in any event to be favoured.

Still it was a bold statement and one that required he be protected from what Hotham had seen as a specious charge of illegal impressment. How else was the navy to be manned without pressed men? If Barclay had strayed outside the strict limits of the law by entering the prohibited Liberties of the Savoy, so what? And who was this damned fellow who had lodged the complaint with Lord Hood only for him to land the problem in the lap of his second-in-command? Pearce was nothing but a jumped-up radical who should never have been given a lieutenant's rank in the first place.

With a client officer in some difficulty he had no choice but to support him; not to do so would make every other captain who depended upon Hotham wonder if they had hitched a ride on the wrong wagon; in short, the obligation went in two directions and, obliged to act, he felt he had manoeuvred with some cunning. He had his letter writer take depositions from a trio of common seamen: O'Hagan, Taverner and Dommet, fellows John Pearce referred to by the nonsensical soubriquet of Pelicans, men who had been pressed at the same time, all of whom confirmed where it had taken place and who had led the raid.

Hotham then sent them all off on a mission to the Bay of Biscay under the command of Henry Digby, a junior lieutenant aboard Barclay's frigate, which meant their depositions could then be safely ignored. Along with them went Pearce and a midshipman called Farmiloe, the former because he would be the chief and most formidable accuser, the mid because Farmiloe had actually been present in the Liberties and so was an equally dangerous witness.

With all those who could harm Barclay out of the way, he set up and staffed the court with officers he could trust to come to the right verdict, and allowing Barclay to present his nephew by marriage, that weak and malleable article Toby Burns, as the main witness. He had been well coached to take the blame for something he had not done, namely to admit he had, on a dark and moonless night, set the Press Gang ashore in the wrong place on the Thames riverside so the illegality could be seen as an error. Barclay, reproached for being over-indulgent to a young and inexperienced midshipman, thus escaped with a reprimand.

If it was generally known through the higher reaches of the command what Hotham had done, no one, Hood or his Captain of the Fleet, Hyde Parker, was prepared to go any further than making him aware they knew it to be a farce of a trial. Hood had confirmed the verdict as C-in-C and sent the papers off to London.

That should have left Pearce high and dry, baying into a vacuum on his return, given Barclay could not be tried on the same charge twice. Nor could Hotham see how any other problems could flow from his actions, assured as he was that once the court martial papers were safe in the vaults of the Admiralty in London, there they would remain and hidden, leaving the verdict unopen to challenge.

Then came Lucknor, a lawyer seeking information on Barclay from the likes of Toby Burns: The only purpose could be to seek grounds to justify an enquiry and that could lead to all sorts of complications. If that succeeded it might not be heard in a naval court but a civilian one and if the evidence of the court martial saw the light of day – a judge could force the Admiralty to divulge it – in such a setting Hotham risked being implicated by association and it might even extend to those captains who had carried out his wishes as judges.

Had the lawyer sought to gather evidence from those who knew the truth of what occurred on that night, Farmiloe and Digby, since they would know that Burns had not participated in the raid? He had to assume it likely, but as serving officers intent of making their way and called upon to damn a senior like Barclay, they could probably be relied upon to be circumspect in their replies and certainly they would be reluctant witnesses. Not so Toby Burns, the one person who could definitely sink his uncle by marriage and that would put Hotham under scrutiny.

The lawyer had hinted that, if Burns had lied at the court martial, the only way the youngster could avoid trouble himself was to turn prosecution witness and plead coercion. The reply, opened by Toomey, curious as to why the lad was communicating with a London lawyer, was so damning it could not be sent and another had been composed by his clerk to take its place. At all costs the spineless little toad must never face a civilian judge for he would sing like the proverbial canary to save his own neck.

Hotham was aware that Toomey, after not much of a knock,

had re-entered the cabin and he turned to see on his face an air of deep concern, held as he joined Hotham by the casements, where he spoke in almost a whisper, a common precaution on a ship of war, where it seemed the bulkheads had ears.

'A copy of the letter I composed has been sent to Pearce along with the suggestion that he find Burns and ask him if what he wrote is all he knows of the matter.'

'Meaning he clearly suspects not.'

That put Toomey, as the originator, on the defensive. 'All the man says is that it disquiets him but he does not say why.'

'We must make sure Pearce will not get the chance to ask.' Hotham grunted, there was no need to add the youngster could not be allowed to see it. 'The letter to Burns?'

'Mr Lucknor asks for various clarifications, really the man is fishing for inconsistencies, which I will of course take care of.'

Inwardly Toomey was cursing. He had seen his actions at the time as merely aiding his master and on reflection he now regretted it, especially since it had not solved the problem. Worse it had put him on a par with Ralph Barclay; such acts as the forging of a letter to conceal a crime came under the heading of conspiracy. If exposure might see William Hotham disgraced it could lead to him swinging from the Tyburn gallows.

'No sign of Pearce yet?'

'He is well overdue, sir.'

'Fellow's a poxed sybarite, Toomey. No doubt he is troughing his snout in the fleshpots of Naples. Still, if he is not returned and Barclay has yet to appear, it gives us a chance to put matters in hand.'

'What do you have in mind, sir?'

There was a very long pause in which the admiral remained deep in contemplation. When he did speak it was in the cautious and hushed tone that had covered the whole of their exchange.

'Something I once considered a pleasing fantasy may have to be made reality.'

Toomey waited for further elucidation but none was forthcoming; whatever it was Hotham was not going to share it. 'I think it would be best to pass on the other letters, sir, to avoid suspicion.'

'Make it so.'

Back in the screened-off cubicle that served as his place of work, Toomey began to assess what had happened and most tellingly how it affected him. Being clerk to an admiral – and a confidant – was a highly sought-after and well-rewarded position and he was determined to keep it, not least given he, too, expected Hotham to supersede Hood as C-in-C. This would, at a stroke, increase his stipend by half to £150 per annum, a sum above the pay of the captain of a fifth-rate frigate, very little of which he was required to spend, given the navy fed and accommodated him.

The position had not come to him without application and effort; he had begun shipboard life as a purser's mate and after much application became a purser, a position he found less than comfortable given it exposed the holder to much financial risk and a real, if rare, possibility of bankruptcy. It did however show his aptitude for letters and numbers, and he had shifted to become clerk to the then Captain Hotham, a much more secure place to earn a wage.

The Irishman had two burdens; one was his own ambition to comport himself as a gentleman, which he would achieve in time by husbandry of his money, something only broken by his very rare, indulgent runs ashore for a touch of debauchery. The other was a dependant family in Wicklow that, being to his mind idle, saw him as the source of all their needs and complained loudly when he often refused to meet their requests.

In so readily aiding Hotham he had been, he now realised, seduced by his own abiding desire to be rated as ingenious, writing that letter when he should have been pointing out to the admiral the obstacles Pearce would have in getting Ralph Barclay, as a serving officer in the King's service, into the dock without any *prima facie* evidence.

Did that lawyer have something they did not know of? Toomey ran the thought through his head for, even if his legal knowledge was limited, it seemed to him that this matter would not be progressing unless Lucknor and Pearce reckoned a case could be made. Were there facts of which he was not aware? If there were he had to acknowledge the only time he would be made so was when it proceeded to some kind of indictment and that was a thought to induce anxiety.

What to do now? The notion of betrayal to save himself could not be included. He had to keep his place, for to be dismissed – and he would not put it past Sir William to do so if he thwarted his wishes or failed to aid him – was to be cast into an unknown future. Would another officer employ him when such an elevated personage had clearly found him wanting? They certainly would not if he helped to ruin him.

There was a very distinct possibility the whole thing could blow up in his face and that of Hotham too, a fact of which the admiral could not be unaware. The three main players in this seedy affair were about to be in the same place. Pearce and HMS *Larcher* would return to San Fiorenzo Bay and Toby Burns was already here. The only person missing was Ralph Barclay and, according to that despatch, his arrival was imminent.

'Whatever you have in mind, Hotham,' he whispered to himself, as the ramifications of that combination ran through his mind, 'it had better be a stroke of genius. Might be best to let Barclay plough his own furrow!'

CHAPTER EIGHT

If asked, the captain of HMS *Semele* would have told anyone who cared to listen that he was not one to enjoy the duty he was now obliged to undertake; it was, however, one he would not shirk. The whole crew were on deck, here to witness punishment being meted out to one of their number. Some would see it as a travesty, the sea lawyer types that plagued every vessel in the King's Navy. Others, and Barclay reckoned the majority, knowing the man had got himself drunk, going on to rudely abuse the premier, would reckon him to be getting what he deserved.

'Mr Penny,' he asked his youngest and brand-new lieutenant, 'this man serves in your division. Do you have anything to say in his defence?'

The youngster was as white as a sheet, showing that he clearly did not relish either being on deck or the notion of witnessing what he was about to watch. That for his commanding officer was telling; he held that a man who shied away from this might also shy away from a full engagement in battle. Unknown to Penny there was now a question mark against his name for, if most aboard the seventy-four gunner had been in the Battle of the Glorious First of June, he had not.

'Perkins has been diligent in his duty, sir, and this is the first time he has given me cause for concern.'

A well-worn mantra, Barclay thought, and one I have used myself but it will not serve. He replied to Penny but the message was for all assembled. 'If a man transgresses, Mr Penny, then he must be brought to a reminder of his duty, for if he is not, bad behaviour is prone to become a habit. Bosun, seize him up!'

It was the bosun's mates who did the seizing, taking some delight in a dramatic ripping of the man's shirt, the replacement for which he would have to pay the purser, and thus added an additional punishment to what he was about to endure. By the time he was lashed to the grating, one clear fact had been established: this was not his first flogging; his back bore the scars of previous chastisement and that got Penny a jaundiced look from his captain; diligent in his duty, is he?

'Carry on.'

The bosun stepped forward and loosened the whip, freshly made for this day's work, which had Barclay eyeing it to see if it was of the right quality and would be painful when employed. He knew that it was possible to be humbugged by the instrument, for the bosun's mates to manufacture one that scarce marked the skin; indeed he had been so mocked in the matter on one occasion.

Given the man at the grating on that occasion had been John

Pearce, more trouble than any common sea lawyer and the swine, moreover, who had run off with his wife, he felt the bile rise in his throat as the first crack of the whip hit flesh. Six times this was repeated and with commendable gusto on behalf of the bosun; he laid in with a will to create huge red weals. The skin broke on the third lash and in his mind's eye Barclay envisaged a different back to that actually before him. Then he glanced sideways at Penny, to see the man's eyes closed.

'Attend to it, Mr Penny,' he growled softly. 'If you serve long enough in the navy you will witness much worse than this.'

'Aye, aye, sir,' the lieutenant replied, opening his eyes, but raising them high over the scene before him.

'Take him down,' came the order as the last of the six hit home, sending blood spraying in several directions, some of it far enough to carry beyond the canvas spread to catch it. 'And I would like my deck pristine, as it should be!'

This order, delivered to no one in particular, was sent out as Barclay made his way to his cabin, Perkins being carried below to be attended upon by the surgeon. Right behind the captain came Devenow, a huge and brutish fellow who had endured more floggings than most, some of them wished upon him by the man he so slavishly attended upon. He was rated as a servant, if that was the correct word for a man who could not serve a tureen of soup without spillage, nor let a bottle pass out of the pantry from which he had not taken a swig.

Devenow always stayed close to Ralph Barclay and not just through admiration for the man he held as near a father to him. The captain, with only one arm, even with his very good sea legs, was at risk of a fall if the deck shifted suddenly and with unexpected strength; his servant was there to steady him. On the rare occasions it happened, such a stumble usually got Devenow a mouthful of abuse.

'The master has just informed me we will raise the mouth of the Tagus tomorrow.'

This observation, delivered as he entered his great cabin, was barked at Cornelius Gherson, his clerk, who lifted his head in response to reveal his absurdly handsome, almost girlish face, which, topped as it was with fine blond hair, had led many a woman a merry dance. Given his preference for the married kind, this had usually been an expensive taste for both her and her cuckolded spouse.

'Then let us pray, sir, there is something for us.'

'My coat, Devenow.'

That had the servant step forwards to take his hat then help his master remove the heavy blue garment, tipped with the twin epaulettes that told all that its owner was a full post captain on more than three years' seniority. Gherson had ceased to look at Barclay, instead cast his eye on Devenow; the change in Gherson's expression was striking, going from supplicant to distinctly malevolent which changed what was handsome to one unattractively surly.

The pair loathed each other, which suited the man who employed them right down to the deck planking; sure that everyone in the world was capable of conspiring against him, including his inferior officers, his naval peers and superiors, Ralph Barclay preferred those who served him to be so disunited that they would never combine in any way which would be detrimental to him.

'You'll boat ashore as soon as we anchor off Lisbon, Gherson.'

'Surely we would want to see if there are any plate ships in the roads, sir.'

'There may be specie destined for the fleet that we can carry that has not come in from the Americas.'

Fat chance of that, Gherson reckoned, and if it had, some other sod would have got the passage of it and thus the reward of a percentage of the value. A greedy fellow himself, and not an entirely honest one, Gherson was quick to lay the label on others for faults he himself had but would deny. Ralph Barclay and he formed a strange combination; the clerk had scant respect for his employer's intelligence and not much more for him as a person, albeit with the full realisation that the man did not care.

Being loved figured low on Barclay's list of priorities; what mattered to him was his career: that he should suffer no blemish on his record, should rise in the service, in time to hoist his own flag and profit from it on the way. There lay the glue that bound the pair together, for Gherson was just as eager that Barclay should prosper as was the captain himself, for he, too, would profit by it.

If Ralph Barclay was hurt by his wife's desertion – and he was – it was as much to do with the potential dent to his standing as the loss of her connubial affections, and added to that he felt cheated by her ingratitude. Had he not taken a slip of a girl from a provincial background and opened up to her a world of opportunities? She had rewarded him by taking up too much of what was on offer, not least the freedom to criticise his actions both as a husband and naval officer.

'I will want a letter composed to be sent off to Ommaney & Druce. They need to be reminded to keep me informed of what they are up to and such types are over prone to think that out of sight is out of mind.'

'Already partly composed, sir,' Gherson responded.

He lowered his head to hide a thin smile as his employer sat down on the well-cushioned casement lockers, Devenow having disappeared to the pantry. The firm served as Barclay's prize agents and looked after his investments, quite substantial now that he had garnered a great deal of prize money since the start of the war. There was a merchant ship taken off Brittany at the very outbreak, still in dispute at the Admiralty court and another rescued from Barbary pirates on his last visit to the Mediterranean, both deep laden with valuable cargoes.

But the greatest boost to his funds came from his very recent participation in the Battle of the Glorious First of June, a fleet action that had led to several enemy capital vessels being taken captive. When the various sums were added up – the value of the hulls, guns and head money for captured sailors – he and his fellow tars, down to the meanest waister, had shared in rewards in excess of £200,000. If he had subsequently fallen out with Lord Howe, the man who commanded the battle, he had been entitled to his share of the proceeds.

Condescended to by those very same prize agents at the outbreak of the present conflict as the impecunious captain of a frigate – Barclay had been on the beach for five years and was in straitened circumstances – he was now treated like royalty when he called upon them to see how his investments fared. Not that he deigned to examine the accounts himself; that was left to his clerk, while he consumed the best claret Ommaney & Druce could provide.

Unbeknown to Barclay, Gherson was working on their behalf, on a commission basis, to ensure their firm made maximum profits from the captain's money, sometimes in very speculative investments that they would hesitate to risk with their own money. What Gherson told his employer – that most of his funds were in safe Government Consols, and what was imparted to him by Edward Druce, the partner he dealt with, were never quite the same.

'I'll be glad to be in the Med, I must say,' Barclay sighed, in what was for him near to a confidence. 'Not only has it been a happy hunting ground in the past, but I will be able to settle my domestic affairs once and for all.'

There was no need to refer to Emily Barclay; Gherson knew all about the captain's troubles in that area and had aided him in recovering his wife on more than one occasion, not without risk to his own person. This was not undertaken out of regard; Gherson had started his naval life as a pressed seaman, only gaining his present position because of his obvious head for figures. It was one he had every intention of holding on to, for a clerk to a successful ship's captain could find many ways to ensure that when any sums were expended, a certain amount, admittedly small, would be diverted in his direction.

But it was the long-term aim that really mattered. Ralph Barclay was not far off the top of the list of post captains and in time, death and disgrace notwithstanding, he would rise to the rank of admiral and, being an active officer, would likely be given some kind of command. These could be exceedingly lucrative – the two West Indies stations and the Far East were worth a king's ransom. None were without reward and regardless of those postings there was a war on and it looked set to last. There was a great deal of money to be made and Gherson reckoned that he could siphon off enough to set himself up for the rest of his life; the notion that he would spend it bowing at the knee to Ralph Barclay was not one he envisaged.

Emily Barclay had made that dream more taxing so he would do anything necessary to thwart her. Added to his financial considerations, he had once harboured designs on the lady himself only to be rudely rebuffed and, unaccustomed to having his advances rejected, as well as her subsequent attitude of open dislike, had her marked in his mind as an enemy. Aware that his employer was looking at him and that some of the thoughts regarding the man's wife might be apparent on his face, he sought to divert any suspicion by his usual method – sycophancy.

'It is to be hoped we find more prizes in the Mediterranean, sir, to add lustre to your already sterling reputation.'

That got Gherson a sour look, the flattery being so excessive Barclay knew it could only be deliberate, seeing it wrongly as his clerk's preferred way of redressing what he clearly reckoned to be a false imbalance in their respective places. He was about to check him when Gherson added, in a less unctuous tone.

'Speaking of your domestic affairs, sir, it may be a place to achieve a solution more difficult to manage than in England.'

That had Barclay's chin slump to his chest, for he was not unaware of what the man was driving at, hardly possible since Gherson had made little secret of the solution he advised to a problem that to his mind was intractable. With his past, which had involved a fair amount of criminality, how to resolve it was as plain as day and notions of morality could not be allowed to interfere. Emily Barclay should be got rid of!

Her husband shied away from such extremes; he wanted his wife to return to the marital home – the bed was less important – for he feared loss of face more than a denial of his rights as a husband; the notion of men laughing at him behind his back as a cuckold ate at his very soul.

'All to be considered, Gherson,' he sighed, for he had not utterly discounted the possibility of what was being proposed, 'all to be considered.'

'It will also be interesting to see how your nephew Toby has fared.'

'One of these days, Gherson, you will take your teasing too far. It is not beyond the bounds of discipline to see a clerk tied to the same grating as the one from which I just departed and for the same reason.'

'It was well intentioned, sir.'

Gherson had replied quickly, having gone pale at the obvious threat, one he could not be sure was false. Ralph Barclay responded with a smile to the man's obvious discomfort, content that he believed him.

'Personally I hope the little turd has been chucked over the side by his shipmates, with a cannonball down his breeches.'

Toby Burns was hunched over his books in the midshipman's berth of HMS *Britannia* and he was worried; it seemed the more he read the less he recalled, for there were few words in his *Seaman's Vade Mecum* or his *Faulkner's Dictionary* that he had not studied a hundred times, yet now it was as if he had never seen them before.

He might have been told that the answers he had been given were those to the questions he would be asked, but fate and his fellow humans had, to his mind, played so many false tricks the youngster had serious doubts they could be true.

He knew in his heart he was not fit to be ranked lieutenant; indeed he could not fathom why it was that Sir William Hotham was so insistent he sit the exam. He was, for a start, too young, added to which he lacked the requisite sea time. Not that what was about to take place was unique; shipboard tales abounded of rules being broken by senior officers, of mere lads being elevated due to the level of their interest, normally a blood relationship to an admiral.

The most scandalous had been the well-reported attempt by the late Admiral Rodney to raise his twelve-year-old son to the rank and income of post captain, an act so brazen it had been blocked by the Admiralty. If they had been sharp, enough examples of official laxity existed to give admirals on a distant station good enough reason to chance their arm.

Then there was the feeling that Hotham was using it as another means to get rid of him, something the lad thought he had been trying to do for months, ever since that damned court martial at which he had been obliged to lie on his uncle's behalf. 'Obliged' was the wrong word, he had been intimidated and had felt insecure ever since, never more so than by the actions of the admiral, who, as he put it, 'was determined to give young Mr Burns every opportunity to distinguish himself'.

Translated from drivel it meant constantly putting him in harm's way. A dangerous mission in Toulon first had reduced Burns to jelly. Several assignments in Corsica followed before the final defeat of the French, twice under the command of that madman Horatio Nelson, the last resulting in a spell as an enemy prisoner in the recently captured citadel of Calvi. And yet here in this berth, he was envied by his peers for the chances that an indulgent admiral had put his way.

If he did pass he might get out of this stinking hellhole, home to two-dozen midshipmen ranging from a lout in his mid-twenties who would never achieve a step up, to a couple of not long-arrived twelve-year-olds whose main contribution to the berth was the noise of their homesick whimpering, that was when they were not bleating about the theft of their possessions.

In reality he dearly wanted out of the navy, which had turned out to provide a life very far from the romantic notions he had harboured the day he boarded HMS *Brilliant* at Sheerness. He found his uncle by marriage unsympathetic, the duties uncongenial, the risk of death or mutilation terrifying and the company of his fellow midshipmen dire. Such a decision would be easier to justify to his family if he had at least achieved the right to a commissioned rank, something that could never be taken from him, not very grand but grand enough.

To them, following a supposed exploit at the very outbreak of war, he was a hero; the notion that he would not continue to serve and would go on to greater feats of glory would be incomprehensible. There was nothing heroic about any of his actions, quite the reverse; his whole reputation was built on invention.

The pulling back of the canvas screen made Toby Burns snarl; he expected to be confronted by the permanently filthy face of the mid's berth servant, a fellow who saw soap and water as mortal sins and who had never been known to use any. Instead there was Mr Toomey, Hotham's clerk, which left Toby wondering if he had ever seen the fellow so far down in the bowels of the ship before. He thought not.

'Mr Burns, I have here some letters for you, from your family I would guess. Also the Board of Examination is about to go into session and is awaiting your attendance.'

Toby shot to his feet, as careful as any other tar to mind his head, took the letters and without examining the inscriptions tossed them onto the sea chest he had just vacated. He took more care to lay down his *Vade Mecum* and *Dictionary* before he picked up his hat, gathered up the journals showing his progress in navigation and other common naval duties, then stepped out onto the open deck. To call it that was a total misnomer – it was airless, dark and the smell of bilge was strong, which explained the rosemary nosegay that Toomey briefly held to his nose; the clerk was used to better air.

'Now let us ensure you present them a good figure,' Toomey said, tugging at Toby's necktie, then his midshipman's short blue jacket like a mother sending a child to his first day at a new school. 'Let us see that hat set on your head, eh?'

Satisfied, he added. 'You are ready for this?'

There was only one reply, even if it was false. 'As ever I will be, sir.'

'The admiral sends his wishes that you do well. Cannot impart them himself, of course, for that would be seen as prejudicial.'

'Of course,' Toby replied, wondering in his innocent way what was not prejudicial about his being fully primed to pass, if indeed that was the case. 'I do hope I do not disappoint him.'

'Never in life, lad. Sent me special to fetch you so you could sense the high regard he has for you.'

Toomey set off with Toby on his heels, up the companionways to the main deck and thence on to the captain's cabin, taken over for the examination. He opened the door and led him past the marine sentry and the pantry to the actual entrance to the cabin, this opened by yet another red-coated Lobster. Four captains sat behind a long trestle table covered in green baize and on their faces they wore the kind of expressions that preceded a good flogging, looking so formidable that Toby wanted to run. He could not, of course, but he felt the need to tighten his alimentary organs lest he disgrace himself.

'Sit down, Mr Burns.'

The voice was somehow familiar and as he peered from his chair he realised this was the same fellow who had sat in judgement at his Uncle Ralph's court martial. As he sat down and looked at the others present he felt a sense of *déjà vu*: they, too, had a familiarity to them, not that such knowledge eased his nerves. What followed was an encomium on what he was about to face and the consequences. It was no light matter to seek to qualify as a lieutenant in the King's Navy; the rank was important and the responsibilities great; was he prepared to fully accept those as well as the honour that went with it?

'I am, sir.'

'You have the reputation of being something of a hero, have you not?'

'An exaggeration, sir,' was the only reply, now an automatic one.

'Your modesty does you credit, sir, but if I allude to your

exploits it is only to say to you that while commendable it is not enough to justify a positive verdict from this board.'

'Yes, sir.'

'Your journals then, Mr Burns.'

The record of his studies and activities were passed over to be perused and it was some time before the first question was posed by the captain on the far right, this relating to his observations, which he no longer had before him, on the defences of the Port of Toulon. That did relax Toby; it was the question on which he had been tutored to concentrate. Not that he replied with confidence; he had been told a nervous tone would be suitable and he acted as had been rehearsed, pausing to look as if he was searching for the right answer several times. It seemed to work, given the understanding nods from the other side of that trestle.

There were questions on how to take on board and stow stores in a way that kept level the keel of the ship, transgressions of the Articles of War, navigation by compass, charts and his sextant followed by the same in the absence of one of those instruments or all three, all responded to with a decent tremor in his young voice, especially on the article of lunar observations. Then came the last; how would he react to an emergency, this finding himself in command of a frigate in contrary winds on a lee shore?

Out it came as stuttered words from memory; he would have a kedge fashioned and dropped astern to slow the inward progress and adjust the sails to keep steerage way without adding to the problem of drifting. A man would be placed in the chains to take soundings, no two, so he would have some idea of the depth of water under his keel, as well as the consistency of the sea bed, giving him the point at which he could seek to drop a fluke anchor in holding ground. The crew would then be sent to man the capstan, to haul the ship off to a position that she could safely lay off.

'Is there anything else, Mr Burns?'

'There is one other thing,' he replied, to be met with a raised eyebrow. 'I would put a pair of armed guards on the spirit room.'

That got appreciative nods and another enquiry. 'Marines?'

'No, sir,' he replied with suitable gravity, 'I fear for safety's sake it would have to be those ship's officers I could spare from other pressing duties.'

The man chairing the examination looked at his fellows to see if they were finished with their questions, before saying, after each had nodded. 'Please await our conclusion outside, Mr Burns.'

On deck it took little effort to see that nearly every other midshipman with whom he shared his berth had contrived to get into a position where they could observe the outcome. The youth they were watching had no illusions, wet behind the ears, newcomers apart, that they might be wishing him luck for if they had any knowledge of seafaring themselves, they knew how lacking this candidate was in that department.

Called back in to receive the predicted result, when he emerged again it was as if there was some method of verbal transmission that bypassed the laws of nature; it seemed they all knew. But that did not lead to congratulations, still less any cheering. The fellow they referred to when he was out of earshot as 'Hotham's bum boy' had, they knew, got his result through cheating.

Looking around, observing the way they failed to meet his eye, Toby felt a surge akin to pleasure; some of these people had made a life he held to be miserable doubly so. Now, if he was not actually a lieutenant until he was placed in that rank of a ship, he was Toby Burns, passed midshipman and naturally a superior; he had the means to make them pay for past slights and to see that revenge given – it was almost worth staying in the navy for!

CHAPTER NINE

The screen that had allowed Pearce and his crew to get off HMS *Larcher* provided only partial protection from what had followed; a continuation of grape shot being fired through a vessel totally consumed by flames as well as a near impenetrable black cloud of pitch filled smoke. Progress up an already difficult slope was hampered by the need to take cover, their captain trying to time each salvo from what he had previously experienced of the rate of fire, which was no more than guesswork.

'You know, Michael,' Pearce imparted with a grim laugh as they cowered behind a new boulder. 'I forgot, as a captain should, to mark the time of the first Barbary salvo or anything that followed. When I face a court for the loss of *Larcher* that will not sit well with the judges.'

'Sure, it's a blessing for you to know you're useless, is it not?'

'Never cease to remind me, friend,' Pearce responded, while looking at his watch as the hand ticked round, first one minute then two, with no further salvo. 'I think our Barbary brigand has decided he is wasting his shot.'

'So we're free to move?'

'Give it time yet, it may be a ruse to catch us in the open.'

'And that would not bar him from any other ideas he has, John-boy.'

Pearce had no need to respond; he knew what Michael was driving at, that a man who had pursued them so relentlessly might not give up easily. There were bays within less than a mile both east and west of the narrow inlet into which they had driven the armed cutter and there had to be a route to the crest from both. If he chose to land men upon them there was nothing that could be done to prevent it.

'Let us move then.'

It was not just the increasing height that opened up a better view of the Gulf of Policastro; the conflagration consuming their ship had peaked and was dying down, while at the same time the sun was going with it. From the first sight of the enemy's upper masts, both brigantines now, they knew them to be still hove to offshore and stationary. Pearce reckoned they had dropped anchor, which did not bode well. Had they sent out boats with a shore party, something that would still be hidden from view?

Scrabbling up through rocks and scrub brush, with loose screed underfoot and only one good arm, Pearce needed Michael O'Hagan more than once to help prevent a fall but at least he was better off than the one-legged Bellam, whose loud cursing filled the air, and he was being matched by the fellow from the *Lazaretto* who needed to use his stick to progress. It was also exhausting work for all, the air being still and hot; if there was a breeze it was not playing on this section of the coast.

In his frequent stops to draw breath Pearce could see how spread out were most of those for whom he was responsible. If they were subject to a pursuit, being in the open was not going to serve, so he shouted to those furthest ahead that they should aim to their right and make for the tower that stood at the highest point of the hills and skirted the shore.

The closer he came the more he reckoned his first thought – that it was abandoned – was correct. A man standing on its uppermost battlements could not have failed to see what had happened with *Larcher* nor the figures making hard work of climbing the slope. But being empty did not render it useless as far as he was concerned; even in a poor state it could provide a place in which to mount a solid defence, for it would not be gunnery but musket against musket and cutlass against scimitar. Even badly outnumbered, behind any kind of stonework they could make the cost of continued battle too high.

Emily, with Charlie Taverner and Rufus Dommet on each side, was well to the fore, though they had been overtaken by the most fleet of foot, the armed cutter's topmen. He yelled for them to wait but to no avail, either because they could not hear or because they chose to ignore him. By the time he and Michael got onto the flat ground before the tower everyone but Bellam and those aiding him were there, most milling around with no common purpose, which led to a sharp command to cease behaving like headless chickens. If there was a clear pause before that was acted upon at least the instruction was obeyed, which allowed him to go to Emily and check she was all right.

'Hot,' was all she said, adding a wan smile. 'And with badly torn stockings.'

'You are not unique in that,' Pearce replied, with a glance at his own shredded calves.

There was no wind up here either, which was surprising: Pearce had assumed that it was the hills cutting it off and there were higher massifs not far off, but there should have been something. Looking north-east towards what were distant mountains, he saw their tops shrouded in dense and billowing clouds, which indicated there might be a change in the weather on the way; shelter thus became doubly necessary.

'Has anyone found the entrance?'

'Round the back, Capt'n, there's a blocked off doorway.'

The speaker, one of those fleet-footed topmen, was on his way without waiting, Pearce following to be shown that which he had described, a stout door set in a stone arch, with a trio of heavy baulks of wood across, several feet off the ground, higher than the height of a man, with no steps leading to it. The rest of the crew had followed his next command: the men carrying axes were to find some timber with which to construct a rough ladder, not too major a task given at this height there was an abundance of trees.

'And we will need a stout lever to get those baulks off.'

Being resourceful was the natural habit of the British tar: aboard a ship each man absorbed so much in the way of varying skills that the order Pearce had issued was not long in being completed. He was soon provided with a set of short rough branches lashed across two long narrow poles, the risers secured with bark stripped from tree trunks with knives. If it looked makeshift and rough it did the job and the carpenter Brad Kempshall, who had obliged his mates to carry his tools, had overseen the cutting of a thicker piece of wood long enough to act as the lever. It therefore came as a real surprise when the first of those stout baulks, subjected to the required pressure, came away with no trouble at all.

Ten feet of timber and as thick as a lintel beam, it nearly knocked the man sent up the ladder off his perch: he only maintained it by pushing it to one side and letting it fall, sending scattering those below, which was just as well; crowned it would have been mortal to the victim.

'They's not fixed proper, Capt'n,' he cried, 'just sat in holes.'

Pearce went to examine the fallen beam and saw at once that it had four stout and protruding dowels set into it at the corners. He then looked up to where his crewman was balancing and was shown the holes in the brickwork in which they had sat, so he ordered him down and had everyone stand back as the other two beams were levered off with the same ease, to crash to the ground. Everyone was looking at him, requiring their captain to make sense of this, in which they were disappointed; he had no more of a clue than had they.

'The door?'

A sailor ran back up the ladder and reached out to push, but to no avail. 'Big lock, your honour. Take some effort to shift.'

'Best you have a look,' Pearce said to his carpenter.

Brad Kempshall called the man down and replaced him, his opinion being that the only way to get past it was to chisel the frame, which he pronounced as near to rotten. Looking at the sky and realising how soon it would be dark, Pearce ordered him to forget a chisel and employ an axe.

'Mr Bird, you and a couple of men with muskets to the other side to keep a lookout. You will not be able to see the actual shore, but anyone making their way up the slope, even taking frequent cover, must give a sign of their presence. Look for a sudden flurry of birds, for any that had been nesting in the bushes will have settled again now the gunfire has ceased and Mr Bellam has finished his cursing.'

The joke being taken with grins cheered him and with nothing to contribute he went once more to check on Emily, sat in the shade of a gnarled olive tree, their quiet talk made over the sound of a flailing axe as Brad Kempshall and his mates took turns to hack at wood that could have been in place for centuries and had been put there to keep out marauders.

'Once we are inside I will feel safer,' he explained. 'We have food, water and are well armed. Even if they do chase us I would say they will see it as useless to try an assault.'

'And then?'

'Once we are sure it is safe to do so, we must find a road to the north that will take us to Naples.'

'You are sure there will be one, John?'

That got a smile. 'This is the old Roman Empire we are sat in, Emily. Were they not famous for their roads?'

'I am never quite sure, John, if I find your being sanguine reassuring or irritating.'

The sound that came then was not of the axe, but a distant rumble of thunder. It had Pearce standing and peering at the clouds he spotted earlier, which had thickened and darkened. 'We're in for a storm, but not for a while yet.'

'Doors open, Capt'n,' came the cry.

'See anything?'

'Place is full of big clay pots, stacked high and full judging by my push.'

It took Pearce time to climb the ladder, having to hook his slung arm on each rung before he could move his feet up, but when he got there he saw the truth of what he had been told. It was obviously being used by the locals as a storehouse, which went some way to explaining those loose baulks; they would need access on a regular basis but still wanted to deter intruders.

The next obvious fact was that there was no room for him and all of his men as well as what were substantial ampoules. It posed a dilemma given it was rapidly heading towards nightfall; even if there was no pursuit the rumbling from the east, plus the now heavy atmosphere, presaged rain, which meant he needed to get them into shelter and, whatever else it must be, this tower had to be sound and sealed to keep out the weather.

Faced with two problems there was only one solution; to move enough of those ampoules to accommodate his crew, so he clambered down and ordered the tower cleared. Immediately as his men got to the door, one great pot was sent flying, smashing on the ground, sending the oil it contained, the produce of the nearby olive trees, spraying in all directions. Pearce lost his temper then; these ampoules belonged to someone and were obviously valued.

'Damn you, treat them as if they were your own!'

No one would look at him then, he hoped through sheepishness so, in a more conciliatory tone, he ordered they should be lowered with care and stacked in such a way under the nearby trees where they would be afforded some protection from the coming downpour, with the additional instruction that it should be well away from the flaring fire that had been started by those not otherwise employed.

Lit in what was still daylight it now glowed, which had Pearce call in Birdy and his sentinels and get everyone up into the chamber, even if enough space had not been cleared; tonight they would have to huddle. Before that had been completed and the rough ladders hauled in, the first sign of lightning ran through the barely visible clouds, soon followed by a roll of loud thunder, which was repeated regularly.

The space was insufficient for all, which led to a great deal of complaint, and that was not aided when the door was jammed shut by Pearce and O'Hagan and they were plunged into Stygian darkness. But if there was much complaint about crowding, odd for fellows who shared constrained 't'ween decks, it was very shortly overborne by another worry: bats. The first cry was one of deep alarm, a near scream, which set off many more as the perpetrators felt the swish of something very close pass their heads, that followed by the sound of animal squeaking and Emily, made aware of what was causing the distress, buried her head in John Pearce's chest with a muffled moan that pushed his back hard into the door.

'You have nothing to fear,' Pearce yelled, but not to much avail. 'They will not harm you.'

'They're of the devil,' came one response, 'and will suck out our blood.'

'You'se dropped us in it again,' called another voice, which was responded to by a number of worrying growls mixed with stifled cries.

In daylight Pearce was sure he could have provided reassurance; in total darkness it was much harder but he tried, telling them how many times he had taken shelter with his father in old buildings and faced the same, even having had such creatures fly around his head on a summer night when sat by the roadside.

'You will feel their passing but never their touch, for they have a way of knowing exactly where you are.'

'If they can see in the dark then they are agents of Satan,' called a voice Pearce recognised as being the one who had cursed him on the deck of HMS *Larcher*, even when it dropped to a low and melodramatic tone. 'And happen they have come to commune with their familiar, I say.'

'The door, John-boy,' came the whisper from nearby, 'best open it.'

'Damn me, Michael, how? I am jammed against it.'

What followed was a series of curses and sounds Pearce took to be blows, but he did find he had room to move, enough to get the door open a fraction and let in air if not light. It took more effort and forced movement to get it fully ajar and just then the lightning flashed and illuminated for a second the interior, showing Pearce a mass of frightened faces; that was those who were not cowering with their hands over their hats.

Pearce saw it as a blessing that the storm was so fierce; the sky was alive, bolts of lightning were striking the ground with scarcely a pause between them, sending up what appeared to be sparks from anything they struck, rocks or trees, in a cacophony of thunder. The light created was enough at least to send the bats back to their hanging perches and when the rain came it was even more illuminating; it seemed to magnify the light from the bolts passing through to strike the ground, now covered with a low layer of steam.

It did not last, passing over and out to sea as quickly as it arrived but, leaving what had been heavy air somewhat cooler and fresher, as well as the wind that had driven it. It also left John Pearce with a decision to make; was it better that his men were outdoors or should he seek to keep them cooped up in the tower? There was no sign of a pursuit and surely, had there been one they would have known by now, quite apart from the fact that anyone seeking to come to attack them would have been drenched and so would be their weapons.

'Anyone who would rather make a bed outside may do so,' he called finally, for under a sky not yet fully cleared they were going to be in the dark even with an open door. 'But call your name first, it must be done with care and one at a time. Also, anyone with a musket leave it indoors.'

That engendered some murmured complaint so he added, in an exasperated tone. 'Ask yourself what use those weapons will be if the rain returns to soak your flints and powder.'

The downpour had doused the embers of the previous fire but the tars soon got another one going by the simple expedient of finding some dry kindling and timber, then setting it alight where the smashed ampoule had seeped its oil into the ground. What they did not anticipate was the way it flared up and the extent to which it would spread; it provided those still in the tower with a short burst of entertainment when it seemed as if the whole landscape was about to ignite.

Eventually matters settled and so did the exterior crew, with Pearce setting a watch from those who remained inside – there were moans of unfairness – until he made it plain they had two advantages; the height with which to oversee the area and the weapons to defend it from intrusion. Sleep, even indoors, could not be much more than fitful and so it was a drowsy and grubby looking bunch that began to study themselves at first light, where they could examine the effect upon their clothing and faces of that desperate climb up from the shore, and with no ability to boil water with which to shave they would have to stay that way.

With daylight the crew, Pelicans and Emily Barclay apart, vacated the tower, so Pearce elected to search for the means to reach the top. This consisted of a well-worn and equally well-cracked stone stairway. Several of the bricks dislodged on his ascent and fell crashing down to alarm those below and when he emerged onto the top it was to disturb a positive colony of nesting seabirds, who set up a cacophony of noise before seeking to chase him away by swirling around his head.

This meant he only got a glimpse of the inlet in which lay the charred timbers of HMS *Larcher*, no more than the skeleton of the keel, being hit by waves that were much more forceful than those he had faced the day before; it drove home that he had been very lucky. More to the point there was no sign of that pair of brigantines, which brought forth a sigh of relief: he and his crew were safe.

'Best come down quick, Capt'n,' called Michael O'Hagan up the stairwell, 'we got trouble here.'

The descent had to be undertaken gingerly, with all that loose masonry, so he was appraised of what he was about to face before he saw the threat: a crowd of over a hundred peasants armed with every kind of agricultural tool that would serve as a weapon lined up just at the edge of the trees; on closer examination it was made up of men, women and children. He could hear them too, a low and angry murmur that carried over the intervening ground to remind him of what he had so recently witnessed aboard ship.

No great genius was required to work out why these folk had come; this tower must have served as some kind of communal storehouse, and not only had he and his men broken into the place, but they had moved some of its contents and destroyed at least one container of oil, in this part of the world the source of heat, light and the basis of their cooking and very likely any trade they undertook.

It was the line of raised muskets that kept the peasants from coming on but that would not serve. Pearce could not contemplate any shooting to drive them away, quite apart from the presence of women and children. These people were citizens of a power allied to Britain and he had no idea how far away he and his men were from some kind of authority that could aid him.

'Michael, the ship's coffer, fetch it if you please.'

'You seeking to buy them off?'

'Tell me another way.'

'Sure I hope they come cheap, John-boy, for it's a bare store of coin we are left with.'

'First I have to get them to understand me. Best I wear my coat too.'

Charlie Taverner was quick with his opinion, this as O'Hagan aided Pearce to dress. 'Never known anyone confused by a bit of coin.'

'I have my money, John,' Emily added; originally pledged for her voyage, the result of her having traded her jewellery in Naples, it had been returned to her by Captain Fleming. 'You may use that.'

Pearce nodded, adding a sad smile, as Michael came with the coffer and he opened it to slip a few coins into his pocket. 'Let us hope it is unnecessary.'

It was a stiff and slow one-armed descent down that rough ladder and an unhurried walk to the line of his men holding muskets, where he issued a sharp order that no one was to think of pulling a trigger before proceeding, Michael, Charlie and Rufus on his heels. He searched the line of faces before him seeking out the man who was their leader – there had to be one – and as soon as he alighted on a suspect the fellow, swarthy and squat, stepped forward, a billhook swinging loosely at the end of his arm, angry shouts and imprecations at his back.

French had no immediate effect so Pearce tried the bit of Latin he knew, only to be replied to in a tongue, a local argot, which to him had no discernible root. So it came down to grunts, the odd word and sign language in which he imparted his regrets and caused utter confusion by trying to describe with his one good hand a naval pursuit and the outcome for his ship, in short their reason for being here.

In the end Charlie proved to have the right of it; a proffered gold coin, a full guinea on which sat the head of King George, once it had been bitten by the few remaining teeth of the peasant spokesman, began to allay the animosity. It took two more guineas, which left Pearce with an equal amount, to find the price for their losses, or at least one that would satisfy this squat fellow, with Pearce well aware he was probably paying well above the need.

'Should have put a couple of balls over their heads afore you spoke to them,' Rufus Dommet opined as the crowd dispersed to make their way back to their homes. 'Would have saved a guinea at least.'

'Whatever happened to that peaceful young lad I used to know?' Pearce asked, with a sigh. 'The one who rarely raised his voice.'

'Sure he joined the navy, John-boy,' hooted Michael O'Hagan, 'and if it has taken a while I can tell you he has learnt to throw a decent punch.'

'Just as I thought,' came the response, 'we are in a service that makes good people bad and bad people worse.'

'Then it's perdition for you, I say.'

CHAPTER TEN

Throughout the night, in-between bouts of sleep and troubled wakefulness, John Pearce had gnawed on what to do next. He had no surety that his enemies had given up on their pursuit, which would mean them heading for Sapri, where they thought he would go next, it being the nearest point of habitation. If that was to be avoided then so was any notion of progressing inland to seek out a road to the north, for the fishing port was on the way, which had him inclined to the idea of making their way north by sticking to the coast.

There would be a coastal path, in his experience of traversing his homeland there always was and he had no reason to doubt that matters weren't the same here in Italy. They were the routes of trade and travel that went back to time immemorial: on many occasions he and his father had used such paths to make their way from one coastal town to another and if they were not roads they were usually better than the muddy, rutted so called 'highways' that were as likely to be home to thievery as any other hazard.

His thinking was also affected by what he had read, from the annals of empire that began with Rome and extended to the writings of those who had undertaken the Grand Tour, not all of them rich and idle youth. The road to Rome was one much travelled by enquiring minds and one of the things Pearce recalled, amongst their accounts of ancient buildings and fine works of art, were their descriptions of the climate of Italy's interior: hot, disease-ridden and, outside of the monasteries and occasional grand edifice, desperately poor.

If it had been a fancy of his father's, his oft-repeated assertion that sea air was beneficial was a hard notion to refute, then there was the other factor to consider: would it be longer in terms of miles? In the dark a look at one of Dorling's charts was out of the question, which threw up another fact: if they showed the coast and the immediate hinterlands, charts did not stretch far inland and tended to be bereft of topographical features other than obvious landmarks such as the tower in which they now sat.

Yet on the coast they could not get lost and would often have good sight of what hazards lay in their path. So it was either make their way with some knowledge of their location or set off towards the high hills immediately north of the place they now were and step into the unknown. As a dilemma it was unresolved when daylight came and that was before any subsequent problem arose. What was obvious, when those over-rewarded locals had gone on their way and while his men made as much as they could of a less than perfect breakfast, was the fact that he would have to decide, there being no hint from any other quarter of an alternative, though he did feel it incumbent to explain his thinking to the warrants.

'As we saw on the way here many of the bays have boats on the beach, which means they live mainly off fish. But it is a fair bet there will be some kind of livestock too, goats or sheep. It also means they must have fresh water nearby for how could they otherwise sustain themselves? So there we have it, potential food and a certainty of water, plus a knowledge of where we are in a strange land.'

Not a word came in reply and nor was there much faith in the looks he was getting.

'And who knows what we might find to aid us on our way?'

'How far will we have to go, your honour?' Birdy asked finally of a man who had yet to work out the answer to that particular question, which meant his reply was somewhat lacking in confidence.

'Think of it day by day, Mr Bird, ten to twelve miles maybe more, with stops at the height of the hours when the sun is at its hottest.' Which was as good as saying it was going to be a long trek and an uncomfortable one, so he added a bit of wishful thinking to seek to cheer them up. 'And I cannot see it as necessary to cover the entire distance on foot, where we can we will seek out a boat.'

'And what boat will that be, John-boy?' O'Hagan asked as they walked away, for he had overheard the conversation.

'A celestial barge, Michael,' Pearce replied, with a gaiety he did not feel, this as he looked at the bright blue sky, with one single white cloud set over a distant mountain north of their tower, a one-time volcano by its shape. 'For which I would be obliged you heartily pray to the deity you so worship.'

As ever, when any reference was made to God, Michael crossed himself.

'At least,' Pearce added, 'if we stick to the coast we cannot get lost. Now let us gather ourselves up and get moving before it gets too warm.'

In the nature of things even the flagship of the fleet was required to replenish its stores, not least to take on water, without which the ship's cooks could not prepare food, so Sir William Hotham found himself on deck as HMS *Britannia* made her way into the roads of Leghorn to anchor. They arrived to the sound of banging ordnance as his vessel saluted the titular suzerain of the free port, the Grand Duke of Tuscany, while representatives of the Empire of Austria acknowledged his rank, position and Vice Admiral's flag.

Boats of all sizes, carrying traders of every description as well as a goodly number of whores, to the accompaniment of flutes and stringed instruments, had long set out to intercept the 100-gun warship. With its crew of over 800 men it would be a source of much trade in all areas, especially if the vessel's captain would allow them aboard – if not the denizens of the port would still manage to turn a pretty coin.

Despite the Articles of War declaring that the presence of non-naval persons on a warship was forbidden, it was a decision left to each captain as to whether such a stricture was observed. Hotham was not a man to relish his flagship being turned into a raucous whore and playhouse, so John Holloway, the captain of the ship, had strict instructions.

'They may trade through the lower gun ports and no more.' The acknowledgement of the order was delivered with a suppressed sigh; Hotham would not have to deal with the consequences of a crew full of pent-up frustration when they were denied their full pleasures: that would fall to the captain and his officers. 'You will, of course, accompany me to the inevitable ball and I would be obliged if you would choose from among our officers men who can come along and behave themselves.'

'Of course, sir.'

'And a strong word to your liberty men too, as well as your midshipman. There has been too much trouble here in Leghorn of late and I do not want to have to deal with any more.'

The story of what had happened with the youngsters from *Agamemnon* had spread and, of course, grown in the telling so that now, as far as the navy was concerned, there was not a bullock officer anywhere in the entire theatre of conflict fit for duty, and to the tars a damn good thing too.

'Port Governor's barge setting off from the quay, sir.'

This was delivered to Holloway, who was obliged by naval hierarchy to pass on to Hotham what he could not have failed to hear. Likewise the response, to salute the Governor with the requisite number of discharges, had to descend through the ranks all the way to the fellows operating the signal gun, which being a swivel on the quarterdeck was also within earshot.

Hotham made his way to the entry port on the main deck and it was a puffed-up admiral that met the Governor as he came aboard, this to the crash of marine boots as the welcoming guard of honour came smartly to attention. Hotham had never before greeted a visitor as a commanding officer and to experience that now was enough to make him both proud and outgoing. So a pompous and overdressed little pouter pigeon of a functionary was treated in the great cabin to the best bottle of claret Sir William could provide, this while the pair conversed in French: Hotham's stilted, the Austrian's fluent.

'An opera performed entirely in my honour!' Hotham exclaimed with *faux* enthusiasm; it was not an art form he greatly appreciated added to which the standard in Leghorn was not of the highest. '*Trop d'honneur, Excellence.*'

After much stilted exchange the man departed leaving Sir William to deal with his next guest, the British Consul Mr Purdey, a very necessary conduit to London through the Foreign Office, one that bypassed the Admiralty and allowed Hotham to reach his political allies and so also a recipient of the best of the admiral's floating cellar, stocked on his behalf by Berry Brothers of St James' street.

Once Purdey left he began to prepare himself with a careful toilet that went as far as a little powder on his cheeks, which were too red from exposure to decades of wind and water. The happy mood was somewhat dented when he saw that Toby Burns had been included in the list of accompanying officers, but he was unable to object; everyone aboard *Britannia*, Holloway included, was sure he was fond of the young fellow, perhaps too much so.

'You found me an interpreter, Toomey?'

'I have, sir, he came aboard an hour past. Fluent in French, English and German.'

'Thank the Lord. I won't have to engage in these heathen

tongues. French is bad enough, but German. Barbaric to my ears!'

The need for German was due to the presence of officers of the Austrian Army; a small garrison kept in the port to preserve order in times made febrile by the Revolution. Toomey, being Irish and considering his concerns, could not resist a bit of mischief to balance out his feeling of disquiet, as well as exclusion from whatever his employer had in mind.

'I believe it is the common tongue of his Majesty and his family, sir.'

Hotham stopped then as the thought registered: a Whig he might be and committed to curtailing monarchical interference in government but it did not do to go lightly insulting the source of so much patronage. He might want to curse the damned Hanoverians, but it would never do and Toomey, by his remark, was warning him to mind his tongue once ashore.

'A convenience no doubt, for Queen Charlotte, who is German born.'

'Most of those attending will speak French, sir.'

'Do some of them good to learn a bit of English,' Hotham growled.

'I am sure every Englishman trading through the port will attend an opera in your honour.'

'You hit the nail, Toomey. Tradesmen is what they are and a low lot to boot.'

'Yet wealthy, sir, especially those who represent the Levant Company. They sit not far behind the Indian nabobs in the depth of their coffers.'

'It takes more than money to make a gentleman.'

Hotham said this as he turned from his looking glass to

face his clerk and seek his approval, which had Toomey quickly adjusting his expression; he thought the remark pretentious. Sir William had on his blue sash and Star of the Order of the Bath, placed there first by the very king about whom he had so nearly been disparaging. His wig was freshly powdered and his coat and breeches were of the very best quality, while his shoe buckles were gleaming silver.

'Impressive, sir, very impressive.'

The chest positively swelled as Admiral Sir William Hotham, acting C-in-C of the Mediterranean, took in a deep breath and squared his shoulders covered with two heavy and flashing epaulettes, to then pick up his naval scrapper, edged in gold thread, and place it with care upon his head.

It was a mood Hotham carried into the Opera House, sustained by the impression that *tout* Tuscany had turned out to meet him. The place positively glittered with titles, decorations, military uniforms from Austria and Britain as well as low cut and revealing gowns on every woman regardless of her age. The performance was pleasant: a Mozart piece about Turks and harems, while the wine served in the interval was excellent and plentiful. The C-in-C was in heaven as well as in deep conversation with a buxom beauty when he was interrupted.

'Excuse me, sir, if I may I would like to have a word with you.'

Forced to turn away from a heaving and very obvious bosom, Hotham was not best pleased to find himself face-to-face with a bullock, a major by the rank badges on his red coat. He was even less enamoured when the fellow spoke, from a face so fused with what seemed to be suppressed fury that it matched his jacket.

'Major Lipton, at your service.'

'Lipton?' Hotham replied, with an air of confusion, in reality seeking time to think.

'You may recall that I wrote to you?'

'I receive a level of correspondence, major, that you could scarcely guess at.'

'Not much of it from men such as myself, I'll wager, or bearing my sort of complaint?'

Hotham was thinking where was Toomey when he was needed. He was the fellow to deal with this, but the clerk, who too had come ashore, had headed off to the local fleshpots. There he would, no doubt, couch with a whore and get as drunk as only an Irishman could, on beverages bought for him by officers seeking to pick up secrets from the great cabin, a habit when he had a rare run ashore as a price to be paid for his otherwise competent service.

Whatever, there was no denying that he had been in receipt of a letter from Lipton, so he replied in what was a somewhat supercilious manner. 'I recall the name now and I also recall that my clerk wrote you a reply.'

The tone was clearly inappropriate, given the increased flush that came to the major's cheeks as well as his growling response. 'And a damned unsatisfactory one, sir.'

'Your language, sir, is unsuitable to address any fellow officer and I would remind you of my rank.'

'While I choose to remind you, sir, of the depredations I and my officers have suffered at the hands of your service.'

'A few over-eager midshipmen,' Hotham scoffed, 'letting off steam.'

'I find your attitude and response offensive, sir.'

Now it was Hotham's turn to display irritation; no one had the right to speak to him in that fashion, although it was only recently he had suffered such from Lord Hood, the memory of which coloured his reaction.

'And I don't give a damn if you do, sir. I am here as a guest of the Governor and as a representative of our country. If you have anything to say to me I would be obliged if you would find a more appropriate place to say it.'

'You decline to compensate us?'

'I most vehemently do. If you get into a scrape in a foreign port who can you blame but yourself?'

'What a low bunch you tars are,' Lipton sneered in a way that indicated he knew he had hit a brick wall. 'Scum to my mind, risen from foul bilge, low-bred scullys to a man.'

'I think you should be grateful, sir, that none of my officers are within hearing!'

'What? You mean I might face a challenge from men of the calibre of that cur, Pearce. If he was here I'd find a pistol and put a ball in him and between his eyes.'

'Pearce, what is he to you?'

Lipton half raised an arm, wincing as he did so. 'You will not have observed, sir, given you're too much taken with female flesh and no doubt your gonads as well as your belly, but I cannot raise this peg any higher than you can now perceive.'

Hotham, confused, merely shrugged, ignoring the insults which on another occasion would have seen Lipton hauled before his military superiors and forced to apologise.

'That, I have to tell you, is to be laid at the door of your

Lieutenant Pearce who, when we duelled, acted in a despicable manner that has left me a cripple and no longer any good to my regiment, one I would hazard is common among your officers.'

'Duelled? You and Pearce duelled?'

'I did, sir, he did not. He played a low trick that no gentleman could have contemplated. If you doubt the measure of the man ask the fellow naval officer he struck immediately after he had sliced me. Added to that, I have every reason to believe he was responsible for the assault on my officers who were dragged from our quarters by a rampaging mob very shortly after our encounter. The two events cannot be unconnected.'

'Major Lipton,' Hotham protested, seeking time to think, 'I have already alluded to the unsuitable nature of the place you have chosen to accost me—'

'Where else would I be granted an opportunity?'

This bad-tempered bullock could not see into Hotham's thoughts and if he had been so able it is doubtful if enlightenment would have ensued. He could not know of the impact the mere mention of the name Pearce had on the admiral's peace of mind – the swine had yet to return to the fleet and every day of his absence seemed to increase Hotham's anxieties – but the emollient tone that he was now subject to did surprise him.

'I will give it to you, sir, by inviting you to come aboard HMS *Britannia* on the morrow at your own convenience. If, as it turns out, I have dealt shabbily with your complaint you will have a chance to air it fully.'

'I must be assured, sir, that there is some point to this.'

'Oh, be assured, major, there is a very significant point,' Hotham replied, as the first strains of a warming up orchestra came wailing out of the auditorium. 'Now, if you will excuse me, the Governor has caught my eye to tell me he is returning to our box, so I must be about my diplomatic duties.'

As Hotham turned away, he noticed Toby Burns not more than a few feet distant. The little toad had had his head cocked at a curious angle and one that told the admiral that he could have witnessed what had been a less than discreet exchange, a mystery to most of an audience without English.

'How much of that did you overhear, Burns?'

'What, sir?' came the surprised response, delivered entirely without conviction.

'You would do well to keep your counsel if you did hear anything and do I have to say that eavesdropping on the conversation of a senior officer is behaviour of the lowest kind?'

'Which I would never dream of doing, sir, I promise.'

'Not worth more than a pie crust!'

With that Hotham stamped off, unaware that behind his back Toby Burns was smirking, partly from pleasure at the thought of someone shooting John Pearce but also from the fact that he had been an avid visitor to the punchbowl. He had also quite obviously discomforted Hotham, which was as rare as it was cheering. The need to go back and listen to the caterwauling of some very fat people was less so and he decided to stay put.

The eagerness of Lipton to make his case was evidenced by the early hour of his arrival, which left Admiral Hotham scant time to complain once more about Pearce and his whereabouts, this from a clerk in the throes of serious debilitation, a consequence of his nocturnal excess.

'Still no news, sir,' Toomey rasped, thinking the name was a curse. 'Given his extended absence it may be that he has foundered and is lost, or perhaps he ran into an enemy vessel and was taken.'

He waited while his admiral contemplated those two scenarios, neither of which was unknown within the service. The sea was a fickle beast and the annals of the navy were filled with vessels that had simply disappeared. Added to which if *Larcher* had been taken the French would be in no rush to make known such a success and no other enemy, like a privateer, would make the information known at all.

'Bad pennies have a way of surviving, Toomey, look at Burns, so if you raise my hopes it only does so marginally. Best show Major Lipton in and tell my steward to fetch a bottle of claret, nothing too fine, after all he hardly merits it. You, I require to go ashore and make enquiries as to whether Pearce was responsible for what happened to Lipton and his officers.'

Having looked away Hotham did not see the grimace on Toomey's face; he wanted nothing more than to retire to a hammock and sleep off his hangover.

'If he was the instigator it will not be the service that pays, if there's a bill, but him.'

'He's unlikely to admit to it, sir.'

'Aye, deceit comes easily to him,' the admiral growled. 'No good asking the Agamemnons either, they would lie through their teeth. Best be on your way, Toomey, and I charge you not to seek to cure your ills with any more drink, do I make myself clear?'

'Yes, sir,' the clerk rasped and nor would he unless there was someone left ashore to listen to his supposed indiscretions and pay the bill.

Hotham stood to receive Lipton, a singular courtesy given their respective service ranks – a Vice Admiral equalled a Lieutenant General – and invited him to sit immediately before asking him to reprise the events of the duel, how it had come about and how it had ended. The details were delivered in a sour tone that the admiral began to see was Lipton's normal mode of comportment – the man was bad-tempered by nature – which led him to assume that the contest with Pearce had not been his first time out, a fact established by a simple enquiry.

There was a boastful quality to the major's tales of duelling as well to the account he was given regarding Pearce; Lipton wanted his listener to be in no doubt who was the superior swordsman and by a large margin, that he had toyed with his opponent rather than finish him off quickly, this to entertain his fellow soldiers who formed an audience. If his tone was commonly irascible it rose to a wholly more ill-tempered level when it came to the way Pearce had bested him, getting agreement from Hotham, even if he felt that facing death – and by the way Lipton described his intentions the threat of that was real – he might have done the same.

'You say, Major, that, while you were being attended to by the surgeon, Lieutenant Pearce struck a fellow naval officer?' Lipton nodded. 'Surely not his second?'

'No, another low guttersnipe who had come along—'

'Sir,' Hotham interrupted, leaning forward to make his point. 'If you wish for a sympathetic hearing from me then you must cease to insult the members of my service. Indeed, if you continue to do so this interview is over!'

'I withdraw any remark which may cause offence.'

With his high colour and disdainful look, the admiral took that to be a lie. 'Did this officer have a name?'

'Taberly of HMS *Leander.* My companions had to get the fellow back to Leghorn since Pearce and his party abandoned him.'

'And who was it who seconded for Pearce?'

'Fellow called Digby, I believe from the same vessel. But can I move you on, sir, to what happened subsequently and the subject of my complaint?'

'By all means do so, Major Lipton,' Hotham replied, though he had to suppress his feelings of distraction, not really being interested. It was the name of Digby that filled his mind, so he missed a good deal of what the man was saying, only really perking up when Lipton made mention of the attempt by Pearce to challenge every one of his inferior officers on the day preceding their ducking.

'Had a trollop in tow and one or two of my men saw fit to let her know of her station. Set the sod off good and proper.'

'Trollop?'

Lipton nodded. 'Damn fine-looking filly by all accounts and English, looked quite the innocent which, of course, she could not be.' That was followed by a snorted laugh. 'Pearce was set on defending her honour, as if she possessed any.'

'Do you have a description?'

That got a shake of the head. 'Never saw the wench myself. Now, sir, to my account of the monies expended on the medical bills, as well as our extended requirement for accommodation at the *Pensione d'Ambrosio*, which you already possess?'

Hotham was just about to shout for Toomey when he

recalled he had sent him ashore. Thankfully he had the other clerk. 'I ask you to wait on the main deck and the funds will be brought to you. Now, Major Lipton, if our business is quite concluded?'

Lipton looked at the claret bottle, half full, as was his own glass and he flushed a deeper red again. He was being dismissed like a man of no account when courtesy demanded he be allowed to stay till the wine was finished. Hotham sensed his hesitation and could see plainly his reaction.

'You will understand, sir, that I have a fleet to run.'

'I swear, Toomey, he would have thrown the wine in my face if he'd had his coin. Angry is not the word.' Clearly amused by the recollection his next enquiry was quite jovial. 'So what did you discover?'

'There's no indication that Pearce was involved in the disturbance. Tavern owner I queried said it was all young blue coats and common seaman. Weren't easy to get that given he spoke little English but I did uncover something else, sir.' The raised eyebrow invited disclosure. 'According to the Navy Board captain that oversees the victualing, Pearce was in the company of a lady . . .'

'Lipton told me as much.'

'Did he tell you that she was recognised by some of our officers, given she was present in Toulon helping to run the hospital?'

'No.'

'It was Captain Barclay's wife!'

'What!'

'There's no mistake, sir, it was her to the life.'

162

'Is she still in Leghorn?'

'Unlikely, given no one has had sight of her for weeks.'

'What was Pearce doing escorting Ralph Barclay's wife around Leghorn, Toomey?'

'What indeed, sir?'

CHAPTER ELEVEN

'The journey had many pleasing moments, Sir William, and I have to say the coastline was most dramatic, with scenic aspects that would delight any man who could apply a brush to canvas. If we did not eat as well as we might, we did find sustenance enough to sustain us and the folk we came across were eager to aid us on our way. As to my crew, they are a fine bunch and as adaptable as is ever the British tar.'

John Pearce found the lies coming easily; he was sat on a shaded terrace of the Palazzo Sessa overlooking the wide Bay of Naples, fully bathed and dressed in new linen. His arm having been passed as healed by a surgeon it now held a cooling drink and life felt restored in more ways than one. What was the point of telling the British Ambassador of the misery he had suffered leading the crew of HMS *Larcher* along that barren and rocky coast?

Why burden him with the tales of a ship's company that began the journey disgruntled and became more so with every day that passed, complaining of everything from the heat of the day, the biting insects at night and the blisters on feet unused to footwear?

What good would it do to tell him that the subjects of King Ferdinand were, when not being outrageously rapacious, the surliest bunch of scoundrels he had ever encountered out of an English gaol and that he had been obliged to threaten violence on more than one occasion to make any progress at all?

Such untruths were as much for his own good as that of Sir William Hamilton; Pearce had no desire to reprise the many incidents that had seen he and his men forced into wide detours to avoid trouble, of food bought at prices so outrageous that he had allowed his men to plunder pens, storehouses and chicken coops, the only plentiful thing available to them the abundance of water from a multitude of fresh mountain fed springs.

There had been, as he had anticipated, fishing villages but they were far from prosperous places, a few ramshackle huts with suspicious men and even more distrustful women who, if they had reached anything above two decades of age, were universally ugly creatures. The young males, even those of tender years, sought to steal everything they could while the girls, if there were any, must have been kept well hidden for fear they would be ravaged by these armed strangers who spoke a heathen and incomprehensible tongue.

Pearce was sure it was thanks to those arms, muskets and cutlasses that they had survived, for the wilds of the region, and they were that, seemed to lack any evidence of law. The folk lived in primitive and poverty-stricken communes – there were no towns of any size until they reached Agropoli – and the impression had been unavoidable that each one preyed upon its neighbours at every opportunity.

'I must say, it seems Mrs Barclay held up passing well.'

There was a definite look in Sir William Hamilton's eye then, the kind a man has when referring to a lady whose looks have entertained his imagination. Pearce knew the ambassador to be well into his sixties yet obviously his appreciations of the fair sex had not suffered from his longevity. Nor did his attitude cause offence; he was a man of a calibre that a coming-of-age John Pearce had encountered in Paris, where men of parts, if they discerned and admired beauty, did not indulge in the English habit of hypocritical denial and disguised approbation.

'And here comes the very lady of whom we speak,' Hamilton said, rising from his chair, 'looking more radiant than ever.'

Emily, as she came onto the terrace, was not alone. With her was Lady Hamilton and given she was a famous beauty it was impossible not to contrast them, one past her full bloom but still very striking, Emily in the first stages of full maturity, well dressed for the first time in a month and, in receipt of a proper *toilette* and expertly dressed hair, simply stunning.

The dress had to be one of Emma Hamilton's and given the difference in their size a needle must have been swiftly employed to have it fit Emily's less fulsome figure, not least in the area of the bosom, which the ambassador's wife, supremely well-endowed in that regard, was much prone to display and was doing so now. Emily had chosen to be more discreet with some strategically placed lace.

'Lieutenant Pearce has been at pains to tell how eager he is to get back to his duties with the fleet. Looking at you of this moment, Mrs Barclay, I cannot but rate him as quite mad.'

'Careful, husband,' his wife responded, but not with any real indignation, this while Emily blushed slightly.

Having observed them previously Pearce knew them to be happy in their relationship; Hamilton was quite ready to accept that being married to a beautiful woman brought with it the attention of a raft of admirers. One such was Nelson, who had charged Pearce with the delivery of a letter to Lady Hamilton, one she had not sought to keep secret from Sir William, who seemed more amused by the action than upset.

Likewise his relationship with Emily Barclay. The fact that she was a married woman and separated from her husband was not referred to and in no way was she made to feel awkward by her state or the obvious relationship she had with John Pearce. Naples was more lax than London in such matters by some measure; indeed, according to Emma Hamilton, irregular couplings were the norm rather than the exception.

Thinking briefly on the two men the contrast was palpable; Hamilton the urbane diplomat at ease in the salon and the company of the fair sex, Nelson a restless sailor whom he had seen in the company of a rather busty opera singer at a ball in Leghorn. Two impressions remained from that observation: the first that Nelson had difficulty in holding his drink, the second that he had scant knowledge of women.

'While I am not eager to have you depart, Lieutenant, I am looking forward to having Emily here as a companion in your absence.'

John Pearce smiled at Lady Hamilton then, but inwardly he was less happy. If the subject of what was to happen to Emily had not been a constant worry these last troubled weeks, it had been raised more than once. She still thought it best to return to England, while he was stuck with a duty he had to perform, namely to get the crew of HMS *Larcher* back where they belonged, added to that he had to find a means by which they could live, wherever that might be, on nothing more than his present pay. It would be easier in Italy than England, but a lieutenant's stipend would not provide any luxury even here.

'I do not intend to be absent long, Lady Hamilton.'

'Nor would I want you to be,' she replied, with a coquettish tilt of the head, one that was not missed by his own paramour. 'Handsome naval officers are a rare commodity in Naples, entertaining fellows in uniform even less so.'

Pearce saw Emily's nostrils tighten, a sign he knew of displeasure. Could she not see what was obvious to him, that what Lady Hamilton had said was mere wordplay, something he suspected she employed with most of the men she encountered? She would have used it on Horatio Nelson and he would have no doubt misread it; he did not, but it was yet another example of Emily's lack of experience of the world, which if it could be endearing could also be exasperating.

'When I get to the fleet, Lady Hamilton, I will sort you out a dozen or so and have them come and worship at your feet.'

'And trough it at my table,' the ambassador said, though it was imparted with good humour. 'I swear I have never seen any eat like seafarers.'

'Which reminds me to ask you, sir, for an account of the expenses I and my crew have incurred. I am sure the navy will happily meet them.'

The good humour evaporated. 'Then you know of a service that is a stranger to me, sir. When it comes to being tardy in settling their accounts, they have a labyrinth into which they are prone to disappear.'

John Pearce was tempted to ask then, if he had got *Larcher* to Naples, would he have funded her repair; it did not seem appropriate to do so but he did feel constrained to make an offer of his own, as being the gentlemanly thing to do, albeit he knew his available funds to be already overstretched with commitments.

'Give me an account, sir, and I will present it in the right quarter. And if they decline to meet it I will see it as a personal debt.' That being waved aside by the ambassador, no doubt on the grounds that he doubted Pearce could meet such an obligation, his guest added. 'And of course I will meet any expenses incurred while Mrs Barclay awaits my return.'

'Nonsense, sir, she is an English lady in need of support and that is a charge upon my duties. Now, I am due at the Royal Palace—'

'While I,' Emma Hamilton interjected, 'must take my daily stroll in the English Gardens.' Waiting for her to issue an invitation to accompany her, something he had done previously, Pearce was surprised by what followed, but not for any length of time. 'Which will leave you and Mrs Barclay with the run of the palazzo, will it not? Do feel free to treat it as your own.'

If Emily Barclay had suffered a slight blush before she went bright red now and was, once they were alone, in no mood to take up the offer which Emma Hamilton had more than hinted at.

'She is a woman with a past, John, and I have to say that it is apparent in her present behaviour.'

Tempted to say something about people in glass houses, Pearce put that thought to one side. 'Everyone has a past.'

'Not like hers! How can you burden me with staying in the company of such a woman?'

'That, if I may say so, does you no credit. I grant she has a past, though I am inclined to ask if all of the sins laid at her door are true.'

'It is said she was a common whore.'

'If she was ever that I would hazard she was an uncommon one.'

'I fail to see the distinction.'

'Whatever her background she has made a great deal for herself.'

'By marrying a man twice her age.' As soon as that was out of her mouth, Emily realised that it was a mistaken allusion; had she not done the same? Slightly flustered and decidedly embarrassed she sought to cover it with denigrations. 'Don't be fooled by all that overt kindness, John, for there are cat's claws at the back of it. What you see when we are with either yourself or Sir William is not what I am exposed to in private, woman to woman.'

'Which is?' he asked wearily.

'Her notion of liking me is mere pretence. Every word she utters has a double meaning and if at first it sounds like fawning there is a less flattering allusion within her words. I suspect jealousy and not just of me but of any woman she feels challenged by.'

'But you are not challenging her.'

'You think you are so wise, John Pearce,' Emily responded, with a tone that made a mockery of the words, 'with your knowledge of the world, which you are forever reminding me is far greater than my own—'

'I do not remind you.'

'You do,' came the reply, with a catch in the throat to go with it, 'and all that says to me is you are unaware of it.'

Pearce moved towards her and put his hands on her shoulders, feeling them shake as he looked down into her dampening eyes, his voice low as he asked. 'Are you frightened, Emily?'

A nod and a sniffle. 'People will talk of me as they do of her, John, and I could not bear to be so compared.'

'Can I tell you what I see?' Pearce did not wait for her to respond. 'I see a lady much condescended to by those who know something of her past, women especially, who will treat her the way you are accusing her of treating you.'

'So you are taking her side?'

'No, Emily, but from what I know of Lady Hamilton—'

'You seem to know a great deal.'

'She came from humble beginnings and has made something of herself.'

'By what route?'

'If it was the bedchamber so be it. How would you have her make her way with nothing but her beauty as an asset? I admit I found myself uncomfortable in her company at first, for she has a manner that is that of the siren. She wishes every man she meets to admire her and demonstrate it to be so.'

'Do you admire her?'

'In many ways I do.' He felt the shoulders stiffen. 'But not in that way. I wish my father could have met her for she is a perfect example of what he used to harangue his listeners about, that they had it within themselves to be masters of their own fate.'

'Or mistresses,' Emily said, and not as a kindly pun.

'Emma Hamilton did not accept that the station into which she was born should be one in which she should remain. If her path to her present position is strewn with less than salubrious acts then she has transcended them now. She is the wife of a baronet and ambassador, speaks Italian, French and German, can play the

171

harpsichord with some skill and keep hanging on her every word men who should know better.'

She looked up to say something unpleasant, only to see her lover smiling. 'I am not one of the latter, I am a man who only has regard for you and I am also one who is to shortly depart this palazzo, which I would hate to do with you and I in dispute.'

'How soon?'

'I have sent word for the crew to assemble on the quay before the Palazzo Reale. Sir William has bespoken and paid for a boat to take us back to the fleet. You have no idea how tempted I am to send them off on their own, but I cannot and even you must be aware of my responsibility. I have lost a ship and someone has to be accountable for that.'

'If you did not return you would be seen as a coward fearful of facing censure.'

There was dispirited quality to that remark, which Pearce felt he had to counter. 'It is not just for my pride, Emily, it is that I have to be able when I see a mirror to look myself in the eye. You cannot ask me to act dishonourably.'

'Am I asking?'

'No, but time is short and if I want to take away with me anything, it is the feeling of how much regard we have for each other.'

'We need to think of the future, John.'

The reply she got was low and husky as he pulled her unresisting body into his own. 'As of this moment, I cannot think of any time but now.'

It was necessary to wait for the return of Sir William and Lady Hamilton before he could depart and Pearce did not miss the look she gave Emily and he, which was followed by the slightest of smiles. There was nothing in his demeanour to indicate that they had taken advantage of her none too subtle offer. Again, it was Emily's reddening cheeks that gave the game away.

'Rest assured, Lieutenant Pearce,' the ambassador said, 'you leave Mrs Barclay in good and safe hands.'

'For which I am grateful, sir.'

'And of course we wish you a speedy return.'

'Very speedy,' Emma Hamilton added, which set off Emily's nostrils again.

'You have my letters?' her husband asked.

'Both yours and Lady Hamilton's.'

Sir William gave his wife a raised eyebrow. 'Nelson?'

'A copy, the original went down with the Lieutenant's ship.'

'If you see Commodore Nelson, please also give him my regards,' Hamilton said. 'He is a fine fellow and, as I have told Lady Hamilton on more than one occasion will, if the Admiralty has an ounce of sense, achieve great things. Now I will wait downstairs by the hack I have engaged to take you from us. Come, my dear.'

Both he and his wife exited, so that Pearce and Emily could say their final farewells. He knew she would cry as soon as he left but there were no words he could employ to deflect that. And why did he feel a bit of a scrub to be going, given he could not do otherwise? Truly, being in love was the most complicated thing he had ever encountered.

On his way through the crowded streets, filled with the odours of a great port teeming with humanity, made up of the smell of cooking, the stink of animals as well as equine and human waste, the nature of Naples driven home by the way everyone seemed to shout rather than talk, John Pearce reflected that commanding a King's ship, even the one he had so recently had charge of, was simplicity compared to keeping a woman happy.

CHAPTER TWELVE

It was strange to be on a ship and have nothing to do. The merchant vessel Sir William Hamilton had hired had its own Neapolitan captain and crew, men with whom easy communication was impossible. If John Pearce felt odd to be idle he could only assume that the same applied to the men he led. They spent a goodly part of their time below decks gnawing on what the future might hold for them, when they were not engaged in a pursuit, gambling, that he was supposed to prevent.

If he ventured into their domain the means by which they wagered and played was quick to disappear, as it would be on any King's ship, ferretted away by sailors who had years of practice at hoodwinking their superiors. It was one of those areas where a wise officer, provided matters were kept within decent bounds, employed the blind eye and set aside the Articles of War; some things could not be prevented and too heavy a hand led to a disgruntled and less effective crew.

The thought of that was wont to bring forth a smile; the men of HMS *Larcher* required no other reason to be at odds with him than the fact that he had lost their ship and, as far as they were concerned, their home, while he was at a stand to know how to even begin to repair that breach. In any event the means to do so was brought to him by his Pelicans, as ever the best conduit of information, able to do so openly on a deck bereft of any of their mates and far enough off to kill the need for formality.

'There's them that says you did us proud to get us out of that scrape,' Charlie Taverner informed him. 'And not losing a soul in the process, too.'

'Same number still curse you for getting us into it, mind.'

Pearce held back a smile as he recalled at one time how hard it had been to get any words out of Rufus Dommet. Now the one-time callow youth, sucking on his pipe, looked quite the grown man, broader of shoulder and more mature in his look, albeit he still had his untidy ginger hair and freckles on skin that would not take the sun.

'There's those you'll never change the mind of, John-boy, no matter what you do.'

'Does it matter, Michael?' Pearce asked. 'I am not likely to be in command of them ever again. I might never be in command of anyone again.'

Rufus pointed with his pipe. 'I won't say the prospect of you lording the quarterdeck pleases many, but there are a fair crowd who worry how they will end up.'

'Sent to this ship and that,' Charlie cut in, making that gesture with his hat, lifting it to reveal his blond crop before setting it back again – that for him denoted the making of a serious point. 'An' that might be the fate for us, too.'

'What would please them,' Michael added, 'would be if they could transfer as a whole, even the warrants, for they have become used to each other.'

'Which I cannot promise them,' came the gloomy reply.

'They was a crew afore the war, John. It would be hard for them to be parted.'

'All I can do is ask.'

'If you was to say right out that you would,' Charlie insisted, 'it would do wonders for the way you stand.'

'Even if the chances are near to zero.'

That got a grin from the one-time sharp, who had made his way in the world by yarn spinning. 'Reckon a smile from one of the Larchers would cheer you, John. What does it matter if it turns out to be so much stuff?'

'Would you accept, Charlie, that I am less comfortable with untruths than you?'

'Sure, most folk are,' Michael hooted.

'Better a lie than an empty belly.'

'A bit of labour might have kept it full.'

'Toil is for dolts,' came the sharp reply. Charlie only realised the effect of what he said just before he heard O'Hagan growl.

'Seem to recall there was a lot you went shy of Charlie, and not just vittels.'

'There being a certain Rosie that you was sweet on,' Rufus added, with a very obvious look of mischief. 'Must have been hard to see her being charmed by Michael here.'

'Enough,' Pearce demanded, glaring at Rufus.

That was an old dispute that should have been long laid to rest: handsome Charlie, when Pearce had first encountered him, had charm and no money, enough of the former to get this suddenly arrived and obviously weary stranger to stand several rounds of ale for him and his equally hard-up companions. Michael, who dug foundation ditches all day for good wages and seemingly drank all night, had what Charlie lacked and Rosie, of whom both were much enamoured, saw a need, coin to compensate her for her affections. It was the one thing that could, when raised, turn these two seeming companions into foes.

'Pardon for the words, mate,' Charlie said with real feeling. 'Weren't talking of you, of which you should have knowledge.'

'You've a runaway tongue, Charlie,' Michael replied, only partially mollified.

'Speaking of what we was afore tomcat time,' Rufus interjected gravely. 'Do you reckon it wise to mislead the Larchers?'

'Don't know if youse noticed, Rufus,' Charlie scoffed, 'but we is Larchers. I ain't saying John can bring it off, all I am saying is that he could try and if he said he would and did that would be no falsehood.'

'An' we could spread the word?' Michael asked.

The response from Charlie Taverner was an empathic nod.

'Be better,' Rufus muttered, 'than always disputing with them.'

The fact of that, which he knew to be true even if he had never actually witnessed it, embarrassed Pearce; that these friends of his were obliged to defend him was something for which he had to be grateful. It was the need that brought him to the blush.

'Well, we will know soon enough,' he sighed, as he saw the

captain's steward approaching, which was enough to cause that sigh to deepen.

The man would tell him his dinner was about to be served, which would plunge him into another exchange of inanities with the master of the vessel, who not only had a lack of English or French, but who would have been a tiresome companion in any language, given his sole topic of conversation seemed to consist of the virtues of his exceptional wife as well as the undoubted genius of his ten children.

The channel between the Italian mainland and the islands of Sardinia and Corsica was a busy one and thus well patrolled by warships of both Naples and Britain, added to which the benign weather and the tedium of exchange with his host meant Pearce spent a lot of time on deck. It was there that he was approached by a party of the crew, half a dozen tars who for some reason had chosen Todger as their spokesman, probably because they reckoned him favoured by their captain.

'Savin' your presence, your honour, but we has come to ask for a favour.'

Well aware, after his conversation with his friends, of what it must be, Pearce adopted a grave facial expression. 'I hope you know that as of this moment I am in a poor position to grant anyone anything.'

'It be more in the nature of a request,' said Pardew, no longer hobbling with his stick.

Silence fell as Pearce waited for one of them to continue, Todger finally giving a nervous knuckle to his forehead before speaking, while what came out was hesitant and mumbling, to which their officer listened with seeming interest, all the while wondering if Charlie Taverner had the right of it; that it was better to raise hopes than dash them.

'Be assured that I feel I owe you to a man for the loss of the ship. If it is in my power to do what you ask I will bend every ounce of my being to that goal.'

Todger smiled, Pardew nearly genuflected, the rest murmuring various expressions of gratitude, all of which combined to make John Pearce feel like a scrub.

'Then we, for the rest of our shipmates, are charged to say that we is sorry for the way we went against you.'

Some might mean it, others would say anything to get their way, but there was no point it stating that. 'The best thing we can do with that matter is let it rest. Now would you oblige me by asking Mr Dorling, who I feel has been avoiding me since we departed Naples, to join me on deck.'

'The warrants feel as we do, your honour,' Todger insisted.

'Where they go is not really in my gift or even that of the C-in-C. They are granted their warrants by the Navy Board.'

Pearce wanted to speak to him on another matter entirely, being well aware of why Dorling was keeping a wide berth, a point he came to when the young master appeared.

'I am aware that you disapproved of my decision to depart Palermo with HMS *Larcher* in the condition in which she existed.' Dorling did not speak, but he would not catch Pearce's eye. 'I assume you noted your reservations in your log?'

The response was a long time in coming. 'Had to write what I held to be the truth, sir.'

'Well you will be questioned both at my court martial and no doubt before by the Master of the Fleet. I can only advise you, Mr Dorling, to be honest, even if you have an inclination to protect me.'

'I am minded to say we was in a hole, not getting from the locals what we needed and I know that consul was tight with his purse.'

'All I am saying, Mr Dorling, is do not put at risk your own career in an attempt to save mine.'

'I won't damn you if that's what you reckon,' he protested, showing animation for the very first time.

Pearce smiled, really to put Dorling at ease. 'Do you need to, given as far as a good number of the crew is concerned, despite what they might now protest, I am damned already?'

'If that will be all, sir,' came the reply, from a fellow who had the good grace to look discomfited for his past attitude.

'What I have predicted will all happen soon. Our captain tells me we are likely to round Cape Corse not long after dawn.'

Which they did, sailing into the wide bight of San Fiorenzo Bay, a perfect anchorage for a large fleet of British warships determined to do battle with the French should they exit Toulon, something that would not happen unseen. There was an inshore squadron of frigates set to keep an eye out for them. John Pearce looked hard for HMS *Victory* and his heart was not lifted by the lack of her presence, for it meant Sam Hood, a man from whom he might just be able to beg a favour, was no longer in command.

Merchant vessels being no strange sight, on his say-so they approached HMS *Britannia* without trouble, unaware of how, when Neapolitans put boats in the water to transport them to the flagship, such activity caused a stir. Pearce was the first up the gangplank and through the entry port to find, and it was unusual, the captain of the flagship there in person to greet him, though there was no other ceremony, no marines as a guard of honour. The senior man's face was a mask hiding what had to be deep curiosity.

'Captain Holloway,' Pearce said, lifting his hat, 'I have to sadly report that HMS *Larcher* is lost.'

'In action or to the elements?'

'Action, sir, of a sort.'

'Then I look forward to an account of it, once you have reported to Sir William.' There was an expression on Holloway's face then, one that said *I do not wish you much in the way of joy in that encounter*. 'I will send to let him know of your arrival, meanwhile your surviving crew may avail themselves of any space that they can find aboard the flagship. I am sure the wardroom is at your disposal.'

'Thank you, sir.'

'Lost his damned ship in action, did he?' Hotham spat when he was told by Toomey who had arrived, how and why. 'Yet saw fit to survive. Bad pennies, Toomey, did I not tell you so?'

'Do you wish to deal with this yourself, sir?'

That brought a deep release of air. 'I am hoist upon my own petard, am I not?'

The man who held the position of captain of the fleet, in effect the executive officer who dealt with such matters, Rear Admiral Sir Hyde Parker, had gone home with Lord Hood, on leave and due to return by the end of the year. In his absence, Hotham had not put anyone in his place, which meant extra work for Toomey and his under clerk in examining the fleet logs. The Irishman took some comfort at that moment from what was a rare event: his employer taking responsibility for his own mistake.

He was dying to ask him what plans he had but Toomey knew that if he did Hotham would demur and might even be angered by the question. Surely he would not go ahead without involving him! He dare not upset the man, not with another competent clerk, the fellow who had come from *Victory*, accommodated on the Orlop deck and in a position to replace him. Time to volunteer for extra labour.

'If you wish me to undertake a preliminary investigation, sir?'

'Of course I do, Toomey,' came the quick reply. 'The less I have to deal with a jackanapes like Pearce the better. Thing is, should we raise the matter of Mrs Barclay?'

After much speculation, it had been agreed that if Emily Barclay was in Leghorn at the same time as Pearce they must have come there together: it was therefore a logical assumption that when he sailed, she did so in company.

'I would suggest, sir, that would be unwise. Disreputable as his behaviour seems to have been it is a private matter.'

Hotham nodded, though he was obviously not entirely convinced, before adding in a conspiratorial tone. 'Damned awkward him no longer having a ship.'

'How so, sir?'

That got a tap on the side of the admiral's nose. 'Complicates my intentions, Toomey, but there will be a way to sort matters out.'

'I hope so, sir,' the clerk replied, silently damning the man. 'I will interview Lieutenant Pearce, sir, and perhaps put forward a suitable date for his court martial.'

Hotham turned, a gleam in his eye. 'To which I will appoint

the judges. I don't care if he sunk a ship of the line, I'll make sure they have his guts.'

If Toomey wanted to know what had happened with Pearce and his ship he could have acquired the details from almost anyone aboard *Britannia*; the Larchers were not long between decks before they were charged to relate the story and it spread swiftly through the various decks and mess tables.

John Pearce was obliged to do his own telling for an avidly listening wardroom, then was assailed by a raft of questions once he had finished his account. Dorling was relating his account to the master of the flagship, as were Mr Bird and the Kempshall twins to their peers. By the time Toomey asked that Pearce attend upon him the whole vessel, except himself, Captain Holloway and Admiral Hotham, knew the story.

'I think I am obliged to explain what occurred to a fellow naval officer,' Pearce said, fingering the letters he had just been given.

'While the man who commands this fleet, Lieutenant,' Toomey insisted, 'has charged me to obtain the particulars, he being too burdened by duty to undertake the task himself.'

Obliged to comply, Pearce spoke for an age, leaving nothing out and several times referring to his logs, making no bones that the decision to leave Naples had been his.

'The court martial will want to know why.'

'The whole port was abuzz with talk of privateers operating between the cities of Naples and Palermo.' Pearce lied, 'I admit to being tempted into seeking a prize before returning as I was ordered.'

Toomey nodded and took the lie without comment – officers

chasing after prizes was common enough – this while John Pearce was wondering what Dorling would have said in his log; there would be no mention of privateers. At the same time he was wondering why he had found it impossible to ask him.

'As a result of being in the waters between Naples and Sicily we came across one of our countrymen, a merchant vessel, in dire need of aid from a pair of brigantines that proved to be from Barbary, which I gave gladly, for had I not done so she would have surely fallen to them.'

'The minutiae, sir?'

Recounted it sounded heroic, even if Pearce made no effort to render it so. He kept his voice flat and told of what happened as well as the result, making no mention of Emily Barclay, this while Toomey wrote various notes, only occasionally looking at Pearce when he felt the need to confirm the truth of what he was being told by meeting his eye.

The clerk scratched away as Pearce recounted the tale; the sight of the enemy, the pursuit and the eventual outcome, none of which Hotham's clerk responded to with even a flicker of emotion, the same when he related the loss of the ship; he appeared to be a dry functionary to his fingertips. Yet the man he was questioning could not even begin to guess at what was going on in the Irishman's mind; as Toomey wrote, he was also testing ideas on what to propose to his admiral that would satisfy Hotham's requirements yet might either stymie his stated intentions or solve the entire matter once and for all. Luckily a glimmer of a solution was beginning to emerge.

'I will, of course, require your logs to show Admiral Hotham and he will no doubt wish to interview you himself.'

'Meaning I will have to repeat everything I have already said to you?'

'Not everything, Lieutenant,' Toomey replied, producing a smile that stood in stark contrast to his previous dry demeanour. 'I will *précis* it for him.'

'I have one request to add to what I have said, not for myself but for the crew I had the honour to command.'

'Go on.'

Pearce looked hard at Toomey as he asked that they be permitted to stay together, trying to see if it had any effect, not that he was obliged. The chief clerk merely advised him to return to the wardroom and await an instruction from the admiral, which Pearce did once he had checked that his men would be fed, this before being shipped to a transport, which doubled as a hospital ship. It was also a holding space for sailors without a ship of their own where, once he had seen the admiral, Pearce expected he would join them.

That satisfied he went back to the wardroom to read his letters; one from Alexander Davidson telling him how close he was to exhausting his funds, the other from his lawyer Lucknor with news of the replies he had received to his enquiries, including a fair copy of the Burns letter, which had him swearing under his breath, it being a tissue of lies. He registered Lucknor's doubt about the way it was composed and decided that was one little swine he would take pleasure in grilling.

'Anyone here know where a Mister Toby Burns is serving?'

The reply came from a marine captain. 'As long as he's not serving here aboard *Britannia*.'

'I was not aware that he did,' Pearce replied, sensing the disapproval in the way that had been said.

'Gone now,' the marine said, but in a manner that did not invite further enquiry.

That did not bother Pearce; someone like Burns would not be hard to find.

Toomey was with Hotham at the same time and, having told the tale of the loss of HMS *Larcher*, he was now listening to the admiral's thinking on the whole problem of Pearce, Barclay, Toby Burns and the London lawyer and getting himself into a real bind.

'Sir William,' Toomey replied, making no attempt to hide his exasperation. 'I hope you see me as a confidant, a man in whom you can repose your trust, indeed have I not demonstrated that to be true on many occasions?'

The response did not come with the alacrity the clerk would have liked, but then with Hotham it rarely did. 'Yes, Toomey, you have.'

'And it would not surprise you to find that I have thought upon the matter that presses on your mind?' A low shake of the head and a look bordering on suspicion. 'Then would it not serve to admit that two heads are better than one? I would therefore take it as a compliment, nay as a necessity, that you appraise me of what it is you have in mind.'

The admiral looked like a man being asked to hand over his purse to a highwayman. Indicating Toomey should come close, he spoke quietly and with some urgency for several minutes, outlining what he had had in mind for John Pearce, now thrown into doubt because he lacked a ship. Toomey's head dropped to his chest as he listened.

With a wit sharper than the man speaking he could see a

number of definite flaws in what had been planned – it was all maybe this and perhaps that – but it had the merit of being action instead of passivity and that was welcome. At the very least the idea had the virtue of separating for some time the people Toomey knew to be a threat and if what Hotham had in mind turned out to be a dud, then it gave time for other avenues to be explored.

As his employer continued, Toomey had one of those flashes of enlightenment that come upon a person only very rarely, in which a plan of action seems to arrive fully formed and he now interrupted his employer, which got him a glare, one he ignored. He began to speak rapidly, which reversed the previous physical positions until eventually Hotham was nodding.

'Sir, you cannot resolve this problem without taking out of circulation the man who stands as a threat to you. To act otherwise leaves loose ends, does it not?'

That was allowed to sink in; there was no need to elaborate on whom constituted the most dangerous loose end.

'Will it work?' Hotham enquired, like a man who had yet to grasp all the essentials.

'There are still elements I have not yet fathomed. Should you agree to what I am saying, sir, and accept the main conclusion of my argument as correct, there is only one fact that you may find hard to swallow.'

'And what, Toomey would that be?' came the less than sanguine reply, accompanied by a direct look; the notion of unpleasant swallowing was not one Hotham cared for.

'Lieutenant Pearce must have a court martial?'

'He lost a vessel of His Majesty's Navy, of course he must, man.'

Toomey let the irritation pass over him; it mattered not that he had stated the obvious. 'For the plan I have just outlined to work, sir—'

'Get to the point, Toomey!'

'At his court martial, Lieutenant Pearce must not only be cleared of any wrongdoing, he may have to be praised to the skies for both his bravery and application.'

'What!'

'It is, sir, as I see it, the only way.'

CHAPTER THIRTEEN

Toby Burns stood on the deck of the transport vessel *Tarvit* idly surveying the anchorage and the fleet. If he had expected to feel different there was no evidence of it. The arrival of several boats bearing sailors was only of mild interest; they were noisy, it was true, but only in passing and he would see no more of them; the accommodation for officers was well separated from both the area set aside to function as a hospital and the space allocated to house officers; given he was at present, the only occupant, it was commodious indeed.

Tarvit had its own blue coats, who also had their own quarters and to Burns these men had a slightly enviable life; transports were much more relaxed than a frigate, ten times more so than a ship of the line. True they had cannon but they were few and the crew they carried were sufficient to defend the ship against anything but an enemy warship. There was none of the bustle and exactness that characterised a man o' war, which to the likes of him made life fraught with too many possibilities for error, while battle was something to be avoided not sought out. Perhaps he should aim for a place on one.

This reverie was disturbed by a set of cries echoing across the bay, arising from the lookouts set on every warship as a matter of course – there were none on the transports, their shouts followed by quarterdecks suddenly becoming busy. The thought that it might be an enemy was quickly dismissed as risible; the French capital ships were tucked up safe in Toulon and no lesser vessel would enter the British fleet anchorage unless they were contemplating suicide.

Time, as ever, stood still which had Toby reflecting on the stupidity of the air of excitement that always attended a sighting, usually dissipated over hours as what could be seen from the tops eventually came in view from the deck and was only very rarely anything other than a let-down. This was no different; indeed he had time to go below and order coffee from the wardroom steward, drink it slowly and think of many other matters before his return to the deck and the sight of a seventy-four beating up on a contrary wind.

Her name was a mystery to him and would have been even if he had sighted her previously – Burns had little interest in ships – but every other deck would have folk identifying her by the great bosom of the figurehead that decorated her bowsprit, every one of which was singular in design. Besides that every vessel had its distinctive features, for if seventy-fours were built to a standard it was in their ability to give battle, not in common construction. Within two cables' lengths of HMS *Britannia* the guns began to echo as salutes were exchanged, followed by the signal that even

Toby Burns knew being raised, telling the captain to repair aboard the flag.

John Pearce was still waiting for his interview so he joined the rest of the wardroom to witness this new arrival, vaguely aware that he had seen her lines before, yet had anyone enquired of him he would not have been able to provide a name. Since no one else on *Britannia* could identify her it was assumed she was new, making her an object of envy for men who sailed in vessels with hulls made loose from years of service.

'I know that Admiral Hotham has an expectation of being joined by HMS *Semele*. Fresh off the stocks as we suspect but I'm damned if I know who has her.'

That declaration from Captain Holloway caused an unpleasant shiver to run through Pearce's body. If it was HMS *Semele*, and if nothing had changed, he had good cause; the notion of Ralph Barclay, as well as some other bodies from past problems, being in the same theatre as he was a very unwelcome one. It would have cheered him a little to know that William Hotham felt the same, at least about Barclay, given the timing of his arrival was not going to be fortuitous.

Charlie Taverner and Rufus Dommet, stood on the forepeak of *Tarvit*, were close to cursing. The seventy-four was no stranger to them; they had served on her until John Pearce managed to get them off and they had no fond memory of the experience or of the man who had commanded her, while an unwelcome thought could not help but surface; right now they were hands without a home and the possibility existed that they might find themselves shipped into this new arrival. What they did not know was the nature of the men for whom they had been swapped. Michael O'Hagan, standing with them, had an inkling of possible future problems but felt it best to say nothing.

It was not cowardice that had Pearce make for the now empty wardroom but the need to think, and his conclusion, once he had calmed himself, was that his only real concern lay with Ralph Barclay. The men he had arranged should be swapped for Charlie and Rufus were members of a smuggling gang led by two brothers called Tolland, villains with whom he had inadvertently become involved because they saw him as the man who stole their illegal cargo. He was also the man who, after a failed attempt at murderous retribution, saw around eight of them pressed into the navy for which they would be even less forgiving.

Four he knew would be on *Semele* including one of the Tolland brothers, for he had arranged that they be swapped from a receiving hulk for his two Pelicans. Being innocent of the primary charge they held against him meant little but so, too, did their possible presence; as pressed seamen they would be confined to the vessel, even in port, and there was no chance at all of his being invited aboard Ralph Barclay's ship. Even if they sighted him and that was unlikely, they could scarcely harm him, though he had no doubt should the occasion arise they would seek to do so.

There and then he decided to avoid Barclay too, not from fear of a man who had already declined his invitation to meet over any weapon he chose, but just to maintain the peace. He was in enough trouble for the loss of *Larcher* without adding to it by becoming a pariah with every officer on the fleet for his private affairs, some of whom would make up the judges in his court martial. Barclay would hear of his presence, there was no avoiding that and should they come face-to-face John Pearce was not the man to duck such an encounter. Yet for the sake of Emily it was best they stayed apart.

The arrival of Barclay aboard the flagship reverberated through the wardroom bulkhead, as whistles blew and marines stamped their boots. Holloway would be there to greet a man well ahead on the captain's list, as would most of his officers. They had no reason to mention his presence so he began to feel more relaxed; that was until the realisation dawned that Hotham could, without consultation with anyone, make Barclay the man who would head his panel of judges. If that happened he might as well resign his commission and forgo the pay that went with it.

The noise died away and the wardroom refilled as the men off duty who had been curious filtered back into their communal space, full of talk, much of it about Barclay, known from past service to several men, not least from Toulon where he had lost his arm in what was seen as an action to admire. He had also taken several prizes since the outbreak of war and that was an occasion for barely disguised envy. Though each speaker had a care how he expressed an opinion, that being the naval way, it was not hard to detect that Barclay was not much loved, with the word 'taut' being employed more than once, which added to allusions his temper was one that carried a short fuse.

It was telling to Pearce that no one asked him: if he was a guest of the flagship wardroom, he was not a wholly esteemed one. The men who berthed here knew of his name and reputation too, knew of the fluke – as they would no doubt term it – by which he had achieved his present rank as well as the opportunities Pearce had previously been afforded by Lord Hood, missions that, given everyone was highly ambitious, could only cause professional jealousy.

The behaviour here was in stark contrast to the attitude he had encountered in the wardroom of HMS *Victory*. Their initial reserve had melted in the face of a need to be appraised of Pearce's good fortune, though it was a tenet that any such berth took its cue from the attitude of the resident premier. Aboard *Victory* that particular officer had held no grudge against him and his inferiors had followed his outlook; here the man was polite but rigidly so.

It might be to do with his father. Anyone who knew of his antecedents would be quick to alert the rest that they were hosting a dangerous radical, not a species much loved in a naval mess. Yet they would never openly allude to it: mutual politeness was an essential component of wardroom life in which some commissions lasted years, few were less than several months.

Obliged to live hugger-mugger with men you did not like and others whose habits – flute playing or constant singing, indifferent manners, loud opinions combined with very obvious personal faults – could drive another fellow mad with irritation. But that must never be allowed to surface if any kind of harmony was to be maintained. Again the resident premier set the tone and enforced the standards, his rule of the wardroom absolute.

Pearce decided to beard the present holder, knocking on the door of his tiny cabin, which if it contained a hefty cannon, at least had its own access to light as well as a private privy. On entry Pearce was greeted with a sour look, which obliged him to apologise for the disturbance.

'Given the arrival of this Captain Barclay, sir, and his presence in the great cabin, I wonder if the admiral will find time to see me today?'

'It is possible he will not, Mr Pearce.'

'I am concerned to ensure that my men are being well cared for.'

The look on the premier's face then was telling; it indicated that he thought that an exaggeration if not downright false. But good manners required him to meet what was a reasonable request from a fellow officer. It had to be dealt with however low he was held in personal esteem.

'You may send a wardroom steward to enquire of Mr Toomey, if he is available.'

'Thank you, sir.'

'I assume,' the premier said as Pearce made to depart, 'that should you be answered in the affirmative you will depart for *Tarvit*.'

There was a terrible temptation then to say no, just to annoy the sod, but it was not worth it.

Toomey was in his usual place, his tiny workplace just outside the great cabin, examining the logs of HMS *Semele* and wondering what this sudden, and to his mind unwelcome, arrival was going to do to the plan he had begun to hatch, for Barclay was not going to take kindly to any apparent favour being advanced to John Pearce. Behind the bulkhead Sir William Hotham, who had emitted a whole stream of damnations on being told what vessel was in the offing, was also somewhat ill at ease, hardly surprising given the knowledge he had regarding the man's errant wife.

He had welcomed Barclay, as he must with apparent enthusiasm, as a fine addition to his command and shared with him, albeit in circumspect language over a glass of claret, a mutual condemnation of Sam Hood and his tenure of command. It was really a low opinion of his actions regarding the Royalist French takeover of Toulon and his support for it. As much at a loss as his clerk on what this appearance portended, Hotham was saved from having to think too hard on it by Barclay's account of his part in the Battle of the Glorious First of June as well as his troubles with the commanding admiral in the Channel, Lord Howe.

Traducing one admiral to another was fairly safe territory given their endemic rivalry. Post captains were not so very different, indeed it was said that if you sought to roast one of either rank on a spit there would be no trouble in finding another to do the turning. Hotham nodded sagely as his visitor outlined the way he suspected Howe had been humbugged by his French counterpart, drawn into a battle with the capital ships instead of doing what was demanded by the situation; stopping a convoy full of American grain getting to the shores of a France close to starvation. If it gained him glory and a great deal of money it had turned out to be a strategic error.

'It is not a ploy for which you would have fallen, Sir William.' That piece of inaccurate flattery was greeted with full and ponderous agreement. 'I have no doubt you would have seen it for what it was.'

'Fellow's too old, of course. I'm told he has to have a chair on the quarterdeck these days.'

'And not all there in the head, sir, as well as a man to see chimeras: Lord Howe had the damned temerity to accuse myself and a quartet of other fine officers of being tardy in our reaction to his orders.' Barclay allowed that to sink in before adding. 'It was, of course, Curtis who was the cause, he who sought to bring us down.'

'Yet here you are, Barclay.' Hotham responded, clearly curious and somewhat suspicious.

Hotham knew very well how the Admiralty worked; if Sir Roger Curtis, a Rear Admiral and the Captain of the Channel Fleet, had put this man under a cloud he would not have done so without the cognisance of Lord Howe. There was a man with a great deal of influence both at court and in the corridors of Whitehall, he being the King's favourite admiral and a rumoured blood relative, albeit on the wrong side of the blanket. How come Barclay had been sent out to serve under him again in what was, by any standard, an area of operations where the chances of success were high? Up against Black Dick Howe he was lucky not to be on the beach.

'I had the means, sir, to prove them both wrong and such was the information I held on the causes of the battle that my request for the Mediterranean was met with swift approval.'

Hotham mulled over the explanation before responding, followed by a moment when both men looked at each other enquiringly, the admiral letting Barclay know when he did speak that his appreciation of the workings of authority was acute; Hotham was a politico as much as a sailor.

'To avoid embarrassment, perhaps?'

'Precisely, sir.'

'Two admirals outmanoeuvred, Barclay,' his host said after a lengthy silence. 'I hope you have not come to pull the same trick on a third?'

That threw Ralph Barclay. He was committed to Hotham's flag, his future depended on it. Why had the sod said something like that? He could not know, and was not about to be enlightened, that it had to do with the plan he and Toomey had for John Pearce, a pitch that Barclay could queer even if his action was inadvertent. Right now Sir William Hotham was thinking of how to deal with such an eventuality.

'You are a lucky officer, Captain Barclay.'

The reply was guarded. 'I have been fortunate yes, sir.'

The admiral, who was thinking the man was quite the opposite when it came to marriage, smiled as he stood up, a sure sign Barclay's visit was at an end yet it was not an expression full of warmth.

'Then I see it as my duty to ensure that such good fortune continues. You will, of course, dine with me this afternoon and I will invite several of those who are of like mind to us. They will be eager to hear of the Glorious First.'

'Thank you, sir. If I may I will return to my ship.'

'Then I would take it as an honour if you allow me to accompany you to the entry port.'

Barclay swelled then; whatever questions had been raised by Hotham's strange remark evaporated; the man who would do that did not lack esteem for his visitor. Everyone stood to attention and to one side as they made their way to the entry port and Barclay was sent down the gangplank to his barge with a wave. On the way back Hotham signalled to Toomey to come into the cabin where he was informed of Pearce's request, to which the clerk had declined to accede.

'At present Mr Burns is accommodated there. I cannot see it as advantageous that they should meet.'

'A word to Captain Holloway. No mention of Pearce by anyone.'

'Captain Barclay is off the ship, sir.'

'But he is coming back, man. How could I not invite him to dine with me and so must Holloway?' Toomey nodded, knowing both to be a common courtesy. 'The question is what are we to do with him following on from today?'

'A cruise would get him out of the way.'

'And how would that play with other captains who have been loyal to me when Hood was in command and have been here for near a year? A new fellow turns up, flush with prize money already and is immediately favoured.'

'Then there is only one other way to deal with the problem, sir, and that is to take Captain Barclay into our confidence.'

'And give him more by which to sink me!' Hotham spat. 'Had you been present earlier and heard what he had to say about some of my fellow flag officers you might suspect, as I do, that Captain Barclay will, in any situation in which he feels threatened, become a most slippery article.'

'He is committed to you, Sir William, and at greater jeopardy than you could ever be, should any inconvenient facts come to light. He cannot be a threat to you but he may act as an ally.'

'How?'

'I would need to ponder on that, sir, and I will do so. But recall that he hates Pearce with a passion and given the information I gleaned from Leghorn it is not only in the article of illegal impressments. What about his wife?'

'That is why he is here,' Hotham exclaimed. 'He must know where she is.'

'I think the only person who will know that, given Mrs Barclay is no longer in Leghorn, is John Pearce and my guess would be either Naples or Palermo.'

'You will have to make these enquiries, Toomey, I cannot be seen to.'

'Of course, sir,' Toomey replied, suppressing a sigh, it being ever thus, while also wondering if there was anyone Hotham did not see as a potential enemy. 'But might I suggest you request Captain Barclay to come aboard at a slightly earlier hour so that you may appraise him of your intentions.'

'There is no other way, I suppose?'

'Best he hears it from your own lips that Pearce is here and in private, from which, if he is after his wife, he will deduce that she is in the region, which obviates the need for you to open on the matter. As for your being at any risk from Captain Barclay in the future, that is a situation that we can deal with should the need arise. Our primary concern must be the furtherance of that which we have discussed already.'

'I have gnawed on this too long, Toomey, it is time to act.'

The clerk approached his admiral and spoke very softly, given there was no more than the overhead planking between this cabin and that of Holloway who, if he was the ship's captain and one of Hotham's close adherents, was not to be privy to secrets. Having spent half the day pondering on what to do, now that Pearce was returned and whole, he had his answers prepared.

'You can arrange Pearce's court martial this very day if you invite the necessary officers to dine with yourself and Barclay. Your intention to shift Captain Lockhart to HMS *Leander* creates room for a series of promotions which could see Lieutenant

Taberly elevated to Post Rank and given command of a sixth rate, with the subsequent movement of other officers into higher armed vessels.'

'That is a major step, Toomey, and in doing as you say I will have to disappoint others who are committed to me. I also have to worry if London will confirm any of my decisions.'

'I would suggest, sir, that given it is your first set of promotions they would hesitate to question your judgement. I have looked at Taberly's record of service and he has the required sea time and age, while the Admiralty will lack any knowledge of virtues only observable by proximity. We can do that without too much trouble and talk of some act of gallantry.'

'Go on,' Hotham said, leaving his clerk unsure if he was in agreement.

'The same series of elevations allow for Digby to be given a non-rated ship with possible elevation to Master and Commander.'

'You have the necessary vessel in mind I hope.'

'I do, sir, the brig HMS *Flirt*—'

'You do not lack for a sense of irony, do you?'

'In which he will be joined by Pearce, to be despatched on the mission we have agreed upon and if you consider the possible outcomes, well, I need hardly elaborate.'

The suggestion required a period of cogitation from Hotham but he finally nodded, albeit with seeming reluctance.

'I was wondering if Taberly, I recall he has the reputation for being a hard bargain, might be a suitable officer to knock the stuffing into Burns.'

'He can knock it out for my part.'

'Added to which if he has been in receipt of a blow from John

Pearce, alluded to by Major Lipton, I would suggest they are unlikely to be boon companions.'

It was necessary to wait while Hotham thought on that, but he declined to be drawn by Toomey's enquiring look. 'Anything else?'

'Yes, sir, I would suggest that the crew of *Flirt* shift with her present captain and the sloop be crewed by those Pearce brought back from HMS *Larcher*.'

'In God's name why, man?'

'It was a request made to me by Pearce that his crew should be kept together as a body, no doubt one made by them to him and that means it will automatically include those three fellows from whom you took depositions.'

'It smacks of overindulgence.'

'Yet it may be the very lever that enamours him to the position in which you intend to place him, given as an inferior officer he would not normally be allowed to take any followers to a new ship. Added to which, think on the course HMS *Flirt* must sail to get to the Adriatic?'

The subsequent silence was long, typical of a man who rarely did anything that could be considered rash and when he decided in the affirmative it was indicated by no more than a sharp nod. With a slight feeling of being underappreciated Toomey felt he had to add something, given he felt Hotham owed him some credit.

'It is a blessing Sir Hyde Parker went home with Lord Hood, sir. Had he been here this would have proved impossible.'

'We are constantly being advised by the chaplain that God is on our side in our endeavours. It is at times like these that I wonder if the man is deluding himself and us.'

Tempted to respond by saying that the work they were engaged in had more to connect it to the devil than to God, Toomey held his tongue.

'I will send word to Captain Barclay at once, meanwhile can I suggest you must grant Lieutenant Pearce a short interview.'

CHAPTER FOURTEEN

If what was coming to him would be less than a pleasure, there was some of that in drafting out the orders that would shift commanding officers from one ship to a higher-rated vessel and, in the case of Taberly, to command of HMS *Brilliant*. Her present captain, Glaister, would shift to HMS *Lutine*, which was a thirty-two-gun fifth rate as well as a capture from the enemy, one of the vessels taken out of Toulon at the end of the siege and thus held to be a plum.

The Master and Commander of the brig HMS *Flirt* would likewise move to a recently taken enemy ship, an eighteen-gun sloop which, if it was unrated, was larger than his present command, taking with him not just his followers but his entire crew to man her. This would act as a double bonus; captains got to love their crews in many cases, often becoming blind to a good number of their faults. The order to replace him was not yet written out, that would have to wait, as would the required signatures that would turn these documents, once written by a better hand than his own, into reality.

There was only one fly in the reading of such a document; Hotham might sign at the bottom but when the letter writer composed the official missive it would be Lord Hood whose name featured at the top. It would read:

By order of the Right Honourable Lord Hood, Knight of the Bath, Vice Admiral of the Red and Commander in Chief of His Majesty's ships and vessels employed and deployed in the Mediterranean . . .

'Enter,' Hotham called, when the knock came on his door, composing his features into what he hoped appeared to be indifference, not easy since he had carried a look of sour distaste and one, given his felling for his visitor, that would have suited him more.

It would never do to be pleasant to John Pearce; if he was the man would smell a rat but neither could he be sullen. Toomey announced the fellow and Pearce entered to stand before the admiral who studiously kept his gaze on the notes Toomey had provided for him. He also had a report from the master of the flagship which told of Matthew Dorling's reservations on some of the actions of his captain, though there was an addendum to say that without his acumen – a strange expression – they could never have avoided capture.

'This does not make for pleasant reading, Mr Pearce, but then the loss of one of His Majesty's ships rarely does.'

'No, sir,' Pearce replied to the top of Hotham's head.

He spoke in a tone that was respectful; he was in deep enough trouble without antagonising a man for whom he had no regard whatsoever.

'It is however not for me to issue a judgement; that will fall to those who sit on your court martial. You have the right to appoint an officer to represent you.'

'I am happy to represent myself, sir.'

Hotham finally looked up, to meet a very steady gaze that had within it a question but that did nothing to disconcert him; he was after all a Vice Admiral of the Blue and his visitor a lieutenant of questionable provenance. That this man doubted his impartiality he knew. Let him do so and be surprised.

'You may be aware that you are not among my favourite officers, Pearce. I find the way you came about your present position troubling, given it undermines the very core of the service.'

'A matter, sir, you would be obliged to take up with King George.'

'I daresay I can leave that to others,' Hotham responded languidly. 'What I will say to you is this, that you will get as fair a hearing as any other officer unfortunate enough to find themselves in the same position. The loss of a warship is serious, but it is also a hazard of our occupation and I am not going to prejudge the outcome by a long and extensive enquiry of my own.'

'Can I ask who will head the court, sir?'

'That I have not yet decided.'

The pair locked eyes: if he could not see into Pearce's mind he could certainly guess at his feelings, one of which must be to damn him to his face and tell him to stick his royally gifted rank up his fundament. What he could never have discerned was his dilemma, the fact that being committed to Emily Barclay and given the constraints on his funds and, noted by Davidson, the legal bills he had incurred in pursuit of her husband, not to mention her continued accommodation in Naples, meant he felt committed to keeping his position and his pay.

'I believe I am allowed to object to being judged by certain officers.'

'You are,' Hotham replied with a knowing smile. 'And just so you don't embarrass the process be assured that Captain Barclay will not be one of the examining board.'

'Then do I have permission to depart the flagship?'

'Why would you do that, Lieutenant, given the court will sit on the morrow?'

'So soon?' Pearce asked, genuinely surprised.

'Why not? It would be too trying to keep everyone in suspense. I'm sure the premier will find you a berth; we are, after all, short on our full complement of lieutenants. That will be all, Mr Pearce.'

Out on the main deck, Pearce stopped to think and he had much to ponder. Hotham he did not trust at all but there was no way he could fathom to have an effect on his judgement or his actions. Should the court find him guilty of taking excessive risks – and he guessed despite the recent assurances Hotham would bend it to that conclusion – he would be denied further employment with the fleet.

In truth any place was in Hotham's gift and he would whistle for anything in that quarter, which would mean he might as well go home, knowing that any chance of future engagement with the navy was just as unlikely there. At least he could badger Pitt and Dundas, the two politicos who had sent him out here in the first place – for some kind of task that carried a stipend, given he felt they owed him a great deal.

The temptation to throw in the towel before he faced the court was strong but had to be resisted; even a lieutenant's half pay was worth something and besides, in his contrariness he would take pleasure in seeing the game played out to the end. Perhaps the outcome he knew to be coming was the best solution: to go back to England with Emily and seek some other means of making a crust.

There were those radical people who thought like his father and had helped both he and his son to flee to Paris from that writ for sedition. The members of the various Corresponding Societies might aid him in finding paid employment, though he had to consider that his irregular liaison might have a similar effect on them as it had had on Captain Fleming; if such people sought to change society it was in the political sphere not the personal.

As to his pursuit of Ralph Barclay, that would wither without funds to pay the lawyer he had engaged and he knew for certain the navy would do everything in its power to protect their man, especially if his suit went anywhere near an admiral; added to which, Barclay was now well heeled enough to fund a powerful defence. The cry of *Semele* from without the entry port, to tell all aboard that the barge carrying the captain of that ship was approaching, had Pearce moving quickly, forced to bustle his way through the folk gathering for the required ceremony.

Ralph Barclay came aboard with his faithful Devenow at his heels to have his wet boat cloak removed before raising a hat to the invisible quarterdeck, the marines being afforded a perfunctory inspection and their officer the habitual praise for their bearing. He then exchanged pleasantries with John Holloway before making his way aft to enter a cabin in which Admiral Sir William Hotham stood in the company of his clerk.

'Captain Barclay, I asked you to come at an earlier hour because I have something to impart to you that will not make for pleasant listening.' He then nodded towards Toomey. 'My chief clerk you will know from previous encounters . . .'

'Toomey,' Barclay acknowledged.

'He has, on my behalf, been engaged in some enquiries engendered by rumours that reached my ears.' He could see Barclay stiffen and the one empty left sleeve seemed to twitch; the man did not like the sound of what he was hearing. 'I refer to what is a private matter and one in which you have nothing but my deepest sympathy. It is also one I would dearly like to have kept hidden but circumstances do not allow.'

There could only be one of those so the response was swift, though it was delivered through a constrained throat, struggling to sound normal. 'If you have knowledge of the whereabouts of my wife, sir, I would be grateful to be told.'

Hotham seemed to visibly grow with relief; he had been dreading the notion that he might be mistaken, that Barclay had no idea his wife had run off with Pearce. 'I wondered if you knew.'

'What information do you have, sir?'

'Toomey will tell you.'

Barclay's eyes swung to the clerk and lost any notion of respect, not that Toomey was fazed by that; he dealt with post captains all the time and if he was deferential he was never humble. His voice was even as he explained what his enquiries in Leghorn had produced, given with a brief description as to what had led to their initiation, all listened to in silence.

'Is Pearce in Leghorn now?' Barclay really meant his wife.

'No, sir, he was sent with despatches to Naples.'

'Then I would suggest that given Mrs Barclay left England on his ship, she will have taken passage with him.'

'It is not that simple, sir.'

'Sit down, Captain Barclay, please,' Hotham said, 'we have matters to relate to you that I would not want to be overheard.'

The admiral sat down himself and indicated that the others should join him; once sat he urged them into a proximity in which, once their heads were leant forward, put them close enough together to make their breath mingle. It also permitted Toomey to whisper and the concentration with which Barclay listened impressed him; there were no exclamations, indeed hardly a blink in those steady eyes as what Pearce had been up to was related.

'And he is on *Britannia* as we speak.'

'He is,' Hotham acknowledged. 'Awaiting his court martial, which I intend to convene tomorrow.'

'Then I ask to be allowed to sit on the panel, in fact I would dearly love to head it.'

'No, Barclay,' Hotham replied, but seeing his guest suck in air for a protest was quick to add. 'And now Toomey is going to explain to you why.'

As the clerk spoke Barclay dropped his head to listen, once more in deep concentration, only occasionally nodding at some pertinent point like the naming of his nephew, though he could not disguise his surprise that Burns was now entitled to the rank of lieutenant if not one confirmed by the Navy Board.

He added nothing and entered no suggestions, which intrigued the clerk who was quick to surmise that the man was being excessively cautious. He was being handed a gift of which he had no part in fashioning and therefore no responsibility, which brought back to Toomey's mind Hotham's remark about Barclay being a slippery customer; even as he spoke the clerk was thinking that was a matter which would require some consideration.

'You think this will produce a result?' he asked when silence fell.

'It is our intention that it should, sir.'

If his silence did not faze the others they would have been less comfortable at what he was thinking; Hotham had no idea that Pearce had a full transcript of the court martial, a copy he could only have got through Samuel Hood or someone very close to him indeed and all Barclay's attempts to recover it had failed. If the admiral found out would he be so keen to still support him? It must have taken some guile to get hold of that copy, which led him to point out a very pertinent fact.

'Do not underrate Pearce, sir. Much as I hate the sod he is no fool.'

The response from Hotham was rather testy. 'If you can contrive a better solution, Captain Barclay, I would be glad to hear of it. We have expended much thought and consideration on this matter and, while I will grant you there is no guarantee it will solve the entire conundrum, it stands a very good chance of doing so.'

'Is Digby essential?'

'Sir William cannot be seen to give Pearce a command, not after the loss of HMS *Larcher*, regardless of how the verdict of the court is worded. Also, as you know, they have served together before on an independent cruise.'

'He might decline the appointment,' Barclay mused.

'We think,' Toomey hissed, 'we have the means to persuade him to it.'

Waiting for the inevitable question, Toomey was disappointed, though that was not the emotion he felt. Barclay did not want to know, which meant he was thinking of any subsequent consequences, a time when he might be asked questions to which he would honestly be able to say he had no idea of the answers.

Again what the man was actually thinking was very different. Barclay only knew Henry Digby as a relatively distant if competent enough inferior, a lieutenant on HMS *Brilliant* and one it had been convenient to get rid of at Gibraltar, the very place where he had pledged his commitment to Sir William Hotham. If he had been efficient he had not made enough of a mark to impress his then captain to the extent that he could form a judgement as to how he would act in the future. And how close was Digby to Pearce? Enough to take the man's mistress, his wife, on board perhaps?

The sigh that Barclay emitted then made his companions curious but they would not be enlightened as to the thought that spurred it; Emily had made her bed and must lie in it and if that took her into an arc of danger, so be it.

'Please do not think I am lacking in appreciation, sir.' That got a sympathetic nod from Hotham. 'Tell me what I must do and I will follow your instructions to the letter.'

'Good man,' the admiral replied, as he heard the sound of stamping boots, a sure sign of other captains arriving at the entry port. 'I know you will struggle to be at ease given what you have learnt but I would ask that no hint of your discomfort be imparted to your fellow officers, with whom we are about to dine.'

'Of course.'

'Toomey, alert my steward that we are ready to receive our guests.'

'Do any of them know about Mrs Barclay?'

'If they do, it is not from anything that has passed my lips,' Hotham replied, standing, which obliged the others to follow. 'I also hazard if they do they will refrain from mentioning the matter, for to do so would be a serious breach of good manners. Now, Captain Barclay, I beg you to partake of some claret and Toomey, I think that will be all.'

Within minutes the cabin was full of post captains, for each had been punctual in their arrival, with Barclay being welcomed and doubly so when these peers of his heard he had been with Howe on the Glorious First. That elevated him to a very special guest indeed and from being rather downcast such was the attention he received that it lifted his spirits to the point that the problem of Pearce and his young wife could be shifted to the back of his thinking.

That did not apply to Sir William Hotham; as he described the battle and fielded erudite questions, Barclay kept an eye on him and it registered what the admiral was up to, engaging certain captains in a discreet way and if he could not overhear all of the conversations he could put together a fair summary of what they were about, aided by snatches he did manage to pick up.

One matter he did register; this was no exclusive gathering of his clients, there were men present who were closer to Hood, Commodore Robert Linzee, very senior on the captain's list and close to flag rank, being one of them. Not that he got chummy with the admiral; when they did speak it was with chilly politeness; Hotham had taken aim at others.

'Can't fault a fellow for going after prizes . . . Master reports his action in the chase as showing great acumen . . . got his crew back to the fleet, which is a surprise on its own . . . seems he saved a very valuable vessel and crew from being taken and at great personal cost . . . took a wound you know.'

Barclay also tried to discern the reaction from the men Hotham was engaging with, not that he had to wonder much. They would pick up from the admiral the drift of his feelings and given they probably had no real idea of any personal animus towards Pearce – his name had hardly been mentioned at Barclay's own court martial and these were many of the same fellows who had judged him – they would know they were being given guidance on how they should proceed.

It was all completed before they sat down to a meal close to the naval heart; roast beef – if not of Old England then fresh from the nearby island – washed down with copious quantities of Italian wines bought in Leghorn, followed by port that induced a feeling of convivial bonhomie. As they made their way back to their various barges it was not the rocking motion of HMS *Britannia* that induced an unsteady gait.

Only one commanding officer was sober, Ralph Barclay, who had been unusually abstemious as, on a different level to his many conversations, he thought through the ins and outs of Hotham's proposal. The conclusion: if he had reservations he was damned if he knew what he could do about them.

'Let the game be played out,' he said out loud, as he sat in his barge.

'Your honour?' slurred Devenow, far from sober himself having put much pressure on Hotham's pantry and his steward – he was big and a noted bully – to provide him with a taste of the wine being served at table.

'Nothing, Devenow, a bit of devilry, only at this point I have no idea who is really Satan.'

John Pearce heard them depart, for it was again the occasion for many a bosun's whistle to be piped but he sought to shut it out from his mind, which was engaged with the paper before him and the writing upon it, a list of questions he expected would be posed. To these he must prepare answers and if some of them strayed somewhat from the truth all he was concerned with was one possible outcome: could those lies be challenged?

CHAPTER FIFTEEN

Was it essential that the condemned man should eat a hearty breakfast? It seemed the junior members of the wardroom thought so if not the premier – he was plied with eggs and ham, a whole pigeon in a pie as well as a suet pudding and as much coffee as he could consume, given he declined wine. If they were not partisan on behalf of John Pearce, some must be quite the reverse, each knew that one day they might find themselves in a similar predicament in which any actions they undertook, regardless of how brave and how right they had seemed at the time could, in the cold light of a courtroom, be seen as wrong-headed and career-breaking.

It seemed the same as Pearce took a turn around the deck to ease his alimentary discomfort; his stomach was somewhat distended though, he wondered if anxiety played a part. Every eye he caught – and that included the common seamen – had within the look a man gives out when he is mentally swapping places with someone in difficulty, usually accompanied by the slightest nod of encouragement.

Could Pearce take from that their approval at least of his actions after leaving Naples, for everyone now knew the story of his adventures? He had to conclude not; their opinion mattered not at all. He also knew of the flaws in the case he was about to present, which rested entirely on who the court would call from the crew of *Larcher* and what they would say.

Dorling would be questioned for certain and perhaps the other warrants, all of whom could blow his defence out of the water but who he hoped might not. But would they question any of the lower deck? It was not impossible; it depended on their determination to convict and he reckoned if they brought the Jeremiahs, who had plagued the ship from Palermo onwards, to testify against him he would be quickly sunk.

The beat of the drum told him that the court was assembling, which oddly took him back to an unhappy recollection; that was the same kind of rat-a-tat tattoo that had heralded the arrival of a tumbril of prisoners from the Conciergerie prison in the plaza, those who had overthrown King Louis: it was named the *Place de la Révolution*. Suddenly he was back in that packed Parisian square, hemmed in by a screaming mob all yelling imprecations at the tattered aristocrats and denounced unfortunates destined to feed both their blood lust and the guillotine. It was not a happy portent.

'Mr Pearce,' the officer of the watch said as he approached, 'the court is assembled and awaiting your arrival.'

'Thank you, Lieutenant.'

Pearce waited for the man to wish him luck but it did

not come, so he just nodded and passed by him, heading for the upper deck cabin vacated for the occasion by Captain Holloway. Again, if you took away the dark blue coats, there was a similarity to the revolutionary tribunals he had witnessed; the stern faces set along the rear of a long baize-covered table, the air of serious intent with Pearce hoping what was missing would be the certainty of guilt and inevitable conviction that had so recently animated the rogues of the Committee of Public Safety.

Having sat down at a small table, on which lay a batch of papers, he became aware that an audience was filing in behind him to occupy the chairs set out to accommodate them. He was obliged to stand up again so the charge against him could be read out, this by a captain the accused knew to be called Linzee, a hardy-looking fellow with a high forehead topped by grey curls.

Linzee was very senior indeed; Pearce had been on a mission to Tangier, which Linzee had led and knew him to be somewhat intemperate but also effective as an officer. Seeking to place him in the Hotham firmament, he struggled to recall if the man from Hampshire – he had a distinct vocal burr – was closely attached to Hotham and he thought not, which rendered his presence a curiosity.

'Lieutenant Pearce, the charge against you is that on the dates listed in the papers before you, you did willingly and unnecessarily risk the vessel under your command, the armed cutter HMS *Larcher*. It is also a charge against you that you disobeyed your orders to return from Naples with all despatch and instead deviated in order that you could profit from the dereliction of your rightful duty, subsequently creating the circumstances that led to the loss of said vessel as well as the lives of several of your crew.'

Toomey, who had undertaken the task of clerk to the court, allowed those words of his to sink in before asking. 'How do you plead?'

Pearce addressed Linzee. 'Not guilty, sir.'

That got a sharply raised set of heavy eyebrows. 'That is a bold plea, fellow.'

'Sir, if you were to separate the charges I would admit to disobeying my orders, but I cannot plead guilty to doing what I consider to be my duty and that of every other officer in His Majesty's Navy, in seeking out and confronting his and our nation's enemies.'

'With your permission, Commodore Linzee,' Toomey asked, to a quick nod. 'You cannot separate the charges since the action in one case led to the entire consequence. You may therefore wish to change your plea.'

'No, I stand to be judged by my actions.'

'Very well, let us proceed. Lieutenant Hotham, if you please?'

He sat opposite Toomey in the position of the prosecutor, at another small desk on which sat the logs of HMS *Larcher* and he now stood up to address Pearce, who was wondering what the name portended for he had to be a relative even if there seemed to be no family likeness. The man spoke to first confirm his name, rank and the date of his commission, which occasioned a great deal of concentration on the trio of captains who made up the bench to see how they reacted, given the circumstances of his elevation were unlikely to be a mystery. There was nothing there but frowns of disapprobation; King George and his whims be damned.

The litany that followed from this younger Hotham was no more than a confirmation of his orders, that he had fully understood them, this leading to query as to his actions in disobeying them.

'If you are prepared to plead not guilty, Mr Pearce, you must have grounds to justify that?'

'It is an unfortunate fact that I cannot call to the court certain witnesses who might be able to give grounds to validate my actions—'

Any hope that such a point would be helpful was quickly dashed and from a very correct Linzee. 'Just answer the question.'

'In my meeting with the Ambassador to the Kingdom of Naples he alluded several times to the losses being suffered by British, Neapolitan and neutral vessels in the waters between the capital of the mainland and the capital of the island of Sicily, namely Palermo.'

'Do you have any evidence of this?'

'I have my word as an officer, no more, but if I may continue?' A nod. 'Sir William Hamilton has requested from both Lord Hood and Admiral Hotham that a squadron of His Majesty's ships should be stationed in Naples to patrol said waters and provide protection against both privateers and pirates from North Africa.'

Linzee indicated that Toomey should approach the bench and there followed a whispered conversation, the contents of which Pearce could guess at. It was Hamilton who had told him of the requests he had made and if his reasoning was somewhat different they were real. The ambassador wished to show support for King Ferdinand in a kingdom unsettled by events in France; no monarchy was immune to revolutionary undercurrents not even King George, which was what had made he and his ministers so afraid of Adam Pearce.

'We accept that such requests were made,' Linzee said eventually, looking left and right to his colleagues to assure himself they understood before nodding to the prosecuting lieutenant to continue, the next question an obvious one.

'Did the ambassador request you to act upon this?'

'He made it plain to me that a diversion in my course might serve a useful purpose.'

Pearce had to hold his breath then; no matter how many times you rehearse a lie to yourself the first time it is publicly aired is a moment of anxiety. Having mentioned missing witnesses he was banking on the fact that this court could no more call Sir William Hamilton than could he.

'How did he make it plain?'

'I don't follow,' Pearce prevaricated.

'Did the ambassador ask you to deviate from your orders?'

'Not in so many words.'

The response came with a touch of theatrical exasperation. 'It would be instructive to hear what words he used, Mr Pearce.'

'I doubt if I repeated them, and accuracy would be questionable in any case from a series of fragmented conversations, if they would have the same effect on you as they had on me.'

'You must try us,' growled the fellow to Linzee's left, a dry stick of a captain who looked to not be utterly well, in sharp contrast to the heartily round and red-faced fellow on the other side.

Pearce adopted an air of troubled recollection as he spun his fabrications. 'He generally deplored that his requests had been ignored, alluded to the absurdly high insurance rates pertaining to the Levant trade and hinted that he would encourage any officer who felt he could detour for a short time to those waters.'

'Was anyone else witness to this?'

'His wife on one occasion, Lady Hamilton.'

It was necessary to hide his amusement at the reaction to that name and if it smacked of disapproval he knew it to be larded with hypocrisy; not one of these men, exposed to the charms of Emma Hamilton and finding her willing to succumb, would have hesitated to bed her. The pause such musing engendered allowed him to continue without interruption.

'The same point was made to me by Captain Fleming of *Sandown Castle*.' As expected that got a facial query. 'He commanded a Levant merchant vessel about to sail to Palermo prior to an onward voyage to England with a valuable cargo and with several passengers.'

'Captain or proprietor?' asked the prosecutor.

'He did not own the ship.'

No one spoke; they all knew that a merchant captain doing such a thing was making a little extra for himself, monies he would not have to report to the vessel's owners and it was such a common practice as to be hardly remarked upon. Nor would he have to record his detour to Palermo and Pearce was suddenly aware that there might be another reason why Fleming had felt it unwise to carry Emily back to England. A normal passenger posed no threat, one carrying a whiff of notoriety might.

'You're suggesting that this Captain Fleming, who is another witness we cannot question, expressed a specific worry.'

Pearce could have kissed this prosecuting lieutenant, who had just made his case for him. He had been about to put forward the same point. 'I am.'

'Did you undertake to aid him?'

'No, but HMS *Larcher* weighed shortly after he did and I decided to adopt his course before turning north and returning to the fleet.'

'I refer you to your logs, Lieutenant Pearce, in which you make no mention of either of these conversations.'

'I do not see them as a place for speculation but you will have observed that I noted the course I followed, which was in the direction of Palermo and in the wake of *Sandown Castle*.'

'Indeed. Now please describe what happened following on from this decision.'

Which he did; the sighting of the enemy and the dilemma with which he was presented regarding the odds posing a rhetorical question. Could he leave a fellow countryman to a certain fate and the brigantines being Barbary that would have been worse than he first imagined?

'I could not, sir,' he said, addressing Linzee directly, 'stand aside even at risk of the loss of my ship. I may have come to the navy and my rank by a route not generally taken but I do most heartily understand the ethos of the service of which I am part. Who, sir, can merely watch while an enemy snaps up a British prize?'

The heads went down to the table then; they were serving under a commander who had done just that in the American War and it would never be forgotten. Invited to continue he outlined the fight and the consequences and his own arrival in Palermo harbour as a victim of both a wound and a blow.

'And I must, if I may, commend the actions of my men in what they undertook when I was not able to give them guidance, being unconscious. They fought like lions according to Captain Fleming.'

'Noted,' said Linzee, with a glance at Toomey.

Then it was Palermo and di Stefano, who Pearce praised for his efforts to get HMS *Larcher* back to sea. 'Tireless is the only word to describe him,' he lied. 'But he was up against his fellow countrymen, gentlemen, for whom sloth and chicanery is a way of life.'

That got a murmur from his rear, quickly killed by a glare from Linzee; damning Johnny Foreigner was always good for a bit of sympathy even if Pearce doubted his own fellow countrymen were much better.

'The consul made it plain to me that despite his sterling efforts I could be stuck in Palermo for months and without any aid in the way of funds. The poor man is up against debts he has already incurred on behalf of His Majesty's Government and could not in all conscience take on the burden of any more without risk to his own position. It was he who suggested it might be wiser to seek aid in Naples.'

There was no need for the prosecutor to mention another absent witness but he did, which led quite naturally to the events that followed and here the questioning took a different turn. The men before and judging him were all long-serving sea officers and they had curiosities they were not prepared to leave to second-hand explanation. Each one began to interrogate him separately and Pearce had a feeling that, Linzee apart, there was a want of censure in their expressions when he gave them answers.

'To have fought would have put at hazard not only the vessel but also the crew who sailed her. If I could not save both I decided it was my duty to save one element who could then, at least, continue to serve against our enemies.'

Another murmur broke out from behind him at what even Pearce knew to be hyperbolic excess, this time let pass by Linzee, as the prosecutor, having established the board had no more questions, requested permission to call Matthew Dorling. That changed the mood of John Pearce who felt he had made a good case and if it was built of falsehoods then there was no way to gainsay them. But the young man who entered now to swear on the Bible to tell the truth could sink him with one name.

If he mentioned Emily Barclay, especially after her husband had just arrived from England, he would be damned as a seedy lothario and his evidence seen as a tissue of lies. In considering his case Pearce had known that honesty was not his best course. He had no idea what Dorling or anyone else would contribute, which left him relying on any residual goodwill they might have; it was a tenuous place to be.

'Mr Dorling, were you aware of the reasons why Lieutenant Pearce disobeyed his orders on departure from Naples.'

'Wasn't aware of his orders, sir.'

'He did not confide in you?' Linzee demanded, surprised.

'No sir, he did not.'

'Did you not find that strange?' asked the dry stick captain.

'It's my first warranted place, your honour, I am a loss to know if what Mr Pearce did was the right thing or a commonplace.'

The man in question, who was both holding his breath and

seeking to keep his face from showing any emotion began to relax; if he had not stated to Dorling his orders there was little doubt that the master knew what they were. The man was not going to desert him and quite clearly he had not noted in his log that Pearce had chosen to ignore them or the reason.

The prosecutor, first making sure he was not about to interrupt a superior, took up the questioning. 'So you did not question the course he set you?'

'I set the course, sir,' came the proud reply. 'Mr Pearce was inclined to trust me in that once I knew his aim.'

Dry stick came in again. 'Do I take you to mean that this officer lacks the necessary skills in that department?'

'He does the best he can, sir, but will, by habit, check with me.'

That got Pearce a sour look from the middle of the bench as Dorling was asked his opinion of the decision to engage a superior enemy, which got the reply, delivered with respect that such judgements were not for the likes of him to question. When it came to the leaving of Palermo Dorling had no choice but to back up the opinion he had written down on the day, that it was a risk he himself would not have countenanced, which had the prosecuting lieutenant looking at Pearce, who stood up to cross-examine.

'Mr Dorling, did you at any time have dealings with the British Consul in Palermo?'

'No, sir.'

'And while we were berthed off Naples you never departed the ship?'

Dorling blushed then and proved he was as adept at lying as his captain. 'No one did, sir, bar the wounded, on your orders.'

'Thank you, Mr Dorling,' Pearce said, before addressing the court, 'I have no further questions.'

Dismissed, Dorling was followed by Mr Bird and the Kempshall twins, none of whom materially added to the case and were quickly sent on their way, which had Linzee check that his prosecutor was done with the witnesses and that Pearce, unlike him, did not want to enter into a closing argument, before he stated that the captains would retire to consider their verdict.

It was only when he stood and was able to turn round that Pearce espied Henry Digby; he smiled at his fellow lieutenant who merely nodded in response. Then he saw Taberly on the other side of the room, who looked at him as if the mere act would kill. There was true hatred there, for which he cared nothing, but the lack of a reassuring smile from Digby did bother him.

He looked straight ahead as he passed them, to be escorted by a marine officer to a cabin on the orlop deck, which normally housed one of Hotham's clerks. The admiral would be beneath the feet of that court, no doubt willing them to damn him and as he considered what had occurred Pearce reckoned he had done as well as he could.

It was not long before the court was reconvened and he was escorted back to his table to sit and immediately stand again as Linzee looked at the paper before him on which was written the verdict. Acutely attuned to the atmosphere Pearce feared the worst for the face was not reassuring; it seemed as if every muscle was as tight as a drum.

'By the power vested in me as President of this Court I hereby declare that it is the decision of myself and my fellow judges . . .' Linzee paused then to glance left and right at two others who seemed to be sitting back a bit and wearing on their faces a look of serenity. 'That the accused, Lieutenant John Pearce, blatantly disobeyed his orders, while his stated reasons for doing so do not justify his actions.'

Time to think of another way to earn a crust, Pearce thought.

'It is however the verdict of this court that in doing so he rendered sterling service to both the navy and His Majesty and that in his action against the enemies of our sovereign he demonstrated both flair and application.'

'Rubbish,' came a hissed whisper, which Pearce thought he recognised as Taberly. Linzee heard it too and barked out. 'This is not a playhouse. Anyone else who comments where they should be silent may well find themselves sitting where the accused has been these last two hours.'

His eyes went back to the paper he was reading from. 'The court finds that in leaving Palermo, Lieutenant Pearce took a calculated risk and cannot be held accountable for the misfortune that befell HMS *Larcher*. In his actions to save the crew he showed commendable skill and sound judgement and he therefore cannot be held to account for the loss of the ship.'

He's not happy was the next thought Pearce had, unlike his fellow judges, who were now managing slight smiles, not very evident ones but contented expressions nonetheless. Had they disagreed? Was Linzee being obliged to read out a verdict he did not approve of, had he been outvoted? The way he read the final sentence certainly made it seem so.

'In conclusion, we find Lieutenant Pearce worthy of a reprimand for his disobedience of his orders, but that it must be mitigated with praise for his subsequent actions. It is the opinion of this court that he should be returned to duty with no stain attached to his name.'

Linzee looked up and glared at Pearce then, his high forehead creased with lines in such a way that left the accused in no doubt that if he could, he would have thrown him out of the navy. The trio stood and disappeared into Holloway's dining cabin without any exchange, even eye contact.

'Congratulations, John,' said Henry Digby, over the noise of scraping chairs and a babble of talk. 'You have a Will O' the Wisp's ability to escape the consequences of your behaviour.'

Having turned, Pearce saw Taberly not far behind Digby and he spoke too.

'You're a liar, sir, to my mind.'

'I invite you to say that in another place,' Pearce replied, his tone cold and measured.

'Fight you? Never and not only because it is forbidden that you be allowed to challenge a superior officer. I have seen your methods, Pearce, and they leave me with only one impression, that you came from some gutter and have the mores of your upbringing. Mr Digby, might I remind you as your superior officer that your duty is aboard HMS *Leander*.'

Taberly spun on his heel and left, Digby sighing and following.

Toomey had come up behind him and when he spoke Pearce turned back to face him. 'Well I am surprised, Mr Pearce. I had you down as guilty.'

'I would like to be a fly on the wall when you tell Admiral Hotham.'

'I daresay he already knows and is now wondering what to do with you. The fleet is short of officers and now he will find he has to provide you with a place.'

In truth, Hotham was in his cabin and smiling as he appended his signature to the orders that would shift a whole raft of people from one vessel to another. Matters were, to his mind, moving in a promising direction.

CHAPTER SIXTEEN

Henry Digby opened the heavy piece of parchment, breaking the Admiralty seal with something akin to bewilderment. Two documents had been delivered to the wardroom of *Leander* – a third had come aboard of which he was unaware – one for Taberly, another for him and while the premier had gone into his cabin to read his, Digby, aware that all eyes were upon him, decided to examine it at the table at which he had just finished his breakfast.

The preamble at the top was the standard identification of the authority under which it had been written, namely Lord Hood as C-in-C, followed by the names of various officers being shifted and as he read on his mind had some trouble taking in what was being imparted.

You are hereby required and directed to proceed on board Flirt *and take charge and command of her, willing and requiring all the Officers and Company of said Brig to behave themselves in the several employments with all due respect to you as their Commander. You will likewise observe as well the General Printed Instructions and also what orders and directions you may from time to time receive from any of your superior officers of His Majesty's Service . . .*

It ended with the usual warning that failure to abide would cause him and those he commanded to answer at his peril, and there was his name and that of the ship, signed by Sir William Hotham.

'My God, I have got a step.'

'To what vessel?' came the enquiry from another lieutenant.

'*Flirt*, fourteen-gun brig.'

'I know her, she's a damn fine ship, fast on a bowline.'

'And will now have a damn fine commander,' essayed another voice.

Digby, raising his eyes from his instructions looked around the wardroom at the collection of faces and he could not fail to see that the last sentiment expressed was not held by all, certainly not by those he called 'Taberly's geese'. Some of that band looked positively miffed but he took more from the smiles than the frowns. The door to the premier's cabin swung open and Taberly yelled for his servant before raking the wardroom with a look that Digby could not fathom. Was it a glare or was it a sneer?

As soon as the servant appeared and entered the cabin the door was closed behind him, but not before those observing heard the order to fetch up his sea chest from the hold and pack his dunnage, with an added and more muffled order to clear out his private store locker.

There was joy in the wardroom, for even Taberly's geese were smiling now there was none in the cabin above their heads where their captain, Frost, was reading his own orders shifting him to HMS *Conqueror*, another seventy-four and one that he was likely to be singled out as being most in need of a full refit; in short he was being sent home and in a vessel that would discharge its officers and crew as soon as it docked at Portsmouth. He was being beached.

If he was an indolent fellow and a less than taut commander Frost did not see himself as such; in his own opinion he was a diligent and conscientious officer who had the good sense to choose the right inferiors, men like Taberly, thus leaving him free to do those things that left his mind clear for reflections on higher matters. Standing, he went to the bulkhead to examine the collection of butterflies therein, something of a passion and right now he felt very close to those pinned to the board and no longer living creatures.

An order to shift was not one to be either questioned or delayed whatever your rank, but when he called for his servants and clerk to begin the necessary packing it was done softly and with a real degree of sadness; his cabin had been his home and now it would be that of another officer and he felt he must be gone before that person arrived to avoid his own feelings of embarrassment. It was only when he went on deck for a deep breath of air that Frost got wind of the other changes and that induced feelings of deep misery. His subordinates were on the up while he was well on the way to a half pay.

That was when Taberly approached and asked if he could use the captain's barge, to which he got a shake of the head. 'But I have been given my step, sir.'

'And I, Taberly, have been given the boot.' The insincere regret with which that was greeted was impossible to miss, but it was ever thus. No one sought advancement or comfort for another in the service; Frost reckoned it was dog eat dog. 'So, lieutenant, you will have to satisfy yourself with the cutter.'

Digby got the Jolly Boat, which in his case was sufficient and he had good grounds to be cheerful for two reasons; first the independence he would now enjoy and second he would get away from a man he had come to hate. As far as Captain Frost was concerned he thought the man was getting what he deserved: let him employ his catching nets at home, where there were just as many butterflies to pursue.

Toby Burns registered the commotion aboard *Tarvit* even if it did not affect him in any way. The draft of sailors who had so recently come aboard were being shipped out and he left his part of the vessel to look over the side and observe them piling into the boats. One huge fellow took his eye, he being so much bulkier than his companions, impossible to miss. Burns was forced to withdraw his head sharply as the man turned his head and looked up.

'What the devil is O'Hagan doing here?' he hissed to himself, before edging forward to look down again, able to observe an Irishman busy exchanging jests with his shipmates, the faces of whom he took note of, reckoning there might be a couple more who had served aboard his Uncle Ralph's frigate.

'They're all off to a brig called HMS *Flirt*,' snorted one of the transport lieutenants, who had come alongside Toby without his noticing and had spoken to him, which was a rare event. 'Damn me they'll have to use their bare fists to defend a ship with a name like that, don't you reckon?'

'Not a berth I would be happy to admit to, no.'

He was not thinking of that really, but the fact that O'Hagan was close to John Pearce. Had he done a bit of ship visiting he might have known that the man he feared was aboard the flagship and had just undergone a court martial, for if Hotham had wanted his proximity kept close that evaporated as soon as he took Ralph Barclay into his confidence. The name was on many a lip in every wardroom in the fleet and so was the verdict of the court, which was held to be remarkable.

'Can I borrow a telescope?'

'Help yourself, Mr Burns,' came the reply as the transport officer moved away.

With that instrument, once he had seen the direction in which the boats were heading, he could pick out their destination, the first fact to register that just as many boats were leaving the vessel as were approaching. It was not a practised eye that looked at what he now assumed to be *Flirt*, a low flush-decked brig lying at single anchor with seven visible gun ports. Another person might have appreciated her sleek lines; Toby Burns could only think of her as being seriously cramped.

Henry Digby and his servant beat his new crew to their ship with enough time to exchange pleasantries with her departing commander, Lieutenant Atkins, and more than that, he got to glance at her logs and extracted good information on the brig and her foibles, as well as an invitation to dine aboard the captured French sloop Atkins was shifting to.

'Have to clean her from end to end first, of course,' Atkins growled. 'Dirty dogs the French when it comes to cleanliness.'

'If the odour of vinegar becomes unbearable, sir, let me entertain you instead.'

'You are aware I am taking my standing officers, Mr Digby.'

'I am, but the men coming aboard are the crew of HMS *Larcher*, newly lost, so I have a full pack.'

'Odd outcome, that court martial, don't you think?'

'Who can fathom the thinking of senior officers?'

'Not I,' came the reply. 'I wish you good fortune in *Flirt*, sir, for she is due some. We have worked her hard but never seen so much as a bag of nails for our trouble.'

Atkins had only just left when the first of the new crew came aboard and from then on there was too much to do, for thinking about his good fortune of whether he would have any in command. The crew had to be mustered and entered to then have read out to them the Articles of War, which promised draconian punishments for offences various and death for quite a few.

Sitting working out the watches, he noted that as with every other vessel in the fleet he was seriously undermanned; but he also noted for the second time several names – he had recognised them when compiling the muster roll – and one in particular, a fellow impossible to miss. He was just about to send for O'Hagan when he was apprised of more boats approaching with a body of a fourteen marines and so was obliged to go on deck to greet their commander, a Lieutenant Grey.

Flirt was entitled to a complement of Lobsters, which eased the under manning somewhat and he found in Grey he had an officer who needed no aid to allot his men to the duties they were there to undertake, such as manning the two four-pounder cannon that took up a fair amount of his cabin space. It was with a bit of chest-swelling pride the first time Digby passed the red coat and rigid attention as he took to the steps of the short companionway that led to his cabin.

Once more sat at his desk, Digby pondered whether it would be a good idea to write to Hotham, or perhaps Captain Holloway to point out that if he had a crew and marines he had no officers or midshipmen to aid him in the running of the ship. Did they expect him to stand every watch himself? On balance he decided it was best to wait.

John Pearce was utterly unaware of his old commander's good fortune or the way the Larchers had been shifted; he was, as he saw it, trapped in *Britannia*'s wardroom when he should have shifted to the transport, there to await whatever fate Hotham had in store for him, probably at best service in a ship of the line; at worst it would be an order to go home. Several times he had sought to beard Toomey and elucidate what was going to happen to him, the only reply he got being that no decision had been made.

The next shock of the day came when the sun was over its zenith: an order to Toby Burns to repair aboard HMS *Brilliant*, Captain John Taberly, there to assume the duties of an Acting Lieutenant, where the order added, he might learn to occupy the rank before it was officially gifted to him. Having become accustomed to the ease of life aboard *Tarvit* he was far from pleased, but the only choice he had was to accept or refuse the appointment, with what consequences in the latter scenario he could not begin to discern.

The reality of his position hit home and hard; if he had got to be a passed midshipman by chicanery he was now about to be faced with carrying out the duties he was supposed to have mastered. Taberly he did not know but other officers aboard *Brilliant* had been more inclined to seek to educate than to remonstrate and then there was a crew, many of whom must still be present. Hotham was dropping him in the steep tub again! As he gathered his possessions it was with something less than eager anticipation.

Hotham was with the youngster's new captain, a courtesy he would have extended to anyone being elevated to a rated ship, and in the rather stilted conversation he was trying to assess the man and was wondering how to broach the subject he wished to raise. Given no opening he was obliged to just speak out.

'You were in Leghorn about a month past were you not?'

Hotham was glad to see the slight stiffening as he responded. 'That is true, sir.'

'And I believe you became involved in a rather unfortunate affair.' Now the man had gone rigid. 'I received a written complaint from a Major Lipton, Captain Taberly, who told me he duelled with a Lieutenant John Pearce, a calling out that you witnessed.'

The reply took several seconds to be volunteered. 'Yes, sir.'

'You did not see fit to interfere and put a stop to it?'

'No, sir, and nor could I have done.'

'Even if it was your duty to do so, duelling being forbidden by Royal Decree?' Taberly shook his head but held his gaze steady, which impressed the admiral. The man would fight his corner. 'I am informed that Pearce did not behave as an officer of the King's Navy should.'

'He did not, sir, if anything he disgraced the service.'

Hotham nodded slowly, before pinning the real point for which he was aiming. 'Major Lipton alluded to something that took place after the fight was concluded.' That caused Taberly to flush deep red as Hotham added. 'You were, I am told, struck by an inferior officer, which you did not report.'

The Adam's apple moved as Taberly gulped, yet there was

nothing in the tone of his voice to indicate the anxiety he must now be feeling; if an admiral could give him a ship he could take it away. 'Since you know the facts, sir, there is nothing more for me to say.'

'It pleases me you do not deny it, but let us move on to other matters. I intend to place aboard your new command a young fellow who has just successfully passed the examination for lieutenant. It does, of course, have to be confirmed by the Comptroller of the Navy Board, which will take several weeks.'

'The name of the young man, sir?'

'Burns.' Hotham watched for the reaction, which came as nothing more than a flick of the eyelids; little passed in San Fiorenzo Bay that did not soon become common knowledge, given the endemic ship visiting of a fleet at anchor. A specially arranged examination for one candidate was so unusual as to be remarked upon, so the name of the sitter was known and that must have led to talk of the way Hotham had favoured this particular youngster in the past.

'He is a young man I fear I have somewhat overindulged. You may hear from others what that consists of. In placing him with you I want you to be sure he is put to his proper duty. As a passed midshipman he may occupy in an acting capacity the lowest of the lieutenant's tasks aboard *Brilliant*, which, by the way, he served on before.'

'Indeed?'

'Suffice to say I want a close eye kept upon him and to be regularly informed of his progress. Also he has been engaged in some questionable correspondence and associations from which I see it as my duty to protect him. In this I will require your assistance.'

'I will be only too happy to assist, sir.'

'Good, Captain Taberly.'

When the man left Hotham could guess what he would do; beard anyone he knew aboard the flagship and enquire about Burns, in which he would learn chapter and verse about how he had been favoured. That should tell him to keep a close eye on Burns. As soon as Taberly left Toomey entered to be told how the interview had progressed.

'That, we can be sure, is one ship John Pearce will not be visiting.'

'I would suggest, Sir William,' Toomey insisted, 'that apart from the orders you will give him in writing, it would be a good idea to talk to Lieutenant Digby in private, as you have done with Taberly.'

'Verbal instructions?'

'Which can be recalled in the manner in which you wish.'

'I am minded to ask Holloway to undertake the duties of captain of the fleet, which will shift a burden from both our shoulders.'

'Until Sir Hyde returns?'

'I have a feeling, Toomey, that Sir Hyde Parker will not wish to serve in close proximity to me. He is too much Hood's man.'

There was a bit of a gleam in Toomey's eye as he responded, an appreciation that his employer was, for once, thinking clearly. 'Which means the written orders come from Holloway?'

Hotham nodded. 'Best send for Digby.'

To be called to the flagship was the last thing that particular officer wanted; he had far too much to do in sorting out his new command, but it was an instruction that brooked no delay and it was with a quick decision that he appointed an experienced seaman called Tilley as his coxswain, his job to take charge of an equally hastily assembled boat crew who soon got their rhythm and cut down on the spume coming in over the thwarts. There was joy too when Tilley yelled out to *Flirt* to tell the officer of the watch, who was coming aboard, somewhat dampened by the ribald comments that came out of the lower deck, the gun ports in association with the name.

A master and commander merited little in the way of ceremony and soon Digby found himself outside the admiral's cabin awaiting instructions to enter, his nerves on edge for the very good reason that folk below the rank of post captain were rarely called to see the admiral. Besides, the whole thing was new to him. It relaxed him not at all to enter and observe that Hotham, seated at his table, had upon it not only charts and papers, but also a bottle of wine and two glasses.

'Mr Digby, I welcome you. And can I say that it gives me great pleasure to promote deserving officers. It is one of the chief joys of command, of which I have to tell you there are precious few.'

Digby was tempted to ask him why the hell he had promoted a sod like Taberly, but it did not lasted long. 'I hope I can justify the trust you have put in me, sir.'

'Did you not do so before, when I sent you to Biscay? That was a mission well fulfilled, was it not?'

That made Digby swallow hard; he suspected, as did John Pearce, that he had been given the task to get him out of the way. What came to mind then was that letter he had got from a lawyer called Lucknor and the question it posed. Who had been aboard HMS *Brilliant* the night Pearce had been pressed and who had been out hunting with the press gang?

He had thought about not answering but finally decided to do so; after all he had been left aboard the frigate. But he declined to say who had gone out with Captain Barclay, pleading lack of recollection, for to do so would drop the then midshipman farmiloe in the potential soup. Realising Hotham was still waiting for an answer, he gave one in the affirmative.

'Hard to go from that and back into a ship of the line?'

Harder than you think was what he reckoned, what he said was, 'I go where my duty takes me, sir.'

'Please, Mr Digby, sit down,' Hotham said, pouring two glasses of wine as he complied. 'Italian, I'm afraid, supplies of claret being hard to secure.'

'I drank nothing else in Leghorn, sir, and found it very palatable.'

'Ah yes, Leghorn. Mr Digby, I have to tell you that I received a complaint from a certain Major Lipton. The name is, I think, familiar to you?'

'With regret, sir, it is.'

'It pleases me that you do not equivocate, which seems to be the manner of too many young officers. Perhaps you would like to explain the connection.'

Digby took a sip of wine before complying and when he spoke he did so hoping the tremor in his voice was not noticeable: about how Pearce had asked him to act as his second, he agreeing on the grounds there was no one else, that no amount of offered apologies seemed acceptable to Lipton though many had been made.

'He is a man of high passions, is he not?'

'Yes, sir.'

'Then it would be hard to hold against an officer the need to aid another. Please know that I asked only for clarification because a certain incident followed on from that encounter and I wonder if you know of it?'

'Incident, sir?' Digby asked, looking perplexed and convincingly so.

'Yes, apparently certain insults were directed to a lady in whose company Pearce was met. It ended with a serious assault on Lipton and his officers.'

'This is the first I have heard of it, sir.'

'Did you come across the lady in question?'

That got a furious shake of the head. 'No, sir.'

'Well, we shall rest the matter there. We both know that duelling is forbidden but I will not make an issue of it. All I will say is you should, if you can, avoid acting as anyone's second again.'

'I will most certainly take that advice, sir.'

'Good. You will shortly receive orders for the Adriatic. There is an important task of some delicacy to be carried out there and I want to add certain facts for you. I wish you to take a message, it will be from me and in writing, to a certain Mehmet Pasha, who holds power on behalf of Constantinople in old Illyria and specifically in the Gulf of Ambracia. You will not know of it.'

'No, sir.'

'Damn fine anchorage I am informed, could hold an entire fleet if we ever needed to seal those waters.' Digby looked at Hotham as if willing him to continue in the same vein, but the subject was switched. 'Intelligence from various sources, not least the Austrians, tells me he's a bit of a rogue this Mehmet and I fear he might be playing ducks and drakes with the French. He needs to be sharply reminded that the power in the Mediterranean lies with the combined fleets of ourselves and Spain.'

Hotham spun round the chart on his table and placed a finger on the gulf in question, a circular bight with a tight set of narrows that suggested an extinct volcano. Beside it lay a map of the surrounding land, with towns and rivers marked to which the admiral alluded, pointing out a place called Koronsia where the Turk occupied an old fortress and from where he ran his satrapy, both of which Digby was to take with him on leaving.

'Greed is at the heart of the matter, of course. He will love money, being a Turk.'

'Can we match the French?'

'I'm damned if I will accede to that. If we proceed in the subsidy line we will get fleeced. No, it must be made plain to him that he is risking everything he possesses and I will give you a letter telling him so. How's your French?'

'Poor, sir.'

'Well in that case we will need to send with you someone who has the facility. You heard about the verdict at Mr Pearce's court martial?'

'I was present, sir.'

'Were you by damn. To support him once more?'

'No, sir, mere curiosity.'

'Well his acquittal presented me with a problem for I cannot just reinstate him to another command and nor do I think he would suit a place in a ship of the line. Too independent a character, which would only lead to another court. He has, as you know, excellent French, which is Mehmet Pasha's second tongue.'

'You're proposing he should come along?'

'Two birds with one stone, Digby. The fleet is short of officers and so are you. Mr Pearce can fulfil a dual role as your premier and the fellow to press home my message to our Turkish satrap.'

Digby did not dislike John Pearce yet he wanted to object; he was a mite headstrong and then there was a gulf between them on many matters, not least religion and that included Mrs Barclay. But there was no gainsaying Hotham, the admiral would get what he wanted.

'I wish to request another person to stand watch, sir, perhaps a mid with some sea time.'

'I fear I cannot indulge you, Mr Digby, every vessel is short.' That got an unhappy nod; he would be obliged to stand watch himself. 'I would appreciate some indication of when you will be ready to weigh.'

Digby was not fooled by the avuncular way that was said and there was, for any naval officer, only one response. 'I will raise anchor as soon as I receive my orders, sir.'

'Then I will write my message to Mehmet Pasha right away and if you call upon Captain Holloway he will present you with your orders. He is now captain of the fleet.'

There was a hard tone at the end of that, one that imparted it was time to go so Digby stood up, thanking Hotham effusively, but he wasn't finished.

'One more thing, Mr Digby, I am all for the taking of prizes and for enterprise and gallantry in my officers. If I admonish you on one thing, while I would not want you to ignore opportunity if it arises, do not let a fellow who has just lost a ship, in a somewhat unconventional manner, entice you into doing the same. There is a difference between being brave and being rash.'

Which was as good a way as any for the admiral to say he was certain the court had got it wrong. 'I will bear that in mind, sir.'

'The primacy of this task cannot be overstated.'

'Sir.'

'That will be all.' As Digby made for the door, Hotham added with the distracted air of something forgotten that should not be. 'Oh, and there will be despatches for Naples.'

CHAPTER SEVENTEEN

'Lied to me about Mrs Barclay, of course, which I will not forget. But I think I can safely say that I have given young Digby certain markers he will not miss. I doubt if he sees a Spanish Plate Ship taking in water he will risk HMS *Flirt*.'

'They are our allies, sir.'

'Irony, Toomey,' Hotham responded wearily. 'Are you ready for the next stage?'

'I am,' replied the Irishman, 'but I still wonder if it would be better coming from you.'

'Don't agree. Pearce knows I don't like him and he also would dearly love to see me forced to justify my actions over Barclay. Anything I offer him will be seen as a poisoned chalice and I think even from you he will be guarded.'

'Hence the despatches for Naples?'

'Exactly, and if it is Palermo I am sure the sod will contrive some way to get Digby to call there. Then Sir William Hamilton may get his wish and find a powerful British warship in the Tyrrhenian Sea, albeit for a very short time, long enough for Mrs Barclay to be found and returned to her rightful station.'

'I cannot see even then that Captain Barclay will find the task easy. Any woman who has run so far will not be biddable.'

'All I can do is give him an opportunity. After that it is up to him how things work out.'

Though he berthed elsewhere, Toomey ate in the wardroom and that was where he found John Pearce, who looked at him in an expectant way to receive in response a shake of the head.

'But I can tell you one piece of news that will please you. The men from *Larcher* have been shifted as a body.'

'Admiral Hotham agreed to that?'

'It is not a subject with which he would concern himself. In the absence of a captain of the fleet I undertook to make it so.'

'Why thank you, Mr Toomey.'

To say that John Pearce was perplexed was an understatement; he had never seen this fellow as a friendly sort, quite the reverse. Also it seemed, right at this moment, the Irishman was somewhat on edge.

'Perhaps a turn around the deck, Mr Pearce?' The clerk tapped his earlobe, which obviated the need to say why.

'If you wish.'

Out on deck the way the weather had changed was very obvious, the ship hauling against her anchor on what was a lively swell. The long spell of good weather was over; there was a blanket of cloud overhead as well as a telling and far from warm wind.

'I hope this breeze does not discomfit you.'

Such a comment, clearly some kind of preamble, only served to make a cautious John Pearce even more wary. 'Not at all. Is it not you who is more likely to have an aversion to the elements, which makes you being here somewhat odd?'

'I admit to the truth,' Toomey answered with a smile that was quickly followed by a frown. 'I have a favour to ask of you.'

'In return for the Larchers?'

'You see through my attempts at subterfuge, sir.'

Not much of that in evidence, Pearce thought, but it was not worth saying. 'What kind of favour?'

'One that involves your knowledge of French.'

'I have a sudden sense that Lord Hood is still with us in spirit if not in person.'

'The reasons are the same and if he were still present he might well ask you for the same favour. There is a mission to undertake in which the facility with the language would be an asset to back up a written message. No, not an asset, a necessity, since it may well lead to some form of negotiation and that requires a degree of discernment.'

That got a wry look from John Pearce; he was unsure if that was a quality he possessed.

'The task is to call upon a certain Turkish satrap who controls the Eastern Adriatic to warn him, or perhaps advise him would be a better way of putting it, that the way he is dallying with our enemies is not only unhelpful but, for him, precarious. The French are making overtures to him and he is, we are told, tempted by their blandishments.'

'You want to demand that he cease?'

'But with some delicacy, for such people can be touchy when

it comes to respect. He speaks no English so there is room for misunderstanding. There was a previous embassy sent by Lord Hood in which that occurred through the use of an interpreter, Mehmet's own man, given we have no one at all who can speak to a Turk in his own tongue.'

'And Lord Hood's envoy—'

'Spoke little French,' Toomey said quickly to finish his sentence. 'The letter he carried from Lord Hood was in French but it was no more really than a means of introducing his man and alluding to his mission. Whatever the Ottoman interpreter said, and who knows if it was accurate, there was so much confusion that the whole thing ended up in some very sharp exchanges. I'm afraid the officer Lord Hood chose was of a somewhat short temper.'

'Foolish.'

'Mehmet Pasha needs to be spoken with directly, not through another, first to reassure him of His Majesty's friendship added to a discreet reminder of the power that represents. It may be that we will be obliged to bribe him, which requires some indication of the level of such.'

'There is another way.'

'Do not think it has not been considered, but Sir William must have the strength to beat the French now snug in Toulon, he cannot have diversions in other parts of the Mediterranean that draw off even one of our line of battle ships.'

'If he's that much of a threat?'

Toomey scoffed. 'The man's a distraction at best, which is why we seek another avenue besides a show of force.'

'There must be others you can ask.'

'True; there are post captains who have some facility with

French but they would not take kindly to being sent away on what is something of a modest task with a potential fleet action in the offing. You are a more fitting person if for no other reason than your present unemployed status.'

The truth of that had to be acknowledged; every sailor in King George's Navy thirsted to be part of a successful fleet action – the Glorious First had made them all jealous – and there was a very high chance of one here in the Mediterranean in the coming weeks.

'So we will send a smaller vessel and a non-post captain. It struck me that if Lord Hood were still present he might engage you for such an embassy. Sir William requires the same service and I wish to suggest to him that you should undertake it.'

'At least this time my court martial is over.'

'Touché.'

'I am pleased you do not pretend not to know what I am talking about.'

Toomey stopped and looked Pearce right in the eye. 'I advise the admiral, sir, but I do not command him.'

There was a huge temptation to ask the Irishman to elaborate then but it was stifled by one certainty; he would not say anything that would be a criticism of his employer, a man upon whom he depended. As well there were certain matters nagging at his attention, not least that this conversation was happening not long after the arrival of Ralph Barclay.

'Mr Pearce, I acceded to your request regarding your late crew in order that you would accept my *bona fides*. I am tasked to solve the problem for Admiral Hotham whom, I can assure you, while he might accept you could be the perfect choice for a problem left for him to deal with by Lord Hood, he will not ask himself. Indeed he may take some persuading.'

'Just as well,' Pearce snapped; it was just as well the sod had no idea he was after him for a conspiracy to allow Barclay to commit perjury, or was that still the case? 'Lord Hood had this in mind, you say?'

'He did, but failed to act upon it prior to his departure. Sir William will dictate his letter to the Pasha using the same quill as Lord Hood, that of Mr Brooks, the under clerk who came from *Victory*, who has excellent French.'

'Then send him.'

'He is a desk man and not made of the stuff required, Mr Pearce. Besides, his duties in the flagship means he cannot be spared. The vessel chosen will proceed to the Adriatic *via* Naples, where certain requests must be passed on to King Ferdinand by Ambassador Hamilton . . .'

Pearce's heart leapt; he nearly repeated 'Naples' and 'Hamilton' but stopped himself.

'. . . before proceeding to the Gulf of Ambracia to meet with Mehmet Pasha. The captain chosen to head the mission is one Henry Digby, who has just been promoted into a fourteen-gun brig.'

'Was that your doing too?' Pearce cut in.

'I thought it might facilitate the conversation we are having.' Toomey paused to give his next words real effect. 'Which is why he now commands the men who were so recently under you.'

'Have you ever read Machiavelli, Mr Toomey?'

'If you are asking me if I have the ability to get done that which needs to be done, Mr Pearce, then I think you have just answered yourself.'

It was the opportunity to visit Naples that was the key for Pearce but he could not say so, and then there were other matters to consider, which required time to reflect. He had to put up some kind of show of reluctance and only one came to mind.

'If I am going to agree then Admiral Hotham must ask me personally.'

'What!'

'If he does not you must find someone else.'

Toomey's shoulders slumped then and he abruptly stopped his pacing. 'You put it high, sir.'

'I put it as I require.'

'I cannot guarantee that he will agree.'

'I am sure Machiavelli would have found a way. I will wait in the wardroom.'

Which he did not do immediately; waiting until Toomey was in the great cabin he sought out the fellow called Brooks, a man he had come across in his dealings with Lord Hood. Looking up from a sheaf of reports it was clear that the interruption was unwelcome; that did not faze Pearce who made a casual enquiry regarding his facility with French. That established he mentioned Mehmet Pasha and asked Brooks if he had ever communicated with him.

'What is it to you?' the clerk asked, adding a sniff of disapproval. 'I do not discuss official business outside the confines of those officers entitled to know about it, of which you, sir, are not one.'

'Lord Hood mentioned a fellow by that name to me.'

'I cannot think why.'

Never friendly to this kind of functionary, Pearce had to force himself to be pleasant. 'It was, I thought, a matter that troubled him.'

'It was,' came with an undertone that it was none of his business. 'Now it falls to Sir William to deal with it. If you wish to know more I should enquire of him!'

'Just showing an interest, Mr Brooks.'

He left the man wondering on that and made for the wardroom to examine what was being proposed from every angle; the thought of Naples a constant intrusion, given he would have a chance of getting ashore and seeing Emily. Henry Digby disapproved of their relationship but then he had no idea she was there, that being a secret Pearce would try to maintain. If he did have to reveal her presence there it would only be with a promise to tell no one.

The person that must be kept from was, of course, her husband. It was too much of a coincidence that he was now part of Hotham's fleet. How could the man think that he could get Emily back? Indeed, he was exposing himself to the ridicule he so feared by even trying. Had he told Hotham of his quest? Did the admiral know of how much trouble Pearce could cause and not just for Barclay?

Toomey had gone to a great deal of trouble to arrange matters, but that only became suspicious if certain other pieces of a very tangled enigma fell into place and Pearce could envisage no way in which they would. Brooks had as near as damn confirmed what Toomey had said so the need for the mission existed; he did have the necessary language skills and was free to be sent.

In the face of no certain knowledge, John Pearce was left with speculation and the prospect of a possible interview with Hotham, so there was a very good chance it would all come to nothing. If not then that would be the time to decide. When the summons came, delivered by a midshipman messenger in a less than discreet manner, he left the wardroom knowing every eye was boring into his back trying to guess the reason.

He entered the cabin to find the admiral staring out of his casement windows and as yet seemingly unprepared to acknowledge his visitor. Pearce took in the nature of the well-appointed cabin: the highly polished furniture, the deep red leather of the chairs and casements, the large bowl of fruit that stood as a centrepiece on the round table obviously employed as a place to work.

The cabin was dominated by a full-length portrait of the man himself in a heavy velvet cloak, the star and sash of his Order of the Bath set against a snow-white waistcoat and breeches. Hotham was a good-looking man, if short, and in his representation confident, his eyes as blue as his admiral's coat, his wig as bleached as the clouds that scudded across the sky behind him, the cheeks full and well fed. The face was, if not pale, free of the ravages of a life spent at sea and Pearce recalled that of every naval representation he had seen – admittedly not many – the countenance of the sitter had been made more pallid than reality. Another feature was the look into the distance, eyes fixed on some object not visible to those it aimed to impress.

Hotham finally spoke without turning around. 'I doubt you have any idea how unpleasant I find this.'

Then let us put you to the test, Pearce thought. 'It is my sincere hope that it is wrenching at your vitals, sir.'

'Sir Hyde Parker told me of the way you used to address Lord Hood. I always swore if you talked to me in a like manner then I would see you keelhauled.' That was embellishment and Pearce took it as such, declining to respond, which obliged Hotham to speak on. 'However, the needs of the service must take precedence over my feelings. I need the same qualities that so impressed Lord Hood and if it must be me who asks you to volunteer for the task Toomey outlined to you then so be it.'

Circumlocution, Pearce thought, and he was tempted to force Hotham to ask in a less equivocal manner. But that would only engender more hot air, so he gave an answer that contained his own qualifications.

'Since I doubt you wish to advance my career in any other way I am near bound to accept.'

'Gracious,' Hotham sighed, in a tone full of sarcasm. 'If it was anything vital you are not the man I would entrust with it. I hope you will be satisfied to deal with Toomey from this moment on?'

'He will be the lesser of two evils.'

Hotham tried to keep the anger out of his voice, but he failed. 'That will be all, lieutenant.'

Passing Toomey, who was sat outside at his work desk, Pearce just nodded as he passed, keeping a smile off his face until his back was square to the clerk. His next stop was to beard the purser of HMS *Britannia* to secure from him replacement possessions for those he had been obliged to leave aboard *Larcher*.

He required a sea chest and one was produced that had, burnt out, the initials of the previous owner; how it had come to be free for transfer was neither volunteered nor asked for. It would be the property of some deceased officer or midshipman and bought by the purser when the poor soul's goods were auctioned.

Pearce needed new linen, breeches and a blue coat that had not suffered from the sun, his own being more sky blue now than navy and these came from the same source. It need not be spilt blood that had caused the demise; life aboard a warship was dangerous, land service more so, while disease and accident carried off more people than battle. When Pearce had what he required the sea chest was near full and the bill amounted to a tidy sum.

'Send the account up to Mr Toomey,' was his cheery response. 'He will reimburse you.'

His next call was on the officer of the watch, to ask for a boat to take him to HMS *Flirt* and a servant to be sent to the purser to gather up his new chest and fetch it to the entry port and, so he would not be in the way, he went to the side and looked out at the fleet. Putting his hand in his pocket he felt the letters Toomey had passed to him, which had him going back to talk to the man stood by the binnacle.

'Before I depart I enquired of a Midshipman Toby Burns earlier on . . .'

The lieutenant on duty did what, for Pearce, was a strange thing; he looked around as if not wishing to be overheard, that followed by the kind of wink that hinted at some shared knowledge, which the fellow it was aimed at certainly did not have.

'Past midshipman, you mean.'

'Do I?'

He was about to ask to for clarification when the mid who had been sent to organise his boat returned and barked at his back in a voice that could have been heard in the tops.

'Boat's awaiting you, sir, and your dunnage is already aboard.'

Pearce shrugged; Burns he could find and deal with on his return.

* * *

'Couldn't for the life of me look him in the eye, Toomey. Not sure if I had, whether I would have laughed or lost my temper at the manner in which he addressed me. The arrogance of the fellow is astounding.'

'He does not lack for self-regard, for which we must be thankful, it being a form of Achilles' Heel. Now, sir, we must discuss and compose the message we are to send to Mehmet Pasha.'

That got a wolfish smile from Hotham. 'I'm beginning to enjoy this game.'

'I urge care, sir, for there be many a slip betwixt cup and lip.'

'There can be none once they weigh.'

Toomey joined the admiral at his table with quill, ink and parchment and together they composed the message they thought would meet their needs, all of it in plain English, signed with a flourish by Hotham before being sanded then sealed, a superscription being added to the effect it was to be opened only by the person to whom it was addressed; *Son Excellence; Mehmet Pasha.*

The next task was to write out special orders for Henry Digby – he had his destination from Holloway – and in these it was made plain that he was to use Lieutenant Pearce as an envoy and to take no part in the negotiation himself. He was admonished that at no time should he risk HMS *Flirt* or the complement thereof and while he was free to take advantage of any opportunity that presented itself on his return voyage, with the caveat of excessive risk underlined, he was to ignore such temptations on his way to the Gulf of Ambracia, failure to do so being at his peril.

'Do we wish to seal his orders, sir, until he is at sea?'

Hotham pondered on that for several seconds before seeing the sense of Toomey's suggestion. Anything that might have Pearce becoming concerned had to be avoided.

Toomey then sealed the document and wrote upon it: *Not to be opened till south of Cap Bonifacio* before calling for a midshipman to take a boat to HMS *Flirt* and deliver it immediately to Captain Digby.

Toby Burns got to HMS *Brilliant* before the return of Taberly and he was aware that his arrival was not met with universal approbation; there were too many who knew Burns of old.

'Turds float and that little guttersnipe is the living mark of truth.'

This was the contribution of one Martin Dent, who had been the ship's drummer boy under Barclay and one of those present the night John Pearce had been pressed; from being Pearce's enemy he had become more than a friend.

'Sure he is that, Martin,' opined Blubber Booth, 'but we are goin' to have to treat him as a gent.'

'Hard, mate,' Martin protested.

'Captain's barge in the offing,' called a voice, 'look lively.'

And the whole ship's company did just that; they had not seen much of Captain Taberly but they had seen enough.

'Holy Christ!' Rufus exclaimed as he looked over the hammock nettings of HMS *Flirt*. 'Do you see who is in yonder boat?'

That had them all looking and it was a welcome sight, for none doubted their still being a crew was the doing of John Pearce; how could there be any other reason than his coming to serve, especially with him coming aboard with a sea chest?

Pearce was examining *Flirt* with a now practised eye, noting her low flush decked lines and the slightly raked mainmast, part of a top hamper that could, for her size, carry a great deal of canvas; everything about her lines spoke of a fast sailing and easy to manoeuvre vessel that, with her fourteen cannon, would make for a formidable opponent to anything near her size.

Closer to her he could see that she had sound-looking scantlings and had been scraped and painted regularly in a blue that went a great way to matching the colour of the sea on a sunny day or the now faded broadcloth coat in the sea chest. His deliberations were set aside as the man coxing his boat called out to announce his arrival.

Henry Digby put aside the unopened orders he had been weighing in his hand to come on deck, alerted to the approach by his new bosun, Mr Bird, so he was by the gangway when Pearce's boat crunched alongside, which earned those men rowing a stream of abuse from a crew who had adopted the brig in the same way that they felt about *Larcher*. The buggers from the flagship were told to mind their ways.

'Belay that,' Digby called, but without much ire. He stood and waited until Pearce stepped out and, covering the short haul from boat to planking by means of the man ropes and three steps, raised his hat to the quarterdeck. 'Welcome aboard, John.'

The informality was noted and not least by the person on the receiving end who thought it boded well for what he needed Digby to agree to. The crew within earshot were just as pleased, the closest those who had taken delivery of the sea chest, for if these two officers were friendly and got on, their life was likely to be easier.

Pearce took in quickly the sight of a man he had not really seen for an age and registered little change. Digby was not as tall as him and had a darker countenance, with the air of being slightly plump in both cheeks and belly, which was odd for he was abstemious in matters of food and drink if far from an abstainer.

'Take Mr Pearce's dunnage to his cabin,' Digby ordered. 'John, I invite you to join me in my cabin for a drink.'

'Delighted.'

That did not last longer than the pouring, added to the fact that Digby, when out of sight of the crew, was far from happy, a sign that Pearce quickly picked up. He distracted himself by a comparison of space, the cabin being larger than that of *Larcher* but a cubicle compared to Hotham's, added to which it was furnished in a very basic fashion: uncovered chairs, a plain deal desk and solid wood and varnished seating on the casements.

'Is there something amiss?' came the eventual enquiry.

'John, while I am glad you are come aboard, I do have a concern.'

That was stiffly put, which meant the reply had to be likewise. 'Which is, sir?'

'Is there any need for that?' Digby responded, now irritated. 'We know each other quite well enough to dispense with honorifics in private.'

Pearce nodded. 'Your request, Henry?'

'First, a toast to the success of our mission.'

That could not be challenged but it did nothing for the tension Pearce was experiencing; he was sure something unpleasant would follow. 'These men have served with you before and may well still see you as the man to look to. I cannot fathom why they were shipped aboard wholesale, warrants included, but the fact that you too are present hints at your involvement and creates a potential problem.'

'They may look to me instead of obeying you?'

'Precisely. I need you to go out of your way to prevent that happening.'

'Then rest assured the first one to make that mistake will face my unbridled wrath, I promise.'

'Good. Now tell me of those I may trust and those who may cause me trouble.'

That slog across southern Italy had not been all waste; Pearce had been able to identify the probable Jeremiahs for they were men who never ceased to complain and they had had no lower deck in which to hide their negations. Now he marked his friend's card with the aid of the muster list, suggesting a few adjustments to break up the watches in a way that would diminish their influence.

'The warrants are excellent and you can rely on them, added to which I will have an ear to the ground for any rumbles of discontent, not that I can see why that would occur.'

'The Pelicans?' Pearce nodded and Digby smiled, showing he did not resent the connection. 'I think I must ask you to unburden yourself of that fine coat you are wearing and change into working gear. There is much to do.'

'One thing: Michael O'Hagan acted as my servant aboard *Larcher*. I would be obliged if he could do so again.'

'Of course,' Digby replied with a look of astonishment, 'though I can scarce think of anyone less suitable.'

'That, Henry, is what makes him perfect.'

The sound of a gun boomed across the anchorage, which had Matthew Dorling knock and enter. The look to Pearce was automatic and quickly diverted by a snap of the head in the direction of Digby.

'Flag has raised our number, sir, with a signal to proceed to sea.'

'Very well, Mr Dorling. Mr Pearce, all hands to weigh, if you please.'

CHAPTER EIGHTEEN

There was no aiming at concealment when Henry Digby opened his orders, this as they passed the channel separating the islands of Corsica and Sardinia. Mr Dorling had been asked only to set a course to the south even if there was no anticipation of a change from Naples being the first port of call. But it did no harm to then advise a destination at another time; it added to the mystique of command.

His instructions had come in a bulky oilskin pouch and consisted of his caution-filled orders as well as a sealed communication addressed to Mehmet Pasha. Another tied bundle contained letters addressed to Sir William Hamilton. For a moment he contemplated calling Pearce in to show him the Mehmet letter then put it aside. Much as he saw him as a colleague he was also his inferior officer and it was, to the captain's mind as he pondered on it, a sound notion to keep in place that distinction.

In the short period they had been at sea Digby could find

nothing about which to complain; quite the reverse. HMS *Flirt* was a true plum, a brig that sailed easy and fast, especially with a crew informal to converse with and superbly competent. They were so well worked up that orders only had to be issued in a normal talking voice to be swiftly obeyed. Called to change sails the topmen were adept aloft, the waisters just as quick to man the falls and with a vessel that handled so well any change of course had been a joy to watch.

Clearing for action went as smoothly as could be expected on a vessel new to the men knocking out bulkheads and storing furniture but that would improve with repetition. He had had the guns run in and out in dumb show and seen that the crews, their messes worked out by his second in command, were excellent in terms of both speed and safety, so much so that they were set to training the less than delighted marines. Fresh from San Fiorenzo Bay, food and water was fresh and more importantly Pearce had made it very obvious by his somewhat exaggerated deference who was in command.

On deck Marine Officer Grey was exercising his men in musket drill and the command drifted into the cabin. With the distance from there to the deck being a few steps up a companionway it seemed fitting for Digby to invite Pearce to join him at two bells in the last dogwatch for some cheese on toast in his cabin. Prior to arrival he put the orders in the secure padlocked coffer that was provided as a container for all the ship's papers as well as the funds he held as the commanding officer.

'We are bound for Naples first, John.'

'Are we?' Pearce replied.

In responding he affected surprise, which he certainly did not need to do. Toomey had mentioned Naples and probably provided the main lever by which he had accepted the mission, the only wonder he had being why Digby had waited so long to pass on the information.

'And then we are off to the Adriatic. Do you know anything of the Gulf of Ambracia?'

'The purser in *Britannia* was a bit of an antiquarian. When I mentioned it he claimed it to be the very sight of the Battle of Actium, where Octavius defeated Mark Anthony in the Civil Wars.'

'I know who fought the battle, John,' he said, a finger on the requisite chart.

That reply being somewhat terse took Pearce aback and he was obliged to recall that, although they had sailed and fought together, he and Digby were very different people. Though he would not claim to be without pride, John Pearce saw it as an encumbrance to be very rarely invoked, while Digby was a man somewhat sensitive about being condescended to. He had come into the navy, unlike so many of his contemporaries, from a relatively privileged background, his father a well-placed divine and with a Baron Digby for a cousin.

That should have made him less of a delicate soul, instead it seemed to feed on what Pearce could only put down to a sneaking air of inferiority which seemed to characterise the man; perhaps his elevated relation had lorded it in the family firmament. Then added to that was their very different outlooks on life and, more vitally, career.

If he had lately come to give some value to his rank, it was not from ambition but necessity and on their previous voyage together he had made no attempt to disguise his disdain for the idea of a naval career. Digby was a man committed to making his way in his chosen profession; he was also deeply religious and that was a subject, like the Thirty Nine Articles of the Protestant Faith, best avoided, given when Pearce pointed out the absurdities of Christian dogma and obscurantist prejudice it did nothing to endear him.

'I'm wondering if Admiral Hotham sees it as a future anchorage.'

Pondering briefly on that Pearce shook his head. 'What purpose would it serve?'

'Look at the charts, John, it is a secure bay and sits just to the north of the route to the Levant, and we both know how busy that is.'

'True, but there's no enemy fleet to oppose us in the Adriatic as far as I know. The main task is to contain Toulon.'

'I said the future, did I not?'

'You may well be correct,' Pearce replied, with as much conviction as he could muster, given he reckoned the notion to be far-fetched, more Digby trying to elevate his mission. But then he had to disguise a thought that intrigued him; was there something in the orders, verbal or written, which had prompted the suggestion?

'Did Sir William hint at such a thing to you?'

The sharp reply of 'No' was a way of saying 'what passed between the admiral and I is not for you to know', immediately followed by a smile to take the sting out of the word. That did not settle Pearce's curiosity, it exacerbated it, and so he adopted an air of indifference.

'I ask only because the instructions I received, admittedly

from Toomey, not Hotham, seemed, when I thought on them, somewhat imprecise.'

The conversation was interrupted by Digby's steward arriving with the cheese on toast and a bottle of wine. The laying out had the two officers sitting in silence but Digby took it up as soon as he was gone.

'Imprecise? How so?'

'Our Pasha in flirting with the French—'

'So they send a flirt to remonstrate,' Digby cut in, clearly very pleased with his pun.

'Droll, Henry.'

'Perhaps they feel the need to flatter him?' Digby responded with a wry grin, Pearce nodding at the self-mockery.

'If you want to flatter such a fellow or, for that matter, remind him of where his best interests lay, you send a senior officer and several warships. That happened with the Bey of Tunis, where Commodore Linzee was the representative with a second-rate lieutenant and *Agamemnon*. Some might see a pair of mere lieutenants as an insult.'

'The admiral obviously feels someone of our rank to be sufficient.'

'Meaning this Mehmet Pasha is not so important.'

'Perhaps,' Digby responded, not happily so.

'Naples, you say?' Digby nodded at the change of subject while he chewed. 'Will we dally there long?'

'Touch, no more, deliver some despatches to the ambassador then be on our way.'

'I wonder, Henry, if you would allow me to take charge of delivery?'

If John Pearce held himself to be fairly adept at dissimulation he was with someone who perhaps knew him too well to be fooled. The consumption of food was abruptly put aside, as was Digby's fork.

'If you ask that, John, then you must have a reason.'

'It was to Naples I went with the crew of *Larcher* and Sir William Hamilton who facilitated our transport back to the fleet.'

'For which I am sure the navy is grateful.' It was the turn of John Pearce to look askance then; was Digby taking the rise out of him? 'Would there perhaps be another reason, such as a certain person I came across in Leghorn?'

'Yes,' Pearce replied, wondering how he had made that leap.

There was a long silence as Digby went back to his food and wine, in which the poser of the question said nothing either, until finally his host looked up. His expression told Pearce he was about to be addressed by the ship's captain and not any form of companion.

'I must decline to indulge you. You cannot be unaware that I disapprove of such a liaison, which goes against the very tenets I hold dear, namely the sacrament of marriage, inviolable to my mind.'

'Even if it be to a brute like Barclay.'

'The tone of that question, John, is inappropriate. You're talking of a highly respected and very senior post captain.'

'Respected?'

'Not loved, I will grant you.'

Digby was trying to be emollient but it was wasted on a man who had only one aim and Pearce did little to soften his tone. 'What I find inappropriate is your feeling that you can judge the emotions of others in a matter of the heart. That surely is the sole concern of those involved.'

'Are you telling me that Captain Barclay is not involved, does it not occur to you that he has engineered that he come out to the Mediterranean because he knows his wife is here? Whether he knows she is with you . . . well that is another matter.'

'So?'

'So he is intent on rescuing his marriage.'

'In which he will fail and I tell you, though I will not explain, he has forfeited any right to his wife's affections.'

'John, I am sorry, I cannot in all conscience be a party to this affair and therefore I cannot allow you ashore at Naples in order that you might meet with Mrs Barclay.'

In case Barclay finds out and checks your prized career, Pearce, harbouring such a thought, was about to tell Digby that, in such a case he might as well up his helm and head back to San Fiorenzo Bay but he managed to hold his tongue. They were two days' sailing from Naples, time to work on his man and, if it came to the crunch, he would go ashore and damn the navy. Then let Digby sail back to Hotham and admit his failure to complete his mission.

'I am, of course, on watch,' he said, standing up to crouch under the deck beams. 'And Grey, by the sound of it, has finished exercising his men. Thank you for the food and wine but perhaps it is best if I be about my duties.'

'If you so wish,' came the chilly response.

Back on deck, stood behind the binnacle, Pearce was distracted by the crew, many of whom had gathered in the prow by the bowsprit as they had at one time on *Larcher*, albeit they were now wrapped in kerseymere against the less than warm weather. There they were bavarding away in the same manner as they had previously done on *Larcher* and snatches of their chatter and joshing floated back to him; they were content, he was not.

With only two officers, Pearce suggested that Mr Dorling would stand watch if asked so they could get some proper sleep and it was he who relieved Pearce at four bells, which sent Pearce below to snatch six hours of rest. When he came on deck again at four in the morning it was to replace Digby, who was yet to get to the point of rating someone a midshipman so they could do the duty.

The exchange of greetings was rigidly formal, very unlike that which had gone before, Pearce lifting his hat, listening to the latest information on course and speed before his captain disappeared. On a night of mixed cloud and stars it was to the latter that Pearce went for diversion. He sent for his sextant and went to work on polishing his lunar observations as HMS *Flirt* ploughed on through a decent swell, the wind coming in nicely over her quarter, all quiet until the men were roused out prior to dawn.

The crew picked up the change in no time; all it took was for both to be on deck as daylight arrived to see there were none of the smiles that had attended the previous morning and the pair came under scrutiny throughout the rest of the voyage. The journey to Naples was not of a long duration and once they raised the dome of the Cathedral of Ischia, the highest point in that island, the mood was set if the weather was not: they sailed past the island through heavy rainfall. That did not change when Pearce asked to see his captain.

'I am intent on going ashore, sir.'

Digby winced slightly at the honorific address, 'And if I continue to forbid it?'

'Then you have a choice, to continue the mission given to me with my presence or deliver your despatches to Ambassador Hamilton then return to the fleet without me, for I will no longer continue to serve in this vessel, which is my right.'

There was real pain in the way Digby replied. 'This is blackmail, John.'

'And I am sorry for it, but I left the lady to whom I have pledged myself here in Naples and I will see her come what may.'

'I could have you slung in the cable tier.'

As an attempt at a threat it failed, made worse when Pearce responded with what – and Digby could not know this – was pure bluff.

'At which point you might find out to whom the crew will be loyal. I saved the lives of these men and brought them to safety. I said I would seek to keep them whole as a crew and I did. I would not want to be the one to test whom they will follow.'

There was no doubting what was going through Digby's mind apart from an imagined flogging; disgrace or if not, it would be such a check on his career that he would be lucky to end up on a transport and not in command of it either. Pearce was feeling like a scrub and took no pleasure in putting his one-time companion in such a position.

'It is not normal,' he added, 'to seek to prevent officers from going ashore if the possibilities permit. And even if you outline the reason, I wonder whether that would be seen as sufficient to abort the embassy proposed by Admiral Hotham.'

'It means that much to you?' Digby asked in a soft voice.

'It does and I must tell you Emily Raynesford, as she now prefers to be addressed, that being her maiden name, is at present a guest of Ambassador Hamilton.'

'Then so be it, Mr Pearce,' came the reply, after a very long pause for thought and a chin resting on the chest. 'You may deliver the correspondence for I will not have my prospects damaged by such an affair. But know this, I expect you to return to ship within the day and to sail on with me to the Adriatic.'

'Which I shall do.'

'But I will never forgive you for this and if you ever thought of me as kindly disposed towards you do not make the same mistake again.'

'Permission to take along my servant?'

Digby just nodded.

They had not been long out of the cutter and on the quay looking for a conveyance, when Michael posed his question. 'Will you be telling me what is afoot, John-boy?'

'What makes you think there is anything?'

'Jesus, you could cut the air with a knife these last two days.'

'Digby and I have had a slight difference.'

'Slight you say, by Jesus, well that's not how the rest on the barky see it.'

'Michael, I don't care what they do and do not see!'

If he had hoped to silence the Irishman by his sharp response it fell flat. 'Spoken in a manner that tells me you are not proud of yourself.'

'How do you conclude that?' Pearce demanded, as they clambered into a hack big enough for them both.

'Save us, do I not know you and can I not see with my own eyes that two fine fellows who were laughing on deck not long past won't now look each other in the eye? Sure now, searching your face I reckon that the cause rests with you and seeing where we are headed I am not fool enough to be lost as to guess why.'

'Digby did not want to let me ashore,' Pearce sighed, holding up the package he was carrying. 'He deduced that Emily must be here, I think from my mere request, having met Emily in Leghorn.'

'Might not have been a guess, happen someone let slip, one of those coves you were so hard on when we was marching.'

'I never thought of that.'

'Could have been anyone, mind, when the captain was acting friendly, just letting on you had a sweetheart. What is to happen now?'

'Don't tell me the crew don't know.'

That made Michael smile. 'In truth and for once, they don't.'

Sweeping through the streets and crowds of Naples, sweeter smelling now than he recalled due to the recent downpour which had washed much of the filth into the sea, Pearce outlined the mission and how it had come about to a friend who seemed to have a frown that deepened with each word.

'You don't seem thrilled.'

'Sounds to me as if someone might be tying knots.'

'Barclay?'

'He arrives and this rears up.'

'No, it was a problem before that, I checked.'

'Have you not thought on the chance it is you he is after, not just Mrs Barclay?'

'When will you ever call her Emily?'

'One day, John-boy, but not yet this one.'

'If he can harm me he will and if he can find Emily unprotected then, given the lengths he went to in London, there are no limits to the possibilities.'

'He will have his tame admiral to help him and from the way you talk he is in the steep tub too.'

Pearce laughed. 'Two things, Michael, of which I can absolutely assure you and I thought this through before accepting the mission. One is that Barclay, even if he has come in pursuit of Emily, would forebear to tell anyone, even Hotham, that his wife has run off. The other thing he will keep silent about is the court martial papers presently in the safe of Alexander Davidson, or of his failure to recover them by downright theft, which leaves Hotham utterly unaware of how much he is at risk.'

'Sure are you, John-boy?'

'Barclay admit he's a cuckold? The man would rather give up his one good arm. Tell his tame admiral that he is implicated and how deep that is. He might as well beach himself and kiss goodbye to his career. Hotham would disown him.'

Pearce chuckled to add assurance to his words, 'Do you not think I have considered all this Michael, looked at it from every angle? I have, I assure you and I know our man. Barclay will keep his mouth shut and seek to find Emily by means other than using Hotham or any other naval officer. As to knots, you have to look at who knows what and as of this moment there is only one person who can see every card and that is me.'

'Would it trouble you if I said that you have not always had the right of things?'

'That I accept, but not now.' He looked at the steep incline that led to the Palazzo Sessa, home to Sir William and Lady Hamilton. 'Time to get out and walk, this thing will never get up the hill.'

In what had to be a flying visit, time alone with Emily was severely restricted. The ambassador had to be indulged with the latest chatter from the fleet, which included the news of the departure of Lord Hood. Pearce was pressed for an honest assessment of Hotham as a replacement for Hood, one he was careful to gild with impressions that went against his own observations; it was not wise, even for someone like him, to traduce the admiral when he had no idea if the words he used would remain confidential.

Hamilton knew little of Mehmet Pasha and so could not add to the sum of Pearce's knowledge. Besides, the old man was eager to get off a subject that clearly failed to interest him and on to one that did: his latest find in his dig at Pompeii, with Pearce having to turn down an invitation to go and observe a wall painted with the most interesting figures engaged in a great variety of carnal activity.

'Sir, I am not on this occasion the master of my own time.'

'Pity. The place I would hazard was an ancient bagnio. Some of the ladies on display are damned fetching even now and it is a fine example of the lack of hypocrisy in the ancient world the way they display their repertoire.'

'A bagnio, places which I try to avoid, sir, in the time in which we live.'

'I never did, Mr Pearce. Can't see how a young man makes his way in life without a bit of paid-for dalliance to show him the ropes. Not that I partake now, of course, quite apart from the restrictions of age there is my position, though I confess to missing the excitement.'

'Your wife led me to believe there was scarce a need in Naples.'

'Aye, depravity is rife, which I believe can be put down to the climate.'

The ambassador engaged him longer than he wanted or could afford and then there was Lady Hamilton, present with Emily for most of the time he spent with her, singing the praises of what she called her charge, praised for her beauty at every entertainment or ball they attended, but in a way that was designed to flatter the giver rather than the receiver. On the few occasions he managed to break eye contact with her and look at Emily he saw that the happiness of which her hostess boasted was not replicated in her face, a truth acknowledged in the half hour they had alone all of which was spent in quiet conversation.

'You are not content.'

'There are many things to cause me to be so.'

'Emily, much as I want to be by your side I cannot do so.' That got a sad nod but no hint of complaint. 'It is Lady Hamilton is it not?'

'I think she tries to mean well, John, it is merely that she cannot help herself. She assumes everyone is traducing her behind her back, referring to her lowly origins and her supposed past debaucheries. Thus she is armed to defend herself even when there is no need.'

'And Naples,' he asked, to get off a subject about which he could do nothing.

'Pleasant enough and, if you discount the level of lawlessness in certain parts of the city, then it is as good a place as any to reside. Added to which, if anyone knows of my station they make no allusion to it in either word or deed.'

'Lady Hamilton did tell me that an uxorious married couple are seen as exceptional hereabouts.'

'Then happen I have found my natural milieu.'

That was imparted in a tone larded with underlying waspishness, which left John Pearce out on a limb; to talk of a movement or any improvement in her present situation was out of the question. To act as if all was well was equally inappropriate and then there was his lack of time; he had to get back to the ship.

'The mission I am engaged on will not take more than a few weeks, hopefully even less. I will seek to return to the fleet via Naples and then we may talk at greater length about what we can do. Now grant me a kiss before I depart and know in your heart that I have dedicated my life to your happiness.'

Back in the hack he was feeling low. Michael, who had been in the Palazzo kitchens and had consumed enough wine to loosen his tongue, posed the obvious question. 'Did you tell Mrs Barclay that her man is now with the fleet?'

'No, I did not. She has enough to concern her without adding that. And he is not her man, I am.'

CHAPTER NINETEEN

In the atmosphere aboard HMS *Flirt*, the man caught in the middle was the marine lieutenant and officer of inferior rank to both sailors, for that was the nature of the different services: as an equal he might have damned them both when he found himself required to be polite. It was to his credit that Grey was an engaging character, slim, good-looking in a slightly foppish way, with fair curls and clear skin, added to an insouciant wit and a drawling manner of speech. He also took added care not ruffle what was an already testing situation.

At first Pearce was surprised at the continuing distance kept by Henry Digby, given it flew in the face of the kind of naval conventions to which the man must have wished to adhere, that before he came to realise he was equally at fault. He was far from sure an apology would achieve anything but there was never a moment when he considered making one.

So Grey found himself pig in the middle, dining alone with the captain, then with Pearce and careful to avoid talking about one with the other, which was a pity for had he done so it might have explained to both the differing attitudes and some reason for the depth of the split. Digby had come from an unhappy wardroom to this with his hopes high, only to find within days of taking independent command that a man, whom he felt owed him a great deal, was challenging his authority in a way only too reminiscent of Taberly, who had constantly undermined him aboard *Leander*.

He might have told Digby that Pearce saw his attitude to the relationship he had formed as ridiculously old-fashioned; Emily was never named to the marine nor was the actual relationship, it was all kept in the area of general conversation. Here they were approaching the end of the eighteenth century and he was serving under a man who could not see the flaws in his deep religious convictions.

For a man who had experienced the intellects of Paris, in the salons of men and women whose fame was not confined by state borders and who held that enlightenment barred the crudities of dogma, it was difficult to accept that anyone could still hold to such tenets. There was no aim on the part of Pearce to deny him the right to his faith; to him that was a matter for each man's conscience. He wanted Digby just to accept that in many quarters it was not shared.

The crew were now wary, which thankfully had no effect on their efficiency. They went about their tasks as they should and when called upon to show skill in their sail drill never once failed to impress. The guns were run in and out daily and as they changed course to round the toe of Italy, Digby allowed them some powder and shot with which to practise proper gunnery, the pity evident in every eye that there was no prize in the offing and it was a dumb show; every vessel spotted might as well be either neutral or an ally for their commander never changed course to investigate.

'I must say, Mr Pearce, if I have to exercise my men one more time on that damned crammed forepeak I shall go mad. How many times can a man bayonet a bag stuffed with tow and be entertained?'

'You are not alone, Mr Grey, in belonging to service full of monotony.'

'Which will soon apply to the food, sir.'

Pearce looked at his empty plate, having just finished their dinner and had to acknowledge that was true; what had been taken on fresh at Naples would soon be gone and the biscuit was hardening and attracting more weevils by the hour. They continued a desultory conversation about some modern methods of preservation being proposed when the cry from the masthead had Dorling send down a messenger to Captain Digby, dining alone, a cry which could not but alert this pair as well.

'Lookout,' Dorling imparted quietly as they came on deck, 'has sighted a merchantman and taken leave to suggest she might be in distress, her upper canvas don't look right.'

'She is right on our course, so we lose nothing by having a look. Mr Pearce, we require more sail, let us close at our best speed.'

The cry of 'all hands' he emitted without the use of his trumpet; Pearce disliked the posing he reckoned such an instrument engendered on such a small ship; best that it be saved for storm conditions. *Flirt* had been sailing easy under courses and topsails, now to that was added topgallants and kites, while the spanker was let out to expose more canvas to take what was fair breeze.

At each addition the deck of the brig canted a fraction more until with all set and closing fast on a vessel now hull up, it became wise to take hold of something to maintain upright comfort. There was joy in this even for John Pearce and that he could see was replicated in the faces of both Digby and Grey, for HMS *Flirt* was a flyer and stiff with it, built to be by the man whose name adorned the brass plaque sunk into the binnacle; Thomas Allen of Dover, Kent.

That the rigging of the merchant vessel was tattered became increasingly obvious the closer they came, ropes flying hither and thither in the wind while what canvas they had aloft was shot through with holes, as was the flag of the Levant Company flying from her stern. The other obvious fact was that she was low in the water, denoting a full cargo. It seemed, if the crew had been engaged in repairs, having spotted their flag flying stiffly to larboard they had abandoned that to line the rail and cheer, not that the sound could be yet heard.

'Aloft there, keep a sharp eye out to the east,' Digby shouted before adding, to no one in particular, 'that fellow was not the cause of his own damage and if they are still repairing it cannot have been long inflicted.'

'Clear for action, sir?' Pearce asked.

'When I decide to do so, Mr Pearce, be assured I will tell you.'

None could miss the angry flush that produced; to be cold and distant was one thing, to openly put his premier down in public was another. 'I bow to your greater experience of battle, sir.'

That made Digby physically jerk, it having been said loud enough for many an ear to catch, even if the wind was whistling in the rigging. The captain might command the vessel but there was not a man aboard who did not know that when it came to combat John Pearce had, by several cables, the superior familiarity and reputation; those who did not know before, like Grey's marines, had been put well in the picture by the crew.

The silence that ensued spoke as many volumes as would a normal conversation, there being no further speculation of what had caused this merchant vessel to be in distress. Clearly she had been in some kind of exchange of gunfire and normally mention of what with and when would have been rife.

Finally, as they closed to within hailing distance, Digby spoke. 'Mr Grey, you will oblige me by forming and leading a boarding party. I need to know what has occurred and, if there is a man still in command, that he be fetched aboard to tell us the details.'

Pearce said nothing; that was an order and duty that should have fallen to him. The fact that Grey was just as aware was evident in his face and his startled blue eyes, leaving the man who should have received the order wondering if he would refuse, an act that would put him, too, at odds with the captain.

'I wish you joy of the enterprise, sir,' came the swift remark.

That had the marine snap a look at Pearce, who nodded, which was his way of telling him to proceed; things were bad enough aboard without another spat adding to the atmosphere. Pearce now grabbed his speaking trumpet and without asking yelled out a question to the merchantman.

'Ship ahoy, your name and port.'

'*Lady Massington* out of London.'

'Is your captain still in command?'

'No, sir, he is below with a wound and the first mate is dead.'

'Is the captain well enough to talk?'

'He is.'

'Tell them to prepare to receive a party aboard,' Digby said, in a manner that implied he felt his prerogatives were being stolen, a command with which Pearce complied. 'Mr Dorling, let fly the sheets.'

The crew of the cutter, with Tilley now confirmed as coxswain, had the boat over the side and manned in short order, even before *Flirt* fully lost way, with Grey and four of his marines quick to board as soon as it was in the water. The merchant vessel had likewise loosened what she had left aloft so that both ships sat riding on the swell, with Digby ordering enough set to maintain a safe distance. Time passed before the marine, having gone below, reappeared on the deck to call over, using another speaking trumpet to tell his commander that the captain was in a bad way.

'I have advised him, sir, that we do not carry a surgeon and so he has requested that we take him aboard for a faster voyage to the nearest port.'

Digby held out his hand for the speaking trumpet, which Pearce handed over. 'Please advise him that my duty does not permit such a thing. Is there anyone aboard who can navigate?'

'I'll enquire,' Grey replied, before disappearing.

'Mr Dorling, just in case, please prepare a course for Gallipoli, which I hazard is the nearest port of any size to where we presently are. Even if they are at a stand, the Gulf of Taranto is just over the horizon and once they sight land they can shape a course by sight.'

Grey reappeared. 'No one claims the skill, sir.'

'Very well, return and report.'

Grey did and if Digby had wanted to bar Pearce from a share of the information he was wise enough to know that was a poor notion. They assembled in the cabin and Grey gave an account of what had happened, first telling that the captain he had questioned did not seem to him to be in immediate danger of expiring. He had a wound to the chest from a grape shot ball but nowhere near his vital organs.

'Three deep laden Levant traders out of Acre and bound for home, sir, two of them French—'

'French?' Digby snarled, '*Massington* should have been fighting them not sailing with them.'

'The captain had put enmity to one side, sir, in favour of mutual security. They intended to part company off the heel of Italy.'

'A lot of good it did him.'

'They were intercepted by two pirate vessels flying the crescent flag—'

'Did they say what kind of vessels they were?' Pearce demanded, which got a jaundiced look from Digby and an impatient one from Grey, who was miffed at again being interrupted.

'No, sir.'

'It matters not, Mr Grey, please continue.'

'The two Frenchies have been taken and *Massington* only got clear because the rogues were too occupied with the other captures to prevent it.'

Pearce, frustrated that Digby had not asked the obvious question, butted in again. 'How long ago since this happened?'

'That, too, is of no account,' Digby snapped as Grey blushed; clearly he had not put a question that would have been the very first posed by a naval officer.

'Sir, if it was very recent we might be able to reverse the situation.'

'We will not, Mr Pearce, for we will not deviate from our course to do so.'

'Which, sir, flies in the face of our standing duty.'

'Do not dare, sir, to remind me of my duty.'

'Am I allowed to say that knowing you as I do, I am astounded to be required to?'

'I daresay you are thinking on the money to be made Mr Pearce.'

'I am minded to rescue some poor souls from a lifetime of slavery and can I also say I resent the imputation.'

'Resent away, sir, and I will tell you, though I have no real need, it being none of your concern, that I have specific orders from Admiral Hotham not to deviate from our course until the mission we have been tasked to complete is over.'

'If Admiral Hotham was here he would do as I suggest.'

'He would not, Mr Pearce, and I might as well inform you that this is a situation for which he was careful to warn me. And, at the centre of that admonishment was the person of you.'

Seeing Pearce lost for words he was quick to add. 'He foresaw that we might be presented with an opportunity and knew what your attitude would be. I am now grateful to have seen your true colours over your affair with Mrs Barclay . . .'

Pearce noticed Grey's eyebrows shoot up; he probably did not know anyone called Barclay but he knew the word affair.

'Had I not done so,' Digby continued, 'I might have fallen for your greedy blandishments.'

'Gentlemen, please,' Grey blurted out. 'You are sailing close to a matter of honour.'

'There's precious little of that in this cabin,' Pearce spat, before he made his way out.

Digby shouted after him. 'Mr Pearce, cross to the *Lady Massington* and deliver to them the course Mr Dorling will have worked out. Tell them we will set them upon it before we part company.'

It was a task for a master's mate, not a lieutenant and the latter part could have been delivered by shouting but he was obliged to obey. As he made it to the deck he was met with dozens of questioning eyes and he could make a fair guess as to what was behind them for the marines who had accompanied their officer had told the tale.

Two deep laden French Levant merchantmen were worth a mint of money and if they were taken they would be lawful prizes. Some members of the crew were willing him to defy the captain and sought to tell him they would back him. Pearce shook his head and made for the cutter, still in the water, taking from Dorling the scrap of paper on which he had written the course.

When he returned to the brig all was ready and the orders rang out that saw them set a course a few points off due north until they were sure their charge had it right. Then Digby had Dorling put down his helm and once more they headed east, shaving the headland of Santa Maria di Leuca to enter the Lower Adriatic.

If the mood between the two senior officers had been frosty, that now permeated through the decks to the whole crew and it was impossible for their seniors not to notice, especially their captain as he took the morning watch. What had been snappy behaviour when called to a duty had become, if not sluggish, larded with effort none more so than the running out of the guns at dawn, even more so with the washing and drying of the deck. Then there were the looks, resentment barely hidden as the drying cloths were lashed on the planking.

Sailing across a grey and windy Adriatic there was constant glancing aloft with the hope that the lookout would spot those two French Levanters, for it was held that not even a swab like Digby could avoid a chase if they came in sight. The man himself could not miss the change in mood, which had him eventually, once they had come in sight of the Illyrian coast, call for Pearce to join him at once in his cabin. It was the 'at once', which presaged trouble and when he entered there was no invitation to sit.

'Mr Pearce, I am minded to think you are turning the crew against my lawful authority.'

'While I would reply that nothing I could do would exceed your own ability to bring that about.'

'That, sir, is insubordinate. I am minded to remove you—'

'How is your French, Mr Digby?'

'I was just about to add that the mission makes my desire to do so impossible, but once it is complete, then I may be minded to act. That, I need hardly point out, gives you time to amend your behaviour.'

'You know, Henry—'

The interruption was a shout. 'Do not address me so, sir. We are no longer on such terms and I would remind you of our respective positions.'

'Aye aye, sir,' Pearce replied with such obvious sarcasm in his tone that Digby flushed deep in those full cheeks, so much so that Pearce thought he might have a seizure. 'If I may continue. No act of mine has undermined you, it is entirely your own doing.'

'I am following orders.'

'Instructions which should never have been issued and certainly would not have been by any other admiral in the navy, most of whom are more interested in the money in their coffers than anything else. To return to the fleet with two deep laden French merchantmen would see us welcomed with open arms, even if this Mehmet fellow has raised the tricolour. Do not accuse me of greed when there are flag officers at large who think only of their eighth.'

'I was expressly forbidden to deviate in search of a prize. Sir William fears that French action in the Adriatic will pull him away from Toulon, no doubt their primary aim in seeking to make an ally of Mehmet Pasha. It was made plain to me the mission was of the highest importance and that nothing should be allowed to interfere with its completion.'

'It was not described so to me,' Pearce responded, looking perplexed. 'It was pronounced as precautionary, not even a shot across the bows, more of a gentle admonition to mind his manners.'

'Then you must not have been appraised of all the facts.'

'Who would you appraise of all the facts,' Pearce demanded, 'the man undertaking the talking or the fellow carrying him there?'

'I do not follow your drift.'

Digby made to continue speaking but Pearce held up a hand and, after a pause, 'You received a letter from London sent to you by a lawyer called Lucknor, did you not?'

'You having asked confirms what I suspected, it was on your behalf.' When Pearce nodded Digby added. 'Why have you not enquired before?'

'Before Naples you might have reacted in a way I would not want. Then you did; subsequently the occasion to pose the question has not arisen.'

'Do you not want to know what I said?'

Pearce looked him in the eye; he had to hide the fact that he already knew. 'I assume you told the truth.'

'I did, but made no mention of Mr Farmiloe and his presence with the press gang.'

'You did not need to, he would have got a letter too, as well as Toby Burns.'

'What is going on?'

There was a temptation to tell him everything; the existence of the court martial copy, his intention to use it to blackmail Barclay into seeking an annulment of his marriage or, if not that, the exceedingly different and expensive notion of a divorce. Of how a refusal could lead to him being hauled up for perjury and how that might impact on the likes of Hotham. As he thought on that some of the certainties that had got him this far began to dissolve, but there was one way to shore that up.

'Did the admiral mention you being in receipt of a letter from a lawyer?'

'No.'

That was good, but still the inconsistencies between what Digby was saying and the way Toomey had spoken to him nagged. 'You say Hotham told you the mission was important.'

'Not important, vital.'

'Would you relate to me his exact words?'

'Certainly not.'

'I was getting ready to offer an olive branch but that would now be superfluous. I will however advise you, given it is Sunday tomorrow and the crew will assemble for divine service, to promise them that should any opportunities arise on the way home, they will not be passed up.'

'I am more concerned at what you will do.'

'Why? It will be nothing except to obey orders and speaking of which, I was told we would be delivering a letter from the admiral to Mehmet Pasha.' A sharp nod. 'Do you know what it says?'

'I assume it to be a warning that if he does not mend his ways he will pay a very high cost.'

'Hotham's clerk told me that our task was to give him a gentle reminder and that was to be the tone of the letter.'

'I see your ploy, Pearce. You are seeking to get out of me what Admiral Hotham said by trickery.'

'Believe me, I am not. What you have let fall so far means that what I was told and what you were told are totally at odds.' Digby said nothing. 'You do not find that strange?'

'I have only your word that what you say is true.'

'I would not lie to you any more than you would lie to my fellow Lucknor.'

'For which you only have my word,' Digby replied, with something approaching a sneer that implied *touché*.

'Not true, Henry, I know exactly what you said for I was sent word by Lucknor about your reply and that of Toby Burns.'

'Do you not look in the mirror and despair of your devious nature?'

'I am beginning to wonder if I might be a mere tyro in that department.'

Silent for several seconds and deep in thought, with his captain looking at him in a quizzical manner, when he spoke it was with no great assurance of tone. 'I need to go to my quarters and fetch something. I then need to relate a lengthy tale to you, which also means that I would like permission to sit down.'

CHAPTER TWENTY

'I am tempted to go and check the level of rum in the casks, John,' Digby said, unaware that by merely using the Christian name he had utterly altered the mood of their exchange. 'I fear I will find it much diminished.'

'In all my calculations I discounted Toby Burns.'

'As I recall he is not a difficult person to overlook.'

The story had taken a long time, punctuated by the regular ringing of the bell to denote the passage of time and it had ranged from Sheerness, through events in Brittany, which Digby knew something about, to Barclay's court martial, which he had realised at the time, or when he heard the verdict, was a farce. That he had not reacted by loud denunciation Pearce had accepted and understood; he would be throwing his career away for he did not need telling that Hotham had arranged matters; had he not been sent away as well?

'I blame myself for not paying much attention to what was said to me when I asked about Burns.'

'Like how in the name of the devil did he ever get to pass that examination?'

'Precisely,' Pearce responded, 'but I claim I was distracted by the fact my boat was ready and those set to row me over waiting.'

'No one in the fleet doubts that it was arranged and there was little surprise given, if it is unusual, it is not unknown. I would not say I followed the career of Burns but he seemed, from what I know, to have turned up in some odd places. He was with Nelson on a couple of occasions and wherever that fellow is, it's bound to be hot work.'

'Now I ask you to look at this,' Pearce said, passing over the letter Lucknor had sent him. 'I will say nothing until you have read it.'

Given it was fairly lengthy another bell rang as Digby read, which told John Pearce he was due on watch in half an hour. He waited until the reading had finished and said, 'Well?'

'There's no truth in it that I do know, not if the gossip that ran through the fleet has any credence.'

'Anything else?'

'Well I know Burns and this seems to me to be a mite above his ability with words, somewhat adult in fact. Mind he tended to stammer when he talked, through fear I hasten to add, not naturally.'

'That is precisely the question raised by my attorney and he does not know Burns from David Garrick.'

'And so would not recognise his hand, John.'

The response was a slow nod. 'Say Burns received Lucknor's letter and realised he was in the soup.'

'Did your man threaten him?'

'Not as far as I know, but he is serving as a mid in the flagship and he panics. There's no Uncle Ralph to bleat to . . .'

'So he goes to Hotham?'

'Who will realise right off that this could go in directions he cannot control. Now I am beginning to wonder if he knows I have a copy of the transcript of Barclay's court martial. Lord, are all my assumptions tumbling?'

'Leading to what?'

'Henry, there are five people aboard HMS *Flirt* who know the truth of what happened in the Liberties that night, which means they know of the lies Barclay told at his court martial. The whole crew of *Larcher* is transferred as a body and the crew of *Flirt* shipped out. Usual?'

'Nearly unprecedented.'

'A crew that includes three of my very good friends, to a ship on which you have the command. A trio that had depositions taken which never saw the light of day. Then I am given a mission to join you in what I am told is something of marginal account. You—'

The hand came up to stop him; Digby did not need to be told. 'I find this very hard to credit, John. You are saying that a senior officer has set up a conspiracy that will put in peril the whole crew of this ship in a bid to lay to rest a personal matter?'

'I can think of no other explanation, can you? Will you now tell me what Hotham said?'

There was still reluctance; it went against the grain but finally he opened up and the description of the mission was at total odds to that with which John Pearce had been privy. Each statement of Hotham's was matched against one by Toomey and they jarred.

'But why are they not the same?'

'I would not be here if the mission had been outlined as one full of risk.'

'Which tells me they don't know you at all!'

'I'll take that as a compliment but I think they might have feared I'd smell a rat.'

'And I?'

'While you had to be persuaded of the necessity to ensure you carried it through. A little blackening of the Pearce name was thrown in with that order not to detour from your heading.'

'Yet we were diverted to Naples.'

The look on the face of John Pearce showed he got to the point of that just ahead of Digby. 'They know Emily is there.'

'Hotham asked me about her. Wanted to know who the lady was who caused so much mayhem in Leghorn. I lied, of which I am not proud and said I did not know.'

'What mayhem?'

'Don't josh me, John. That Lipton fellow and his bullocks. A mob of midshipmen and tars gives them a severe ducking the day after your duel and you pretend not to know of it. Lipton complained to the admiral and he very decently agreed to forget my part as your second.'

'Henry, I have no idea what you are talking about,' Pearce insisted, there being no chance he was going to admit to what had happened with Lipton and his bullocks, it being less than edifying for his sense of self-respect. 'I admit some of those officers insulted Emily but if they suffered subsequently it cannot be laid at my door.'

'Then who?'

'Does it matter now? It just underlines what we have been

speculating on. It seems our admiral knows a great deal more about things that we can only guess at.'

'You do realise this presents a dilemma?'

'Only if I am right and Hotham has deliberately sent us into danger.'

'And how do we establish that? It is all very well speculating but I cannot act on that. I have my orders.'

Tempted to scoff at what he saw as Digby being boneheaded, Pearce held his tongue, this as the eighth bell of the forenoon watch rang out to call him to his duty. 'I shall think upon it and so shall you. There must be a way to establish, if not the truth, something that informs us of what we are really being required to do.'

Nothing of much value came to mind as Pearce cogitated throughout the watch. Off the starboard beam lay the shoreline of old Illyria, which before that had been ancient Greece. They were in waters replete with history of battles, victories and losses with the whole of what had once been Attica, then Romania, now under the heel of the Turks. A quick check of the charts told Pearce they would raise the Gulf of Ambracia the next day and that would require Digby to decide how to proceed.

'John, I require you to come below. On the wheel, give out if anything occurs that requires an officer on deck.'

'Aye, aye, sir,' he replied as the blue coats disappeared, before saying to a nearby mate. 'It's John again, matters are looking up.'

In the cabin Pearce was immediately invited to sit and Digby looked at him for some time before he spoke. 'You will not require that I tell you how troubled my thinking has been, John.'

'No more than mine.'

Digby picked up and dropped a sheaf of papers on the desk. 'My orders, which are very specific. You may read them if you wish.'

'I can guess what they contain.'

'They contain no room for deviation and if I do not fulfil them that will be nothing less than a complete dereliction of duty, for which I could be court-martialled.'

'I know it is not easy.'

'Easy? It is damned impossible, John, and before you tell me we have good grounds for suspicion might I remind you of who I will be obliged to explain myself to if we return without the answer Hotham purports to seek? No less than the man himself.'

Pearce shook his head and to cover the silence that followed he leant across and picked up the orders, not with any intention of reading them but to give time for Digby to move on to the next obvious point. 'And if we do proceed we have no idea of what we might face.'

'A Turkish Pasha right on the periphery of the Ottoman domains.'

'You reached a similar conclusion to me. At such a distance the touch of Constantinople must be light indeed.'

In putting the orders down Pearce saw the still sealed letter with the wax impression of the British Crown, Digby following his eye. 'Hotham's letter to Mehmet.'

Pearce picked it up and weighed it as if it were a gold ingot before looking at the superscription; there was Hotham's name and rank plus the address in French to the Pasha.

'I wonder what it says.'

'That we will only find out when our fellow opens it and perhaps not even then.'

Pearce emitted a humourless laugh. 'It might be an invitation to string us up from the nearest yardarm.'

'That is not funny, John.'

'I don't think I intended it to be.'

'From what I can gather Hotham knows no more than we do about our man.'

'He does, this is the second time an envoy has been sent.' Given the look on Digby's face he was obliged to add that he had checked with Hood's under clerk. 'You were not told? It was presented to me as a bit of a misadventure, in which there was some misunderstanding, which means that there is some kind of record of what took place.'

'And Hotham would have it.'

'This all becomes more bizarre by the hour.'

Pearce waved the letter again. 'It may be referred to in here.'

'Which means if we read it, then it cannot be delivered and if it is nothing more than what it is supposed to be, where does that leave us?'

'Not necessarily,' Pearce replied, standing to crouch, his look one of deep thought. 'If I may be allowed a moment.'

'Leave the letter, John.'

'Of course,' he replied, tossing it over, which had Digby examining it, as if by doing so he could see through to the written-on side.

Out on the lower deck Pearce sought out Charlie Taverner and dragged him away from his duty of acquiring the dinner for his mess, taking him up onto the deck and the forepeak.

'Charlie, have you ever opened a sealed letter?'

There was a moment when Charlie adopted the air of a man being accused and clammed up, a legacy of a less than lawful life, but it was John Pearce to whom he must respond. 'Weren't my skill, but I know how it's done.'

'Tell me.'

'Well you takes a hot blade and you slip it slow twixt seal and paper, but the trick is never to let the heat mark the letter.'

'And how do you avoid that?'

'By using another bit of paper, one that you can singe. Parchment be best.'

'Would you feel confident doing it?'

'What are we about, John?'

'Doing right, Charlie.'

That got a grin from handsome Charlie and a tip of his hat. 'Can't be part of that, mate, it would ruin my repute as the best sharp in the Strand.'

'I'm serious.'

That wiped the grin off his face and had a hand on the Taverner's chin. 'Best to practise on what don't matter.'

'Good thinking. Have your dinner and come to my berth when you're done. And, Charlie, not a word to anyone.'

'Weren't necessary to say that, John.'

'I mean it, not even Rufus and Michael.'

The aim, related to a dubious Henry Digby, was finally agreed with one caveat; Pearce had to be sure of success. When it came to a sharp blade there was none more so than a razor and to make sure his was at its best Pearce stropped it for an age. He had also arranged for Matthew Dorling to take over his watch, which the master did with seeming willingness and when he spoke Pearce found out why.

'Never did thank you for shifting us whole, Mr Pearce, and here's me got a bigger ship as easy as kissing my hand.'

'I don't think I thanked you either for not dishing me.'

'Couldn't see you go down, your honour.'

'Even if I deserved it? We should never have left Palermo in that condition.'

Dorling grinned. 'Might still be there.'

'Which would have made you a happy man, seeing that you had found yourself a warm bit of flesh for comfort.'

'Didn't want to be outdone did I, your honour?'

It was clear from the slightly quizzical look that Dorling had that he had no idea how that sally would be taken; it could be seen as highly insubordinate.

'Well said,' was the reply he got.

Charlie came as required and to the look from Pearce he replied that no one had any notion of why he was entering the berth and nor would they know why the screen was immediately pulled closed behind him.

'They'll be peering.'

'Let them.'

'And taking wagers as to what I is about.'

Pearce had a set of sealed blank letters on his sea chest and an open lantern too, into the flame of which Pearce put the blade of his razor, which after a while began to send out a slight smell of burning metal.

'Happed they'll think I'm payin' for my errors at the stake,' joked Charlie.

He was on his knees with a blank sheet of parchment that had come from Digby's private letter case and it was immediately obvious that he was struggling, with melted wax going everywhere.

'You were right about practise.'

'Not the sort of thing you learn in the Fleet. Breaking into houses, yes, and passing off tin as gold, but this is clerkish crime.'

'Let's try another.'

'Won't do much for your razor.'

'If I am right and we fail I won't need my razor.'

That got Pearce a sharp look from Charlie, who was so busy with that that he singed himself, emitting a yelp, which had Pearce begin to chuckle. 'I wonder what they'll think when they hear that, your nosy mates.'

'Don't even make a jest of it.'

The next attempt was better and then Pearce decided to have a try, on the grounds that he could not ask Charlie to take responsibility for the one that needed to be opened and read. That had to be him or Digby and he knew Henry would not do it; no doubt seeing it as a sin. If Charlie had been cack-handed he seemed no better and it was only after half a dozen false starts that he began to get it anything like right. The floor around them was full of messy waxwork and discarded parchment, a lot of it burnt at the edges, bits that had to be stamped on to kill the flames.

'We have to go to the real thing,' Pearce said, 'and, Charlie, you can be no part of that.'

'I get a whiff that you don't trust me.'

'I am about to attempt something that could see me strung up from the yardarm. If you're sure you want to join me, I won't stop you.'

'Taken as intended, John.'

'Back you go to your mess.'

'What do I say to them? 'Cause they's bound to press.'

'Tell them we were raising Satan. That should shut them up.'

'Smells as if that could be the truth. Happen they will treat me as a wizard.'

Entering Digby's cabin he encountered a man deep in concern for he had been subjected to the odour of burning for quite a while.

'I have the way of it now, Henry, trust me.'

'Do I have a choice?'

Pearce shook his head, laid the lantern on the desk and opened the door. His razor was now blue metal instead of silver and still warm. Digby handed over Hotham's missive which was laid flat on a bit of canvas to ensure it did not slip away.

'I require you to hold it, Henry, like so, with your fingers nowhere near the join.'

Digby spread his fingers and took the clench required while Pearce heated the blade. A new piece of parchment was ready and that was laid just so, at the point where the wax met the heavy paper, with Pearce talking, as much to ease his own anxieties as those of his captain.

'If you get it right, Henry, the parchment gets hot enough to slide under the wax and separate it on its own.'

The concentration was acute from both men as Pearce applied the blade, sliding it fraction by fraction, always with the metal kept from the actual letter. The point at which it parted was a dangerous moment for, folded hard, it sprung up like a fairground jack.

'We have it, I think.'

Digby went to pick it up, but Pearce stopped him. 'Wait till the wax is fully cooled.'

When the time came Digby unfolded it, once, twice, the third and fourth time until it was flat, criss-crossed with the creases of its previous state.

'This is in English!' Pearce cried.

'Is that significant?'

'Time to find out.'

CHAPTER TWENTY-ONE

Both men had been prepared to be surprised; what they read gave them a real shock. Hotham's letter was a rebuke to Mehmet Pasha for the way he had treated another British naval officer, one previously sent to seek to put an end to what were termed 'his depredations on the trade routes between the Levant and the nations of the coalition fighting the Revolution'; there was no mention of the French inducements.

That this Turk should threaten a British Officer at all was an insult to His Britannic Majesty King George; to then imply that he could have him thrown in his dungeons and whipped till he learnt some respect was more than that, it was a flagrant breach of the norms of civilised behaviour and a threat to the good relations between Great Britain and the Porte.

The letter demanded a full apology and some token of redress and if that was not forthcoming for such high-handed actions then the admiral in command in the Mediterranean, named on the superscription, would have no choice but to send the firepower necessary to chastise him, with the added peril that he would, should he fall into British hands, be sent to Constantinople to face those authorities whose official policies he chose to ignore.

'This beggars belief,' Digby groaned.

If Pearce shared that sentiment he was more concerned with thinking through the ramifications. Who was this Mehmet Pasha and what was he like? Not a pleasant fellow to say the least if what was written was true. Depredations on such a busy trade route could be read as piracy, which would be just as frowned upon by his own political masters as by any British admiral. Left to continue it would curtail any traffic at all, which would damage the Ottoman Empire as much as those with whom it traded.

He tried to imagine the scene when this letter was handed over, which is what Hotham would have done. Did the Turk have English after all? It mattered not, for if he had an interpreter speaking to him in his own tongue whoever was standing before him would have no indication of what was being translated, unless he could read it in the reaction.

'If Mehmet wanted to chastise an envoy sent to parley with him, what would he do to one sent to threaten him?'

'If Sir William could not be sure he could guess,' Digby responded.

'He's been clever, Henry.'

'How can you call what is sheer criminality clever?'

'Because it is, perhaps too much so for Hotham. It may be that Toomey is the author of this affair.' Seeing Digby about to explode, Pearce laid a hand on his arm and sought to quiet him, not that what he had to say was in any way reassuring. 'You call it criminality but what has been done?'

'He has laid a trap in which someone could be severely injured, even killed. Since you were set to be the victim I cannot fathom how you can react with such composure.'

'Would it shock you to know that there are parts of this for which I have admiration? Our admiral has done his duty, or that is how it would be seen if it were ever examined. You do not agree?'

'I cannot, John.'

'Mehmet, I think we can assume, is indulging in piracy, for which his base is admirably suited. So Hood sends an officer to warn him to desist, which is rejected with scarce a hint that he fears anything or anyone. We can also take from this letter that whatever our fellow is up to it is not the policy of the government he is supposed to obey. That makes him doubly dangerous, since where he is placed, on the very edge of the Ottoman possessions, must make it hard for them to check him. In short, he is acting as an independent power.'

Pearce was slowly shaking his head but it was in wonder. 'What does Hotham do? He could just ignore Mehmet and let the insurers in London bear the brunt of the problem, yet Ambassador Hamilton told me that they are imposing exorbitant rates on the Levant trade, a fact of which the Admiralty must be aware. The City of London is not shy of seeking to have its own interests protected.'

'This is a deliberate attempt to rid himself of you.'

'And perhaps you too, Henry, for if I had gone ahead and ended up in trouble I am sure you would not just sail away and leave me to my fate. You would feel obliged to effect a rescue even if the odds you faced were against you.'

'You are implying that he is prepared to lose both this ship and the crew, John. Surely not even he would stoop to that.'

'Henry, he must know you had a letter from Lucknor. What else he knows I do not want to even guess at.'

'He must be exposed.'

'I can't see how. Who are you going to bring the matter before and what are your grounds to claim a conspiracy? Hotham is the C-in-C and you will be obliged to report to him should you return to San Fiorenzo Bay.'

'Lord Hood—'

'Will not be returning to the Mediterranean, Henry.'

'How can you know that?'

'Trust me, I do. Even if you could find a higher authority, and I'm damned if I can think where, what can you accuse him of?'

'The Admiralty, the Sea Lords.'

'Who will deduce that Hotham has done his duty. He has sent a warship to this anchorage with a message threatening Mehmet Pasha which, if he is engaged in piracy, will be seen as the proper action to take, doubly so if he has insulted the King's Majesty. Lord Hood might have done the same, though I take leave to suggest he would have sent a more powerful force.'

It was with a woeful tone that Digby drew the conclusion. 'But Sir William can claim he could not do that for fear of the Toulon fleet.'

'I told you it was clever. You were given information in private by him, I was tempted in private by Toomey, yet from what I can read your actual sailing orders came from Captain Holloway.'

That got a nod of sheer misery, for it was obvious what he was being told; there was no proof of any conspiracy and if his orders were tightly worded that would also be seen as correct procedure to rein in a man who might be tempted to deviate from his instructions.

'It may be a stroke of genius but what do I do now?' Digby growled, holding up his orders, 'given I have no intention of going through with this.'

'In strict contravention of your orders?' That was followed by a grim smile. 'So even if you fail to accomplish the mission on which you were sent Hotham can see you ruined and if you then accuse him of anything it will be seen as sour grapes.'

'I do hope,' Digby said, clearly exasperated by all this calm exposition, 'when you are telling me this, there is somewhere in your thinking a possible solution, John.'

'Nothing comes to mind that will save you.'

'What about you?'

'I am not in command, Henry, and if in the backwash I am tainted, then I have considered leaving the service many times. You, I know, have ambitions I do not share.'

'Which I might as well chuck down my privy.' There was a pause before Digby roused himself. 'The first thing to do is to shorten sail, I have no desire to open the Gulf of Ambracia any quicker than necessary.'

'You intend to go there?'

'I must, but not to enter the bay and send you off to God only knows what fate. You have often impressed me, John, with your sanguine belief that matters which look grim will somehow resolve themselves. You did so in La Rochelle. I hope and pray that this is one occasion when your tendency to think in that manner rubs off on me.'

* * *

Neither man slept well, while being on watch provided no enlightenment. But once Divine Service had been read – Digby was a dab hand at that part of his duties, good for both a rousing sermon and enough fire and brimstone to satisfy the most hell-fearing tar – with Matthew Dorling on watch duty, the two could get together to search for a solution and it was Henry Digby who made the first suggestion, though he was at a loss to say with certainty why he thought it a good idea.

'A reconnaissance?'

'Just that, John. We will keep *Flirt* away from the shore and out of sight and send in the cutter to look into the bay and see what we face.'

'This is leading somewhere.'

'It is leading to a way out of our dilemma, perhaps.'

Pearce was sure Digby was thinking on the hoof but he was not one to decry a trait to which he was himself prone. A nod got his captain continuing, which he did, but not till he had produced a map showing the land surrounding the gulf.

'We sail and approach Koronsia, which is the Greek name for where Mehmet has his fortress and the centre from which he runs the country.'

'That must be an old map, the Turks have been there for centuries. Why the Greek name?'

'It is what Hotham gave me.'

'Then I would be disinclined to trust it.'

This got Pearce a glare telling him to be serious; not even an admiral would be able to forge a map. 'What I have in mind is that we approach Koronsia with all proper respect, salutes included and then we invent some kind of insult to our national flag.'

Pearce responded with a slight smile. 'Go on.'

'Being insulted I decide to show our Turk that such an act cannot go unchallenged, an insult so serious I have no option but to employ my cannon to check his impudence.'

'Which makes the notion of me subsequently landing impossible.'

'Correct.'

'Ingenious.'

'But I am loath to enter his lair without knowing what I might face. Is this Gulf of Ambracia defended, for instance, for I have no information to tell me ye or nay? Does Mehmet possess any kind of vessel with which I would then be obliged to deal, for it would never do to be caught in confined waters by anything that could match us?'

'And if this course is followed then you can return to Hotham and say the message could not be delivered.'

'Exactly.'

'We are not the only pair on this brig.'

'No,' Digby acknowledged; there was a crew who would be quizzed. 'But I am hoping that our imagination can contrive an excuse for opening fire that will stand up to challenge. Well, what do you think?'

Pearce had to be careful for he, in command, would have just put up his helm, sailed back to the fleet and damned Hotham to do his worst. But he was not Henry Digby.

'I think it is high risk but I also think it forms a basis from which to proceed.'

'Then I request that you take the cutter and look at what we might face.'

'Readily, let me have that map and I will study it for a place to come ashore.'

'I will see a mast stepped into the cutter.'

'No, Henry, this is better as oar work.'

'It will be a damned long haul, I intend that they should not see our topsails. I assume they will have a tower of sorts and they certainly have battlements on that fortress.'

'"Damned" Henry? I am not sure if I have ever heard you employ the word.'

If Pearce needed proof that his captain was feeling more sanguine about things it came now in his response. 'I have been exposed once too often to you and your ways, John.'

'That aside, Henry, you can get in close in darkness and shorten our journey, then get back out to sea before first light. Mr Dorling will work that out in a trice. If we can get ashore ahead of dawn then we might be able to camouflage the cutter and stay for the whole day.'

'Sound thinking. What about rejoining?'

'That too must be in darkness, but with *Flirt* far enough inshore to show a light that we can pick up, yet one that will not be seen from the shore by a sentinel.'

'You think he has those?'

'I would not be willing to wager on the lack of them. Somehow I have this Mehmet fellow down as a cautious cove.'

It was not just a simple matter of distances. There was the sea state, which was benign now but may not remain so. Then there were currents that would affect progress, either aiding or slowing a rowing cutter, which was not a boat built for speed. Pearce was obliged to disappoint Mr Grey who was keen to participate along with his marines.

'We are not going to do battle, if anything we are set to avoid it.'

'Then I must do no more than register my protest.'

'Noted, Mr Grey.'

Next, Pearce had to select those he was taking with him, Michael O'Hagan being the first on his list, which meant the other Pelicans had to be included to avoid pique. Tilley would cox the cutter and out of the crew he knew so well it was easy to pick men he was sure would obey any order he gave without question and also be sharp-minded in themselves.

He had one of the brig's swivel guns fitted in the bows and loaded, with a cover over the muzzle to keep out water, which if it added weight also added firepower, it being a weapon designed to discharge grapeshot. Every man would be armed with knives and cutlasses, while muskets would be wrapped in tarred canvas to keep them dry and laid in the bottom of the boat.

Half a barrel of powder came from Sam Kempshall along with sacks of lead balls. Ash from under Bellam's coppers would serve to darken faces white enough to reflect overhead light, while a packet of biscuits and some small beer would be taken along as sustenance.

The man in charge was equipped with his pistols, his sword and a sketchbook with which to make quick drawings of what he observed, these to be studied prior to any attempt to enter the gulf under a truce flag and he had a small telescope to aid him in surveying the anchorage. On setting off they would row hard to close the distance then more carefully to avoid creating the kind of phosphorescence that could be picked up by moon and starlight.

That the sky was a mixture of cloud and clear had to be

accepted; to seek to row ashore in stygian darkness was to risk too much, though Pearce had a compass. They needed some light to pick out a spot at which to land and also to avoid any underwater obstacles that might lurk on their course. Most of that would come from the stars, given the moon was waxing and no more than a thin strip hanging to the north-west.

'I wish you Godspeed, John, and know that, even if it does not meet with your approval, I will pray for you.'

'Do not doubt that I am grateful.'

'There is nothing we have missed?'

Pearce laughed. 'Only the ability to see into the mind of men like Hotham.'

'Even having seen his sinning ways, I still cannot do that,' Digby said in a sad tone, before calling out to let fly the sheets and bring the brig up into the slight breeze.

Pearce was last into the cutter, now manned by eight rowers and ten more tars, enough it was felt to take on any unexpected enemies and check them so they could make an escape, a fact which did not escape the glowers of the marine lieutenant.

The other worry was a pursuit by something under sail, but Pearce reasoned any such vessel had to be inside the bay and would need to get out through the narrows before they could mount a chase. If they did ,that was when he would employ the swivel gun.

The time came to switch the oarsmen and also to slow their rate and weight of stroke, for anything too heavy threw up high spouts of displaced seawater. When the sky clouded over enough to hide the stars, leaving him with the tin strip of luminosity at the edge of the clouds, he called for the oars to be shipped; the shoreline was low-lying and relatively short on vegetation and he wanted to see where he would touch bottom for it needed to be sandy not rocky.

The first hint of light began to tinge the eastern clouds right in front of Pearce; they had cut it very fine and still he could not see a line where wavelets were coming ashore, so it was time to abjure caution; nothing could be worse than to be out at sea in daylight.

'Haul away, lads, let's get our feet on dry land. Michael, man that swivel and if you hear a sound let fly at it.'

The speed picked up and at last Pearce saw that for which he was searching and it was close, for he could hear the tell-tale lapping of water on sand, thankfully not the hiss of rocks or pebbles. It seemed no time at all until the bottom touched sand, at which point every man leapt out of the cutter to first lighten it then to haul it further inshore where the swivel gun was lifted off its temporary mounting.

Getting up the beach was hard going even if it was a shallow rise and soon they and their craft were in some low bushes, where they could find concealment. There they stayed while the light in the sky slowly increased until it became full daylight. Now Pearce could see about him and reckoned on his luck, for in easy sight lay the rear of a fortified bastion which, covering the narrows, had to have cannon.

A slight change of direction might have had them run ashore beneath the guns. Somehow he would have to find out the number of cannon and their weight of shot for that was the route of entry and exit for *Flirt*. Also, was it only one side fortified, or both?

Raising his head he looked into the gulf, surprised to see four pairs of high masts, two close and two further off. Extra elevation was risky but had to be tried and that showed him two deep-hulled merchant vessels bearing the scars of a fight; even if he had never before called eyes on them he knew them to be those that had sailed in company with the *Lady Massingham*.

What made him so certain was the sight of the two other vessels riding at anchor on the far side of the anchorage, a pair of brigantines with lines too familiar to cheer his mood, even at a distance. Michael had joined him and he was looking with the same sense of astonishment.

'I think we now know who that fellow we came across escaped from, Michael, just as we know now and for certain that Mehmet Pasha's true game is piracy.'

'Can't see proper, John-boy, but what is that hanging from the yards of them merchantmen?'

Pearce swung his small telescope to where Michael was pointing and what he observed brought from him a gasp of breath. 'They're bodies, Michael. I reckon two of the men from those captures, one for each, and they have been hanged.'

'Holy Christ,' Michael swore, before crossing himself.

CHAPTER TWENTY-TWO

For John Pearce the day was spent crawling through undergrowth, which covered the narrow spit of land that formed the southern arc of the bay, to get to points where he could get sight of those things he needed to record, in this accompanied by Rufus Dommet who had the slimmest frame and the least weight of the Pelicans. There was no need to say that Michael O'Hagan was left in charge of the others; no one would argue with him. If he found a convenient spot he would rest his back against a thick bush and, alternating the use of his telescope with a piece of charcoal, sketch away.

By midday he had a drawing of the far from formidable fortress and the buildings that surrounded it, many too close to aid in defence, quite the reverse, which implied it was no longer expected to withstand an assault and had become a place of administration: probably had any cannon stripped out. Not far off from the walls, across an open square, lay a small harbour, containing mostly small inshore fishing boats though there was one bigger vessel that looked like a barge.

From every angle those two swinging bodies were in sight, moving on the slight motion of the ship, as were the brigantines that he was wont to think had been built to haunt him. There was more activity on the pirate vessels, the normal duties on a ship at anchor, with practically none at all on those two merchantmen. Where were the crew; ashore in Mehmet's dungeon or secure below decks and why hang two of them?

The hardest to observe were the two round stone bastions on either side of the entrance to the gulf with cannon that covered the anchorage, presumably the same weight of shot as those pointing out to sea and covered the narrows. He had to assume a deep water channel running down the centre of those narrows but there was no way of telling if it actually lay to the north or south of the middle, which was not a positive. If Digby did enter the gulf, and Pearce would be advising against it, running aground would lead to utter destruction.

Tired and dusty, Pearce entertained a solution that horrified Rufus. He began to strip down to his smalls, preparatory to swimming out to a point where he could observe both batteries and the muzzles of their inward-facing cannon, to try and guess at their calibre, for it could not be more than that.

'What if they spot your head in the water?'

'We have not seen a soul on this bank, not even a fisherman and those ships are too far off to allow anyone to spot me from the deck.'

'And if they have eyes aloft?'

'The only ones I can see,' Pearce snapped, 'are dead.'

Rufus was still unhappy that, should the alarm be raised, he was to race back to the rest of the crew, hidden with the cutter and get it out to sea. 'And take these sketches with you.'

It was necessary to slither down the rough sand to get into the water which, at this time of year, December, was far from warm as he made his way out from the shore to a point where he could observe the shore embrasures of both bastions. Pearce knew he was taking a risk, but those cannon lay at the heart of the defence of Mehmet's gulf, a place in which he clearly felt secure and with good reason; short of a ship of the line blasting those batteries to pieces, nothing could get in that he did not want to and then there was the getting out. Thankfully there was even less activity around the cannon than on the anchored ships.

Next he lay on his back to float and fixed his eyes on a point on shore, the flagstaff that bore the Crescent and Star of the Ottoman Empire, aware of movement towards the gulf entrance; there was a current and a noticeable one flowing outwards, no doubt fed by rivers from the surrounding mountains, which would act to slow any vessel seeking entry. That established, he very gently made his way back to the point where Rufus Dommet was waiting. If it was a cool figure who came back to shore it was one covered in sticky sand by the time he rejoined Rufus; he had to slide uphill. Once he was handed his coat he extracted his watch to check the time, not that it was utterly necessary, the state of the light told him it was time to get ready to depart, especially since he had a long crawl back.

The two had just begun that when a series of screams rent the air, not loud, for it was too far off to be that, but echoing. Pearce stopped and trained his telescope on where it came from, one of the French merchantmen. The knot of bodies soon filled his glass, several turbaned men dragging another across the deck, a sailor by his garb, where they put a rope around his neck, before turning to face the fortress.

A swing of the telescope showed a substantial figure of a man on the battlements and he, too, had a similar instrument, albeit much larger than that which Pearce held and it was fixed on that merchant ship's deck. Around his large frame were what seemed like some kind of court and examining him Pearce could see his clothing shimmered even in the lack of sunlight, which had him think the garments would be lavish and costly.

The portly fellow, and he was well larded, lifted his hand and Pearce swung his glass to see the poor soul who had been struggling to get free hauled up off the deck to kick and jerk as the life was squeezed out of him by slow strangulation. Sighting back to the man who had waved ,it was obvious he was laughing as he turned to address his companions, several of whom bowed.

'Mehmet Pasha, I'll wager and that's what Hotham had in mind for me.'

'Poor bastard,' Rufus said, for if he had not the power of a telescope he had eyes to see the final death throes of the hanged sailor, the last feeble kicks of those legs.

Pearce was still examining the man who had caused this, probably for mere entertainment and it seemed he had seen his fill, for he turned and walked out of sight, once more with bows to mark his passing. Then, with shudder, he resumed his slow and careful progress.

They got the cutter into the water as soon as darkness fell and with just enough light for Pearce to see the pointer on his compass, allowing him to set a course. Rowing into what seemed an endless nothingness induces a strange feeling of embarking on a journey with no end and, given it took several hours before they saw a winking lantern, it was not without concern; if they did not meet with HMS *Flirt* they would be in a bad place.

Closing fast as the sky began to lighten again, the sails made dun-coloured by wind, water and the sun, voices called out to bring them to the gangway, where they disembarked to slaps on the back from their mates; Pearce last out, his hand aided by Michael O'Hagan, issued a quick request.

'A bucket, Michael, if you please, over the side and filled. Rufus, take care of this sketchbook.'

'Mr Pearce, John, I bid you a happy return and am eager to hear what you have observed.'

'There is scarce enough light to see, sir, but I must tell you my body is covered in sand which renders me unfit for anything.'

That said and his pistols and sword handed to Charlie Taverner, he began to undress which got many a chuckle from the crew, who fully expected him to do what they had seen the man do before, which was to dive naked into the sea.

'Please feel free to get under way, Henry, and when I am clean and in decent clothing I will join you in your cabin.'

Finally disrobed, Pearce allowed O'Hagan to douse him in seawater several times until every trace of sand, which had driven him mad with itching for hours, was removed from his body.

Grey had been invited to attend on the two sea officers as it was held by Digby that, being a Lobster, his opinion should be sought on anything that might involve fighting on land: not that there was as yet a plan. What was obvious to the meanest intelligence was the plain fact that if those two redoubts at the entrance remained functional then any thought of doing what Digby had suggested was doomed.

'You only have so many men, Mr Grey, too few to subdue a pair of stout bastions.'

'The trick, captain, would be to subdue one and turn the guns on to the other.'

'Simple to say, not easy to accomplish.'

Grey looked at Pearce as if he had just blasphemed, which reminded him of the odd situation in which he found himself. Normally the man thirsting for action he was trying to dampen the aims of another he knew to be desperate. Digby had to do something; he could not just admit failure and then face the consequences or the man who had sent him, an admiral he could not touch.

'You say the batteries are not heavily manned, sir?'

'Not that I could see. They anticipate no threat from the sea that would not be obvious for some time before it could get within range.'

'And there were no torches lit last night?'

'No, for we would not have landed so close if we had seen them.'

'Lax, Mr Pearce, wouldn't you say?' Grey replied with a quizzical look.

'Only if the force they are required to deal with is overwhelming. Besides that the cannon are set in embrasures and I assume most of them point out to sea.'

'Even stout walls will not withstand the blast of a thirty-two pounder at close quarters.'

'The size is only a guess.'

'No matter.'

'Henry, you are proposing to sail into that gulf with those cannon manned, when you do not even know if they will respect your truce flag. Once inside you are going to open fire on Mehmet's old fort and then seek to get back out again, relying on Mr Grey and his Lobsters to have neutralised the cannon and this when you cannot be sure of a safe channel.'

Digby was looking at the top of his desk and when he lifted his eyes there was a real sense of doom in them. 'John, it pains me to say this, but if you want no part of what I must do then I will need to find a way to get you ashore somewhere safe, a place from which you can make your way . . .' the pause was long, '. . . to Naples.'

'You are so determined on this you will risk destruction?'

'I cannot see another way.'

'There are two well-armed brigantines in the anchorage . . .'

'Vessels *Flirt* can fight!'

'One perhaps for you are much better armed, two is another matter and whatever course you adopt might I remind you it is not only your own life you are risking.'

'I had expected more support.'

'I will support you in anything that can be achieved but not an approach that smacks of madness driven by despair. To take this brig into that anchorage is suicide. I also doubt if the crew were told of your aim they would follow you.'

Pearce paused and rubbed his temples, watched in silence by the others. 'But . . .'

'Yes?' Digby asked, his desperation undiminished.

'In search of a rich prize . . .'

'What are you thinking?'

'What if we went in but *Flirt* did not?'

'To what purpose?'

'To cut out those two French merchantmen.'

'Now I think you as mad as you are claiming me to be.'

'No. We got ashore in the darkness and I can assure you if we struggled to get the cutter off the beach, we managed, and the slope on the inshore side was of the same incline. The cutter is our largest boat and we have two more that we can get into the water with enough men to get aboard the cargo ships and cut their cables.'

'They must be guarded.'

'Against what? The only threat they face are the crew they must be holding as prisoners, whom our friend Mehmet seems intent on stringing up for entertainment. There is no threat from outside the gulf for they do not know we are in the offing. You were probably too far out to even be spotted by fishermen.'

'You reckon we could surprise them?'

'I doubt they are as sharp as they should be and what backs that up? There was no sign of those sentinels I was so concerned about. Mehmet and his men have allowed complacency to replace watchfulness, for they cannot see where any threat could come from by which they would not be well warned.'

'We have no idea of numbers.'

'If I can get aboard with the same number I took in the cutter I will wager it will be Mehmet's men who will be well outnumbered. Mr Grey, if you can do as you have suggested then you would have to subdue both batteries so we could sail those merchantmen out, but I must add they are made of more robust timber than our brig and could probably withstand a bit of a pounding.'

'And if we fail to cut them out, John, and are required to flee?'

'Then as long as our marines control one battery we row out right under their guns, for in that case depth of keel is of no account.'

'That still does not solve a certain problem.' The sideways glance at Grey was enough; he had not been appraised of Hotham's treachery. 'And that to me is central.'

'Henry, I have had a long and exhausting day and it is now the middle of the night. I beg you for some sleep and while I am doing that if you wish to cogitate further on alternatives then who am I to stop you?'

'I, too, am in need of sleep,' Digby said, taking the solution offered. 'Mr Grey, you, too, have been up for too long.'

'And the watch?'

'You trusted this crew, John, I am content to do likewise until Mr Dorling comes on duty. We are set on a circular course so let us leave it that way. If anything untoward occurs let them call our attention to it.'

No amount of cogitating could keep John Pearce awake but he did dream and they were not all of a happy hue, so when he awoke he was far from refreshed. There was a way to alleviate that and once up he went on deck, disrobed and dived naked over the side to stroke hard in the water, a mixture of warm currents and others of icy but invigorating chill. Whatever they were it was an aid to clarity.

Back aboard, dry and refreshed, he could face Henry Digby, who looked as though he had not slept a wink. His eyes were puffy and his cheeks drawn, without much in the way of colour and he was given to rubbing his face hard as Pearce began to talk.

'The problem.' A nod. 'You approached the Gulf of Ambracia and took a precautionary look in without trying the narrows to find two merchant vessels you thought had been taken illegally in the anchorage, these espied from the tops of HMS *Flirt*. I know you not to be averse to going aloft personally.'

'Why did I think that?'

'Damage to their hulls and upper works as well as the presence of a pair of brigantines identified by yours truly as those he fought and ran from in HMS *Larcher*, thus a reasonable conclusion since they are known to be pirates or at best privateers and not British Letters of Marque.'

Now it was fingers kneading Digby's brow.

'Therefore the notion of taking one of His Majesty's warships through the narrows, past double batteries and with two well-armed brigantines within an unknown allegiance, seemed risky until matters could be clarified.'

'And how do I do that?'

'You send in a message demanding to know the name and designation of the merchant ships, which you suspect might be from our own country since they fly no flags.' Pearce laughed. 'In French, Henry, if you are challenged, though it will not need to be seen.'

'Not amusing.'

'It will tease Hotham.'

'I want him shot not teased.'

'Settle for what can be achieved. You receive in reply the most insulting response and you are fired upon by the batteries protecting the narrows when you approach too close. You'll have to falsify the log, of course, time of shot etcetera.' That got a hard look. 'Do not pretend to me it is not done.'

'And then?'

'In response to what is an insult you decide that Mehmet Pasha needs to be taught a lesson, was that not the gist of Sir William's message, which you were obliged to open being unsure what to do?'

'Was I?'

'Of course and here it is as evidence if the event is examined, irrefutable proof that there was no other way to act commensurate with the dignity of our sovereign and the navy. I would like to see Sir William Hotham deny the very words that he wrote or had Toomey write for him. Henry, this turns the tables on him and makes him a victim of his own machinations.'

'I still return empty-handed.'

'Not if you have two fat French merchant vessels in tow. Even if we do not manage to cut them out the mere fact of attempting to do so will look like the behaviour of a committed and dedicated officer. You can then recommend that a strong squadron be sent to destroy Mehmet's base.'

'How did I send in my message?'

'By a fishing boat.'

'You really think anyone will believe that provides a reliable means of communication?'

'Why not?'

'And where is this insulting reply?'

'Henry, I have yet to write it. Now let's get Mr Grey out of his cot so we can start planning.'

'You thought all this out when you were supposed to be asleep just to save my reputation?'

'Saving your reputation will be a welcome addendum to the taking of those two prizes out from under Mehmet's nose. What is really driving the notion for me is the amount of money they will fetch when they and their cargo are sold.'

'So you are greedy.'

'No, Henry, I am needy. I have a battle to fight every bit as important to me as getting out of this hole is to you.'

'Barclay?'

'He's a rich man. I need to be the same to contest with him and make happy the woman I love. And before you frown I will repeat it is none of your business.'

'You castigated me for the notion of the risk I was prepared to take by sailing into the anchorage to bombard Mehmet's fortress. Is this so very different?'

'Perhaps not, but I hope it shows that we are both desperate enough to risk it. What do you say?'

'I say I have no choice.'

CHAPTER TWENTY-THREE

Grey was still sulking; having been told, nay ordered, that he and his men should discard their red coats and gleaming webbing. It seemed his youthful dreams of glory, of some magnificent action in a blaze of bayonet and scarlet, had suffered a serious setback. Pearce finally agreed the garments could be taken along and kept out of sight until the proposed action was at its height.

'We do not want to alert Mehmet Pasha to who it is that is attacking him. If there are no torches lit on those batteries you will have to set them up and your red jacket will stick out and tell him it is Britannia.'

'Surely he will guess.'

'No, he will be left guessing. He may well have enemies of whom we know nothing and then there are his own Turkish masters who must distrust him. Confusion is an asset, let us not throw it away. You can of course appeal over my head to Mr Digby.'

Grey shook his head at that; he knew that Henry Digby had

ceded any leadership of the cutting out expedition to the man who had proposed it. Indeed the ship's captain seemed in something of a fog, whereas his premier was in his element, issuing orders and making arrangements for various eventualities.

Who would man which boats, added to who would command and where; what weapons to employ; the timing of the assault, which would, in darkness and of necessity be hard to coordinate. Then there was the ship itself, which would have to come inshore to drop off the fighting men then take up a risky position to back up Grey's marines. HMS *Flirt* had to be also available to evacuate the marines and to take aboard those who survived in the face of total failure.

Two other factors had to be in place, enough of a wind to aid an exit. Even if it was small, the fall of the tide in the Adriatic would create a stronger outflow current and aid the enterprise. If he sensed impatience Pearce paid it no heed, he consulted the tidal charts as the ship sailed up and down many miles off shore and well out of sight of land, this maintained until he felt the wind shift into the east with the kind of force that would be required. Nothing less than a stiff pennant would do.

Final preparations included the writing of letters for those with the skill. Dorling had command of the ship while the action was under way and it was to him that Pearce handed his letter to Emily. The master had orders that the integrity of HMS *Flirt* was paramount – most of the crew would still be on board to man the cannon and sail the ship; if it looked as if evacuation was impossible and that integrity was threatened he was ordered to get her out of danger.

The sentiments Pearce expressed were heartfelt and true,

acknowledging that he would leave Emily in a less than good situation but with his own confidence that she had the strength to cope. In addition was a note to be taken to Alexander Davidson as a sort of last will and testament, saying that any funds he had remaining or still to come in should be for the sole use of Emily Barclay neé Raynesford. That, after a repeat of his regard, was sanded and sealed.

Digby had asked about the letter Pearce had undertaken to write, purporting to be from Mehmet Pasha and downright insulting; the response had been that it could wait. If the raid were a success it would be written; if it failed such a thing was likely to be superfluous.

'You do realise I might be put in a position where I must lie under oath.'

When Digby said that, Pearce wanted to ask him if he anticipated being struck immediately down by lightning. He forbore, the man was not in a good frame of mind, evidenced by the question. Digby was worrying about his immortal soul when he ought to be concentrating on keeping alive his corporeal being.

'Captain, I calculate that the conditions we need are as good as they are going to get and that we should proceed to action.'

'How very formal, John.'

'What we do is your decision.' Raised eyebrows questioned that, so Pearce added. 'I will not give the orders, Henry, you must. What we do has to be seen as coming from you.'

Digby nodded slowly, further proof to Pearce that what he had suspected was the case; his captain had little faith in what they were about to attempt but he stood up, picked up his hat and followed Pearce on to the quarterdeck where he addressed the ship's master, who in truth was waiting for what Digby said.

'Mr Dorling, put us on a course for the southern arm of the Gulf of Ambracia.'

The cry of 'all hands' went out and quicker than normal the ship came alive with hurrying bodies – they, too, had been waiting in anticipation. The topmen went aloft to let out the reefs in the maincourse that had curtailed their speed, the youngest and most nimble making for the topgallant yard to set those telling stretches of canvas.

Below them the waisters hauled on the falls to bring round the yards so that they took what wind they could. *Flirt* was going to have to tack and wear into the teeth of the easterly breeze to make the correct landfall and at the right pace to bring them there in darkness, while leaving enough time for the proposed action to be carried out.

'Tilley?'

'Your honour.'

Pearce indicated that Digby's coxswain should come close and he leant forward to whisper. 'Mr Digby is in low spirits, Tilley, and I fear he may not act with the speed required in a tight spot.'

'He's lost his colour right enough, Mr Pearce.'

'Feel free to nudge him or even push him if it becomes necessary and at worst take over the ordering of your boarding party.'

'Not sure I can manage that, your honour.'

'I am, Tilley, and do not doubt yourself when others have faith.'

That got a touch of the forelock. 'Aye, aye, sir.'

It was a laborious haul to hold their course, an endless shifting of yards and sail adjustment to get the most out of the brig, with

Pearce eyeing his watch at intervals, while examining the slate to try and calculate how they were faring.

'You're fretting, Mr Pearce,' Dorling said softly, 'which I say is a waste.'

'Can't help it. Action is one thing, the wait for it another.'

'But a joy if we succeed.'

The tone was posing a question; Dorling was no more certain than Digby.

'If all goes well we will have complete surprise. I doubt there is any plan in place to cover what we are about to attempt, which means a lot of fighting men running around to no purpose and leaders having no idea how to command them. The wind is right, the current is favourable and if the marines do their job the way out will be secure.'

'Best keep that last bit quiet, your honour. Never do to go telling the lads they are relying on Lobsters.'

If it was getting increasingly gloomy as the day turned to night, there was still enough light to see Dorling's grin. 'Best shade the binnacle lantern, Mr Dorling, while I make a round of the ship to ensure no one is showing a light.'

There were lanterns below, but Pearce had ordered canvas to be draped over the closed gun ports so that nothing showed through the edges. He passed most of the men who would be taking part in the assault, they asleep, which he wondered at, sure he would not have been able to do likewise. Even Lieutenant Grey was snoring gently. Back on deck when he got there it was full night and if there was again a mixture of cloud and clear, the former scudding was not drifting, showing a higher wind up above.

'Would that proceed anything untoward?'

Dorling looked aloft though he would scarcely need to; as a very experienced sailor he had seen much and heard more, the latter the accumulated knowledge of centuries of lore. The master had one thing Pearce doubted he would ever acquire, the kind of innate understanding that allowed men such as he to see over the horizon and foretell the coming of various sorts of weather, good and bad.

It was not just the sky, it was the sea itself; its colour, the way a certain current would shade that differently, the rise and size of the waves and the rate of run. Pearce often wondered if their noses were as vital as their eyes and ears for he had many times seen Dorling sniffing the wind as if it carried for him some sort of message.

'Nothing pending, though it might turn more foul on the morrow. By my reckoning, Mr Pearce, we will raise the shore at around four bells in the next watch.'

'We will need to shorten sail close in.'

'Accounted for.'

Ten at night, Pearce thought, perfect. Eight hours of darkness and the certainty by that time most of their putative opponents would be at their slumbers. There was nothing he could do so he decided to try to sleep, with no confidence that he would succeed.

'Time to rouse out, John-boy.'

That whispered suggestion, accompanied by a gentle shake, brought Pearce out of a very lubricious dream and there was a certain amount of immediate guilt that Emily was not part of it. Still dressed he raised himself to rub his eyes, with Michael indicating a bowl of water he had fetched to douse his face into wakefulness. He emerged to find the whole lower deck buzzing, no doubt, O'Hagan speculated, about how they would spend the money they would gain from tonight's exploits.

'Some of them may not come back, Michael.'

'And sure don't they know it, but within each soul sits the assurance that if there is to be a fall it will be visited upon another. Mr Dorling requests your presence on deck.'

'Mr Digby?'

'Already there but as silent as the grave.'

Michael was right; Digby stood, his knees giving gently with the motion of the ship, hands behind his back, eyes set forward into what was near total darkness. The only sound was of creaking timbers, stretching cables and the soft call of the leadsman in the chains. As he looked aloft Pearce saw, and that was only faintly, that they were now under nothing but topsails and if they were making progress – it was impossible to tell – it was a snail's pace.

'Boats are in the water?' he asked Tilley.

'Two bells past, sir, and right ready to be hauled in.'

'Swivels rigged?'

'And loaded, your honour.'

Digby should have said something, even a quiet word to pass around would have done, for this was no occasion for a rousing speech, more for a touch of Harry in the night. Lacking that it fell to Pearce and had to be phrased to do its job.

'May God go with all of you and bring you back safe. Pass it on.'

He heard Dorling order the spikes to be pulled and that would, very quickly, let fly the sheets and bring the brig to a halt. It was reassuring the way the raiding party went about their business then, getting the boats alongside and loading them with their equipment, carried out in silence, the marines as ghostly as the tars without their coats and webbing.

'Time to go to your boat, sir.'

Digby seemed to wake from some sort of trance and when he moved he spoke to the master. 'Take good care of my letter, Mr Dorling.'

It came to Pearce then what Digby had done, nothing more than a written condemnation of Hotham and his inexcusable actions. If he were killed the words of a dying man would carry great weight; they might even scupper his adversary. Pearce got in another admonition to Tilley, this time more emphatic, to mind his captain.

'All ready?' A murmured reply from men in boats alongside. 'Haul away.'

As they began to row HMS *Flirt* disappeared, to take up station just to the south of the narrows but just too far out to be visible. There she would wait until it was time for her to take part. The boats were rowed in with great care and at no pace, with nary a word spoken. They hit the same stretch of beach at which Pearce had landed previously. This time it was deliberate and calculated by Dorling.

They were again run ashore to be dragged up into the undergrowth. When the light from the stars permitted, sharp cutlasses were employed to create a path, no axes for they were too noisy, this while Pearce checked with Grey that his men were assembled and to run over once more what they had to do.

This got an exasperated whisper in reply. 'I know my orders, Mr Pearce.'

'Mother hen, Mr Grey, can't help it.'

It took at least an hour to get the boats over the spit and into the anchorage, time in which Grey and his Lobsters crept towards the southern battery with him going forward to reconnoitre; there were no lights and no sign of activity but he was sure that even if he was asleep, someone had been left to keep watch.

Pearce waited – Digby was still silent – until the sky cleared enough to show the two merchantmen and, with all three boats in a line, he ordered them to shove off and dip oars. Those still in the shallows pushed to give the craft initial momentum before clambering aboard to hushes from their mates to stow the racket.

'I'll stow my boot up your arse,' hissed one dripping wet tar, who got a gentle clout from Michael O'Hagan with an order to stay silent, one a smiling Pearce was certain would be obeyed. His friend was no bully, very much the reverse, but few would question him if he advised anything.

Several times there had to be a whispered command to stay the boats with dipped oars. Enough light was needed to pick their spot for boarding, using the chains in the bows where there were aids to clambering, bowsprit rigging and holds in the hull. When they came alongside it was without a tell-tale bump of wood on wood. Bare feet make no noise and Pearce got ten men aboard the first Frenchman before their commander and they were thus able to aid him in his climb, helped by another half-dozen following, something Digby did with more alacrity than he had demonstrated for days, which had Pearce wondering if it was the prospect of success or of his demise that animated him. Whatever, there was nothing he could do, he had his own Frenchie to board.

Again the movement was carried out with care and if the

distance was not great it took time to cover. In his mind's eye he saw Digby's party silent and hidden as best they could be in the merchantman's forepeak; they would not move until he did and his party would have to adopt the same tactic to give the now lightly manned boats time to get into position.

'Lantern?' he demanded.

'Got it, your honour.'

'Unshade twice, yes.' The positive reply was of the same ilk as that previously given by Grey, slightly irritated: Pearce did not care, he was not going to fail for a want of worry. 'Haul away as soon as the boarding party is clear.'

Michael O'Hagan had been the first man aboard their target vessel and it was his hand that hauled Pearce aboard, to step gingerly onto the deck. He could not help looking aloft as the cloud cleared for a moment, to see the silhouettes of those hanged bodies still in the rigging. Then he ducked down so that his shape was invisible against the bulwarks, with only his head up high enough to look across the anchorage and wait for the signal to tell him that his boats had taken up their station.

A sudden commotion across the water had him standing up and peering. That muffled sound did not last, it turned to a shout that told Pearce his comrades on the first Frenchman had been either spotted or had moved too quickly; there was a fight going on.

'Move, lads!' he called.

Pearce hauled out his sword and one pistol then began to run along the deck towards the stern and the captain's cabin, where he was sure that whoever was holding the command for Mehmet Pasha would have laid his head; to neutralise him was Pearce's task.

339

Others made for the companionway that led below to seek out and capture or kill any enemies they could find.

The yells from Digby's merchantman were now ringing round the anchorage, seeming to bounce off the water and be multiplied by the effect. As Pearce approached the great cabin door it swung open to reveal that the interior was crowded; there would be no men below, they were all in front of him. Worse, they were greater in number than those following him.

'Someone, get below and bring up our men!' he yelled, before discharging his pistol into the face of the leading enemy.

Well to his rear Lieutenant Grey had heard the faint sounds. His orders were to wait till he was certain that the attack had been discovered but then he also knew that orders sometimes had to be adjusted. He called to his marines to move forward which they did, muskets at present and bayonets gleaming as they caught the light.

The pace was steady and by now the gap to be covered no more than thirty yards, while the wall at the rear of the redoubt presented little problem if it was undefended. With cupped hands one man aided another up onto the parapet prior to leaning down to first retrieve his weapons before hauling up his mate. By the time Mehmet's gunners emerged from their stone hut they were obliged to face a line of marines who were immediately ordered to charge.

Pearce could only hope for that to be so, he was too busy with his sword trying to prevent any of his enemies getting out through that cabin door, for if he could keep them bottled up his men, once they were a whole party, would have the numbers to win. Nor could he do anything about Digby and his men; they must fend for themselves against what he assumed would be the same numbers as he faced.

The men still in the boats of HMS *Flirt* had got into the position Pearce had designated for them, lined up off the bows of those two brigantines, vessels quickly coming alive as the reverberations of three battles filled surrounding anchorage. The decks came alive with bodies, all peering into the gloom to try and make out what was going on.

Tilley had, as instructed, not only kept an eye on his captain but stayed right by him, yet had been unable to prevent him from moving before the signal came from Pearce to seek to take over the ship. Digby moved forward well before he should have, ignoring a whispered admonition from his coxswain that was decidedly insubordinate. He made no attempt at silence, his shoes rapping a tattoo on the planking. Tilley had no option but to follow and have the rest of the party do likewise. Within a blink they were fighting a desperate battle.

Nearly every man aboard those brigantines was now on deck and the men manning the boats heard the first set of orders being bellowed out. If they did not understand the language they understood the nature and after a call to each other, so their actions would be coordinated, those manning the swivels pulled the lanyards attached to the flints.

The roar of the guns was in direct disproportion to their size but the effect was deadly; the grapeshot swept the side of both brigantines and, judging by the noise that followed, did terrible mutilation.

Pearce was now surrounded by his own men and with an arm aching from use was able to step back and let them deal with his foes, still in the main trapped in the cabin and only able to engage one at a time. That was when he discovered a few had slipped out of the casements and up onto the poop. Luckily he saw the movement at the top of the twin stairways and could counter one while alerting his men to the other.

Grey's marines had done a terrible duty; there was not a single one of Mehmet's gunners still alive; if they had not taken a close range musket ball they had been bayoneted multiple times. Now he had two of their cannon hauled from their normal embrasures and set to fire at the parapet wall, both loaded and fired on long lanyards, he and his men taking shelter in the casualty filled stone hut. The blast removed masonry that had been in place for centuries and it came apart like chaff, stone splinters flying in all directions.

'Right, reload,' Grey ordered almost before the noise had died down. 'The range is seven hundred yards precisely as dictated by the charts. Let's give those sods over the narrows a present they were not expecting.'

'Axe men to cut the anchor cables,' Pearce yelled, as the heat of his battle began to wane. He looked over the side to see his boats returning, they having fulfilled their function, which was to slow the unmooring of those brigantines.

'Topmen aloft and get some canvas showing.'

A rush to the rail showed him that was already happening on the other merchantman and that was the point at which Grey's wall-destroying cannon spoke, the crashing sound echoing right across the water like a wave of air.

'Mr Pearce, we have found the French crewmen.'

'Then let them out and I will get them to work, the more hands the better.'

Lieutenant Grey was in ecstasy, preparing to fire over what was at minimal range an enemy whose guns could not reply, for they either faced out to sea or covered the inner anchorage. That there was panic across the water was in no doubt but that was multiplied after his first deadly salvo, which turned parts of their protective stonework into stone nuggets.

Dorling had raised sail as soon as the commotion broke out and now HMS *Flirt* raked the opposite redoubt with a full broadside, this just before Grey put in his second salvo. The marine lieutenant was standing on what was left of the parapet, now in his scarlet coat, a telescope to his eye as he examined the effect of his shot; the redoubt opposite was deserted, the gunners had run away.

'That's a damn tempting fortress yonder,' he said, languidly. 'I think we have time to put a few balls into her stonework.'

Both merchantmen were now hives of activity. They were still fully rigged for sea albeit damaged, but they had sailed in and they had the ability to sail out, now aided by a crew of French sailors to whom Pearce had pointed out their swinging in the rigging comrades. Nothing more was required to get them working like men possessed.

'Brigantines are unmooring, your honour.'

'Nip and tuck it will be. I never reckoned otherwise.'

The groaning of timbers told him his vessel was moving and a glance over the side showed her consort was just ahead, which would have her as the first.

'Michael, see if there is any powder and balls aboard.'

The merchant vessel did not have more than four useable cannon, but that might just be enough to deter those brigantines, with very little way on them, to come too close. The booming sound of cannon fire had him looking to Grey's bastion but not for long; a ball he had fired demolished one of the houses set against the walls of Mehmet's fortress, which had Pearce wondering where the larded sod was, for in his heart and he was not ashamed, he harboured a desire to slice open the bastard's gullet.

'Anyone spare, cut down those poor sods hanging in the rigging and put them below.'

The wind was billowing in the canvas, the outflowing current driving both hulls. Ahead were the trio of boats rowing fast to get outside the anchorage, there to take off Grey and his marines once their task, not yet completed, was done. The first Frenchie entered the narrows which had Pearce holding his breath; was the deep water channel where he had hoped it would be? For if the first merchantman ran aground there was precious little room for him to get by.

A glance over his shoulder showed both brigantines on the move and they would sail twice as fast as any lumbering trading ship. Then they fired their forward cannon, which must have been hauled right round to bear, the case shot flying through the rigging in an attempt to disable Pearce's ship. It might have worked without the current for some of the sails were holed. Luckily no one was hurt.

The blue lights burst above to hang in the sky and illuminate the whole anchorage, which showed people running in all directions ashore. It also lit up the fortress battlements and there was the man Pearce thought to be Mehmet Pasha.

'Fetch the bodies of those we have slain and toss them overboard so that the swine can see them.'

Just then Grey fired another salvo at the fortress and, having adjusted his range, this time he hit the upper walls. When the dust cleared there was no sign of Mehmet Pasha or any of the entourage who attended upon him.

Digby's ship was through the narrows, though he could see no sign of his captain. That mattered not, now it was for him to follow, which he did, all the time under fire from those brigantines who now had only their bow chasers to use and his wide stern to aim at. As he passed Grey, still on the parapet looking studiously untroubled, Pearce raised his hat, to have his salute returned with a rousing cheer. Now he did wish for a speaking trumpet, to both congratulate and encourage.

As soon as his stern was clear of the cannon facing into the anchorage, the marine gunners blasted out at the chasing brigantines and if they did not strike the great spouts the balls threw up was enough of a warning to haul their wind or face being holed below the waterline. Their thin scantlings would shatter with one shot from a thirty-two-pounder cannon, land based and well able to alter its range.

Pearce was out in the open sea now, with Dorling manoeuvring to cross his stern and close off the narrows to any vessel which sought to follow. Grey fired one more salvo at the brigantines, which removed part of the bows of the leading vessel, rendering unfit for sea, before spiking the guns and heading for the beach where the boats were waiting to take him off. That was when the real cheering started, and it spread to all three ships.

EPILOGUE

It was not until well after dawn and the transfer back to HMS *Flirt* that Pearce found out what had happened with Henry Digby, related to him by Tilley.

'It was as if he wanted to take the blade, your honour, and if we had been one more step behind he would have been skewered more'n once and I doubt still having a breath. As it was we had to fight them swabs over his body and it were a close run.'

'Where is he?'

'Laying in the cabin of the *Eliza* or somewhat, which is the name of the ship we brought out. One of the *grenouilles* had a bit of training in barber work and has bandaged him up.'

'We must, if it is possible to move him, get him on board *Flirt*.'

The look that he got told Pearce that Tilley was not going to recommend it, which had him back in a boat and crossing to examine the casualty, having first spoken with the French crew of what was the *Eliza*. He told them the same message he had given to those aboard the vessel he had brought out, *Le Jeune Eugene*; they would not be harmed if they behaved and that they could go ahead and arrange the funerals of their less fortunate mates. Then he went into the cabin to find the man who had tended to him nursing Digby.

'*Le capitaine, il est endormir?*'

The fellow nodded and responded in a soft voice while Pearce questioned him as to what state the patient was in, which was something of a bad way. Digby had a deep wound to his body which had gone through his upper chest, with the tip of the sword exiting below his shoulder. If there was an indication that no vital organ had been damaged there was no certainty, added to which he had lost a lot of blood until the wound was stemmed, that not having been applied until the merchantman was well clear of the narrows.

Asked if he could be moved the response was a firm shake of the head. Whatever else Digby required, he needed the services of a proper physician. The fellow tending him was quite clear he lacked the skills to properly care for him. What that implied was simple; it could not wait until San Fiorenzo Bay and that probably meant Naples as well. Boating back to *Flirt* he went into the conclave with Dorling and it was decided to change course from the toe of Italy and head for Brindisi, the nearest major port on the mainland.

Progress was not and could not be swift with the two merchant vessels setting the pace and weather that was far from clement, heavy wind and a swell with constant bouts of lashing rain which had them wallowing along. It also had Pearce regularly soaked as he boated from one vessel to the other, finally rewarded when Digby came round and was able to talk, feebly but with enough sense to admit that what Tilley had said was true. At least he could assure Digby there was no sign of a pursuit; either through losses of manpower or damage to at least one hull by Grey's cannon, those two Brigantines had been dealt with. It was the melancholy that was the problem and the reasons that lay behind it.

'Let us not examine the ins and outs of that now, best get you well and then you can see that it was not the right course to follow.'

'I know you think you have another, John,' Digby said with breath that was gasping. 'But I am not sure I am so sanguine.'

'I have only one question to which I need an answer, Henry, am I free to act as I wish in the matter of these two merchantmen?'

'You are in command now.'

'This has nothing to do with command. I am not inclined to seek to sail these vessels all the way to Corsica so that Hotham can dispose of them. The only other destination is Gibraltar and the Prize Court there, which means fees to pay and no doubt a bit of chicanery in the final assessment of value.'

That got a wan smile; Digby would naturally mistrust Prize Courts in general and especially those outside England, staffed as they were with placemen who saw their prosperity as riding very high above that of sailors.

'In addition we would have to crew them and with enough men to ensure the French do not have the strength to retake them, which leaves your ship so short of hands as to be emasculated.'

'So?'

'I propose to sell the prizes in Brindisi and make a distribution right away.'

'Which will delight the crew.'

'It will infuriate Hotham, given it is sailing pretty close to the wind to act in that fashion, it may be illegal in fact.'

'A judgement for a court, John. If it discomfits Hotham you have my full support.'

'Then let us make it so. We can get you proper medical aid and I would suggest a place to convalesce until you are fully recovered.'

'What about the French sailors?'

'They won't be the only men of their nation to serve King George. I will swear them in. The good ones will accept, the others will desert and if they do we will be well shot of them.'

'They'll fetch a tidy sum, I reckon, our captures.'

'True and if my share is scarce enough to match the wealth of Ralph Barclay it will go a long way to aiding my cause.'

Digby became so animated that Pearce had to gently stop him from trying to rise and if his voice was weak there was no denying the vehemence of the words he uttered.

'If you need more, you may call upon my quarter share. If the only way to bring punishment down on Hotham is through Barclay then I am your supporter.'

'Rest, Henry, and I will come again.'

'Grey, did he do well?'

'He did magnificently, even our tars are praising the Lobsters.'

'That is the world turned upside down indeed.'

'How much do you reckon they're worth?' Grey asked, when told of the intention as well as the fact that if he did not mind a soaking he could visit his ailing superior.

'I looked at the manifests and had a word with the one surviving mate. It's all spices and silks, with oils for perfumes too. I would be disappointed by less than thirty thousand.'

'Which means . . . ?'

'A round thousand for us and the warrants at least.'

Grey swelled with anticipated wealth but Pearce had a fly in the ointment. He had avoided reminding Digby of an upsetting fact; if Lord Hood had been superseded, Hotham would be entitled to an eighth of the prize value.

'Land ho,' came the cry, which meant they were close to reaching Brindisi. John Pearce was less concerned about that: he was wondering which was the quickest way to get to Naples: by land or sea?